THE MUMMY

The Mummy

Nael Roberts

2016

THE MUMMY

THE MUMMY

Copyright © 2016 by Nael Roberts

All rights reserved, without limitations the rights under copyright reserved above, no part of this publication may be reproduced, stored in or introduced into a retrieval system, or transmitted, in any form, or by any means (electronic, mechanical, photocopying, recording, or otherwise) without the prior written permission of Nael Roberts, the owner of these works and the Characters within. This is a work of fiction. Names, characters, places, brands, media, and incidents either are a product of the author's imagination or are used fictitiously and bear no resemblance to anyone living, dead, or undead.

All Art work is digitally painted by Trevor Storey and the rights are owned by Nael Roberts. (2016)

All Concepts: Nael Roberts

THE MUMMY

THE MUMMY

1.0

THE MUMMY

THE MUMMY

Books by This Author

1. Shadow Behind the Sun (sci-fi) 1987

2. Legacy of the Vampire (Book One of the Vampire Chronicles) 1988

3. Vagabond Banquet (Book Two of the Vampire Chronicles) 2013

4. Fall from Grace (Book Three of the Vampire Chronicles) 2013

5. Fires of Eden (Book Four of the Vampire Chronicles) 2014

6. Communicator Chronicles (Compendium of The Vampire Chronicles) 1988-2014

7. Echoes Through Time 2014

8. Echoes from the Past 2015

9. Echoes of Death 2015

10. Echoes Trilogy… 2014 - 2015

11. The Mummy 2016

THE MUMMY

THE MUMMY

Dedication

Marion Eddy Storey,

To Egypt, for its beautiful sunsets, and mysterious places.

THE MUMMY

THE MUMMY

Prologue.

The unknown stranger watched the eerily sinister fog that was both dense and unnatural as it embraced the port on that cold December evening. He scrutinised the cargo ship as it sailed slowly into the harbour, an unnatural silence compelling the vessel forward to relinquish its uncanny cargo that repelled those on board, who understood the significance of its presence. The journey from Egypt had taken almost six weeks, and in that time the ship had been plagued with unnatural events, and now it was here, in England, at such an advantageous time in history.

The world had become obsessed by the discovery of the ancient young king's tomb in 1922, and now anything appertaining to this ancient world was both beguiling and intriguing to all those who took an interest in history's forgotten age. The rumours of curses and death followed those intrepid enough to set foot upon the hallowed ground of the ancients, both blessed and cursed by the high priests, for the safety of their masters, in their desire to attain true immortality.

It was aboard this vessel that the dark elements of an ancient Egyptian prince and his priest were placed, bound for London. They had travelled through the rough seas, buffeted by the torments of nature until they eventually found restitution, here on these unimaginable shores of this sceptred isle.

There was a cold, empty silence that hung in the air as the vehicle that had been waiting patiently on the dockside was unceremoniously ushered forward and loaded with the large boxes containing the sarcophagus of those once entombed. Their very presence offering an unnerving atmosphere to those unwitting custodians who were entrusted to deliver this precious cargo to the British Museum, and so, were commended to drive through the early hours of the night to ensure delivery and preparation for their examination on that following morning.

It was either with intention or ignorance that both the driver and custodian, ignored the noises that were periodically omitted from the rear of the truck. It was as if shallow voices were drifting upon the wind and escaping into the cold night air. As they progressed, the dark countryside gave way to the partially illuminated suburbs of outer London and its very occurrence brought with it a relief of presence, for both parties felt that the introduction of light into their dark predicament brought a little solace and a restitution to their uneasy souls. Some distance behind followed a sole stranger, silent yet vigilant.

It was almost 4:00 a.m., by the time the vehicle stopped at its destination. There, outside of the delivery entrance of the Museum, stood six healthy porters who unloaded the Sarcophagus and urgently ensconced them into the protective darkness of the Museum's cellar, to be discovered that very morning by the enquiring eyes of the head of archaeology, Sir Henry Karvahill: eminent scholar, male chauvinist and arrogant child to Lord and Lady Walter Karvahill, businessman, high court judge and prosecutor to the crown.

The doors to the museum were closed to the general public and would be that following day, the only people allowed access were those granted that privilege by Sir Henry himself. Proceedings were to begin at 9:30 a.m. sharp, and until that time, the ancient artefacts were to rest and acclimatise to the damp atmosphere of this green and pleasant land. A dense fog had been rolling across all areas of London, down the streets, across gardens and into blind alleyways, bring with it an unnatural presence that whispered of foreboding dark secrets, and ancient lies. The city was awakening, but the night remained master of the world below, bring with it a presence that was neither welcome nor comforting, for these artefacts brought with them a sinister manifestation, something otherworldly. The dense clouds overhead foretold the probability of snow, but this was never assured, and nature would only show her hand at a time when it pleased her, and no other.

THE MUMMY

Chapter 1.

The Great War had been over for almost ten years and the Roaring Twenties were living up to their designated name, as prosperity lavished the land with the newfound wonders of this new age of enlightenment as picture halls displayed the virtues of this unfettered prosperity that washed across the world. This was even more apparent for those individuals who lived in this desirable district of London. However, for Lady Abigail Cornwall, life for the past eight years has primarily been a conglomeration of study, work and endurance, peppered with slight smatterings of longingly desired sleep. Since her father's retirement, some five years previous, she had felt the pressure to work twice as hard as others, not only to prove, but also maintain the faith that he had placed in her, his only daughter, in this male dominated world.

Abigail had always wanted to follow in her father's footsteps; he had journeyed to Egypt a multitude of times, but these were all undertaken long before she was born or while she was an infant and placed in the welcoming arms of her loving grandparents, thus allowing her mother and father to undertake their adventures to this distant and passionate land. Egypt had always held a fascination to her, even as a child, the tales recanted to her by her mother at bedtime would fill her dreams with colour and wonder and fuel her fervent imagination which would compel hours of day-dreaming and dark restitution from her tutors, as she was a constant traveller within the country of her own lucid imagination.

Here she was, on the eve of undertaking her new position as assistant archaeologist to the eminent Sir Henry Karvahill, Senior Archaeologist at the British Museum, and she couldn't sleep a wink. Even though the hall clock reminded her that the night was gradually creeping forward and daylight was only a few hours away, her mind was in a constant turmoil and driven by her own tentative aspirations. She allowed scenario after scenario to turn over in her mind until she felt as though the pressure of her thoughts were about to suffocate her own imagination. And so, she rose from her bed, as awake now as she was when she lay her head down on her pillow almost five hours previously and made restitution with the forthcoming morning, as it was plainly evident that sleep truly evaded her.

She pensively rubbed her eyes, and pulled on her dressing gown before she made her way quietly out of her bedroom and down the stairs and into the kitchen that was situated at the rear of her home. Lighting the stove, she filled the old kettle, which was one of her mother's favourite possession, as it held so many special memories for her, and placed it gently over the hungry flames, as she then sat at the table and allowed her eyes to become accustomed to the inky blackness of her nocturnally embraced surroundings, whose only glimmer of life was emitted by the fames that offered a gentle, but soothing, yellowish glow.

Abigail allowed her head to fall a little forward, as if captured by the essence of sleep, as her mind drifted quietly onto a sea of deep contemplation, floating upon the pensive thoughts of possibility. She understood the considerable dilemma that was presented before her; the thought of being a sole female undertaking such a substantial role in a male-dominated world, filled her with both trepidation and hope. From her earliest memory all that she wanted to do was to be observed as an equal; a woman in her own right. Honoured for her educational prowess and not for her gender or birth-right. For her intellect was also her downfall, as she knew that gaining a first at Cambridge, outshining her fellow male counterparts, placed her on precarious ground, upon which, only a man could find sure footing. Her credentials would be besmirched and sullied for years to come as whispers of fraternisation or corrupt accreditation would haunt her in this patriarchal chauvinistic world.

It was the sound of the kettle's whistle informing her that the water had reached boiling-point that brought her mind back to reality. Smiling half-heartedly to herself, she stood and walked over to the range. Turning off the gas, she lifted the kettle and placed it safely onto one of the cold burners. After searching for her mother's favourite tea-pot, which she dutifully filled with three heaped teaspoon amounts of their best Indian tea, she poured in the water and allowed the tea to fuse and grow in its potency as she gathered the strainer and a singular tea cup from the cupboard overhead, and placed them on the old kitchen table before her.

From outside of the house she could hear the horse-driven milk cart meander along the street as the gentle sound of bottles clanking together highlighted the imminent delivery of cold fresh milk.

"Is there another cup of tea in that pot?" Lord Cornwall enquired as he stepped into the dimly lit kitchen, drawing his dressing-gown chord tightly around his waist.

Abigail turned and looked at her father.

"For you? Always," she replied with a smile.

"I went to put that book back into your room, but when I couldn't find you, I realised that you must have been downstairs," Lord Cornwall stated. Realising his daughter's confusion, he elucidated. "The detective one which I borrowed, the one about the sleuth who had a doctor as an assistant, I found it very intriguing."

When his daughter did not reply he asked her a direct question.

"Are you nervous about your newly acquired employment?" he asked as he sat in the old leather chair by the fire.

"A mixture of nerves and excitement," she replied. "All those years at university striving to attain an excellent education and subsequent qualification, and here I am, in a presenting situation that I thought I'd never be at in my lifetime, and I feel like the new child at school, full of misguided anxiety and unfounded dilemma."

Lord Cornwall smiled.

"Your mother would have been very proud of you."

Abigail paused for a moment in her endeavours and offered her father a warm smile as she took a second cup and saucer from the overhead cupboard.

"She always wanted a better education, I recall her saying that the only way to enlighten yourself as an individual is through a good education," she said.

"That, and stay away from idiots," her father emphasised with a smile.

Abigail looked at him with an air of slight confusion, realising her dilemma, he elucidated upon his cryptic words.

"Your mother always thought that if you surrounded yourself with ne'er-do-wells and intellectually inferior individuals, instead of allowing your individual intelligence the arena in which to shine, their counterpart's general presence draws you down to their lesser enlightened level and you become homogenised into their dark thought process and eventually mirror their social and educational standing. You become a victim of collective individualism, a lost voice drowned in the politically driven seas of the general masses."

THE MUMMY

Abigail smiled.

"Lay down with a dog and you'll probably catch fleas," she stated, paraphrasing her father's previous sentiments.

"More succinctly put," he replied as he reached out his hand and accepted the hot cup of tea offered by his daughter.

Looking over at the tea-pot that sat on the stove, he smiled.

"I see you have given your mother's favourite tea-pot an airing," he stated in a jovial manner. "Your mother purchased a special Egyptian tea in Aswan, the locals used to brew a hibiscus infusion called Karkade, it was said to be the favoured drink of the pharaohs, far too sweet for my pallet. But your mother loved it, and upon returning home, insisted upon it being poured from an old English bone china tea-pot, which she had made and painted with ancient Egyptian motifs. She maintained that she couldn't start the day until she had at least two cups of the wretched stuff."

"It's now my favourite tea-pot," Abigail replied with a smirk, as she sat on the small sofa that resided opposite her father, the warm glow of the moonlight peering through the window illuminated her delicate features.

Lord Cornwall smiled and lowered his eyes. Realising his emotional dichotomy, Abigail looked at her father as a sense of deep concern washed over her.

"Are you alright?" she sensitively enquired.

"I'm fine," he replied, with an inkling of pride and emotion in his eyes. "It's just that you look so very much like your mother, sitting there with your tea and bathed in the soft light from the moon; it's as if time has allowed her to return to me for one last time. This moment has stirred so many memories, it reminds me of the time just after we were married, when we would sit, as we are, in the early mornings, contemplating our future lives together. We would discuss how many children we would like to have and what career your mother would choose. Would we remain in London, or relocate to the countryside next to her parents in Gloucestershire? It was a magical time for both of us." Lord Cornwall paused and looked tearfully about the room. "This house not only holds shadows, but ghosts of memories that I choose not to forget."

Abigail reached forward and gently caressed her father's hand with her fingers.

"You miss her as much as I do?" she whispered.

Without replying, he offered his daughter an accepting smile and a gentle nod of understanding.

"It's at times like this when we could have both benefited from her wise intervention," he stated. "It was bad enough when you went off to university. Thank the Lord that you were able to reside with your Aunty Mordred for the duration of your education, otherwise your time away would have been unbearable, and worry would have sent me to an early grave." He laughed to himself as fond memories danced through his mind. "She always loved you like her own, your Aunt Mordred, and, as she never had any children of her own, I suppose you were the next best thing," he stated.

"I don't think Aunt Mordred ever grew up," Abigail highlighted. "It was like living with an overexcited child, it was an adventure being in her company and something, I consider, that I would have gladly continued with, had this eminent employment opportunity not presented itself to me to end my own delightful dilemma."

Lord Cornwall smiled, as memories rallied in his mind.

"I always thought that name was so dour for someone so vibrant and full of life," he stated.

"Mordred?" Abigail enquired.

"Yes," he replied, nodding his head.

"I never really thought about it, I've always known her as Aunty Mordred. It could have been worse, they could have given that name to mother," she stated with wide sarcastic eyes.

Lord Cornwall laughed.

"That was a privilege kept for the first born daughter," he said. "A family tradition."

Abigail's eyes widened in horror.

"Were you going to call me Mordred?"

"Your mother wanted to, but I persuaded her otherwise. By the time you were born, both of her parents were dead and it seemed a little redundant to continue with that family traditions, and there wasn't really anyone left to object to our decision," he explained.

"Didn't mother have a brother who lived in the colonies?" she enquired.

"Edmund," Lord Cornwall highlighted. "He lives in New York, he must be some age by now, I think he was a good ten years older than myself, and I'm sixty-two."

"Last time I saw him was at…" Abigail pause for a brief moment and smiled emotionally at her father. "… Mother's funeral."

"And that was almost ten years ago," he highlighted in amazement. "Where does the time go?" he asked rhetorically, as he shook his head. "And here you are, my daughter, professional archaeologist, working for the British Museum. Your mother would have been as proud as I am," he stated with a broad comforting smile.

Abigail placed her empty cup and saucer onto the floor next to her feet.

"Are you worried about entering the work force?" he enquired.

"A little," she replied. "But not as much in relation to the work, more to do with the reputation of this Karvahill character. I understand he's a bit of a bully, and he's only achieved his position in the museum because of his father's pedigree and credentials."

"Pedigree! Hardly. As I've always said, judge a person by their actions, not their reputation. And if you discover that his dark reputation has foundation, feel reassured that you have probably forgotten more in the field of archaeology that his arrogant mind could ever wish to recall. See this employment as a stepping-stone. In a year or two you'll be off to Egypt on one of those expeditions that your mother and I so fondly undertook, and I'll be receiving post cards covered in sand and extoling the delights of your adventures on those dark shores," he said.

"I hope you're right," she replied with a smile.

"We are only limited by our dreams," he stated reassuringly.

"I wonder if my employment has anything to do with your previous connections with Sir Henry's father?" she enquired.

"I hardly think so," he replied. "Walter Karvahill was no more than an honorary member of the House of Lords, whereas my title was hereditary. He only ever cultivated my friendship when he was proposing some law or paper. To him I was a squanderer, a social scoundrel. Instead of dynasty building, I committed the most heinous of social crimes and married a woman for love, rather than social standing or political improvement. He even tried to marry his son off to one of those rich American heiresses, the likes of which have so recently flooded our land, seeking social respectability through marriage and title."

"I would have thought that being more of Henry's way, cold and cultivating," Abigail stated. "Marry for wealth, thus ensuring that the foundations of your own political and social desires are steadfast and assured."

"If I understand Walter Karvahill, then I will understand his first born. They both desire status, and both father and son would desire Henry to marry a titled English lady, who offered both social standing and prestige. They are both ruthless with regards to their social aspirations, and nothing and nobody will stand in their way. Walter was the son of an ambitious barrow-boy called Lechmere, who worked in the Bethnal Green area and sired more than twelve children. And Henry, or Sir Henry, as he likes to be called, a title neither bestowed nor honoured upon him, has neither ethically nor morally transcended that social barrier and still perceives himself as an emotional vagabond, who can bully his way out of any presenting situation."

"I pity the poor filly who he proposes to," Abigail stated with a cold shudder.

Her father turned to her with a dark smirk upon his lips.

"What?" Abigail enquired.

Realisation dawned upon her and an expression of shock swept across her features.

"No!" she cried in amazement.

Lord Cornwall smiled and nodded.

"Both Walter and Henry visited your mother and myself on the eve of your eighteenth birthday and callously requested your hand in marriage, they made it sound as though they were purchasing a bale of cloth, rather than a human life."

"Thank God you declined," she stated.

"I didn't have the chance, your mother chased them both from the house, something Walter Karvahill has never forgiven me for," her father began, laughing uncontrollably to himself. "Your mother always attained incredible insight for she knew that Henry was very much like his father, who had the crass ability to throw his money at a situation in order to attain his own desired outcome, and, several times during his not so illustrious career, this flagrant disregard for his own finances, had almost cost him everything he owned, for he has been on the edge of bankruptcy on several occasions." Lord Cornwall paused his recantation and allowed the atmosphere to soften. "Your mother also had your best interests at heart, for she knew that you were 'different,' and so she knew that if you were to fall in love with a man, it had to be for the right reasons. It had to be because he was an individual who enjoyed and relished in your girlish madness and did not demonstrate or impose his own idiotic manner, or endeavour to force you to conform and be what society classed as 'normal'." He paused for a moment, contemplating his next words. "I know it's unkind to gossip, but it would appear that the apple did not fall far from the tree. I was in Huntsman's, the gentlemen's tailor in Saville Row, and because I'm a regular and trusted customer, they are a little more 'liberal' with their conversation, and an assistant let it slip that Sir Henry had amassed a rather considerable slate, which hadn't been settled in over a year."

"Why didn't you tell me about his visit and proposal at the time?" she cried.

"As your mother put it, he was a whole load of fuss about nothing," he stated.

"I do hope I live up to her expectations," Abigail said, looking at her father wistfully.

"Whose?" he enquired.

"Mother's," she firmly stated.

"Your mother's only expectation was that you should be happy, that's all. She used to say that if you could find an ounce of the happiness we shared, then she would feel that your life had been truly blessed," he detailed with a smile.

"Then I have already surpassed her wishes," she said.

"I suppose that's where you get your aptitude for foreign and ancient language from, your mother could speak fluent German and French with a little Norwegian thrown in for good luck. She had a hunger to learn, to her, every day was always brimming full of possibilities," he said.

Abigail laughed.

"Yes, but mother's abilities were fitting for this modern era, mine are attributed to a language long since forgotten, and if it hadn't of been for Jean-François Champollion and the discovery of the Rosetta Stone, we would have remained in the Dark Ages in relation to deciphering those Ancient Egyptian Hieroglyphics that litter the ruins on Egypt," Abigail stated with a smile as she leaned forward and kissed her father gently upon the forehead.

"And one day, you will see them in the flesh, so to speak," he declared.

"Small steps father, let me get tomorrow out of the way and then we can plan my conquest of the world of archaeology," she stated with a smile.

"I'm sorry," he replied. "It's just that I'm excited for you, with this adventure ahead. A whole new world of possibilities."

"And it is both you and mother I have to thank for this, for affording me the opportunity to be myself. For allowing me to step proudly into a man's world, and for that, I can never thank you enough," she said.

"I fear that your battle has yet to begin," he stated. "All we did was focus your abilities and direct you as best we could," he said.

"But you did more than that. You treated me as a son. You didn't fetter my wings, but allowed them to stretch and reach to the heavens," she highlighted.

Lord Cornwall laughed.

"As I don't have a son I wouldn't know, but what I can say is that I have a daughter, who fills me with a pride that would uplift any father. After your mother died, you gave me a reason to live, and the strength to continue. Now, when it is your turn to require support, I am only to humble to offer you my love and respect for all that you have achieved. I am, and always will be blessed."

"I think that is a pleasure we both embrace," she whispered as she leaned forward and kissed her father gently on the cheek.

Chapter 2.

Abigail had washed and dressed early and procured a cab to deliver her to her new place of employment, just prior to the time requested in her letter of engagement. Although it was winter, she had left her home modestly dressed in anticipation of any physical undertaking she may be required to endure during her first day of work. As the cab pulled up to the front of the Museum, Abigail was startled at the lack of public interest in its proclaimed exhibits. As her eyes searched the signage on the exterior of the building, they observed a notice highlighting that the museum was closed to the public for one day, for what was referred to as, 'administration duties'.

Alighting the cab, she stood for a moment, marvelling at the splendour of the exterior of the building monumental facade, glistening from a recent unannounced and heavy downpour. As she admired her surroundings, her senses highlighted the impending approach of another cab, and she duly stepped slightly to one side as it drew level with the steps of the building that led up to the museum's entrance. As she did so, she moved directly into the line of a deluge of water that was displaced by the vehicles wheels as it approached, and was subsequently sullied as the dirty water splashed across her shoes and the lower portion of her dress.

As the door to the vehicle was opened by the chauffeur, its occupant stepped out into the bright winter sunlight, his attire consisting of mournful, emotionless black, contributing to his supercilious arrogant self-righteous demeanour. Conceitedly observing Miss Cornwall's predicament, he looked her up and down with derisive eyes.

"I do hope you will endeavour to dress in a little more appropriate attire in the future, after all, your dour presentation reflects negatively upon myself, and if that were so, then we would have to have a rather deep and frank discussion regarding this unwelcome situation," Sir Henry coldly stated.

As he made to walk up the steps he stopped and turned to Abigail.

"Sir Henry Karvahill, your employer," he stated with a sardonic smile. "And why are you not wearing a stole, or a winter coat?" he sharply enquired. "If you begin your engagement with a sickness record because of your own lack of insight, then it would not bode well for your future employment."

Abigail smiled.

"All educated people understand that a common cold is reliant upon cross contamination, rather than temperature. But I thank you for your consideration in relation to my welfare," she curtly replied and returned to him a rather lacklustre and pernicious smile.

Pursing his lips, Sir Henry turned and walked impatiently up the stone steps towards the museum's main doors.

"Don't worry, it's not you, he's like that with everyone," a voice highlighted from behind.

Abigail turned and smiled at its source.

"No, I can assure you, it is me," she knowingly stated.

"Allow one of us to demonstrate to you a little social grace, I'm Sir Henry's assistant, Johnathan Pringle," he stated with as he reached out his hand in friendship.

"Abigail Cornwall," she warmly replied.

"Any relation to eminent Lord Cornwall?" he enquired.

"My father," she replied.

"Oh dear, you're 'that' Abigail Cornwall," he responded with a smirk. "Don't worry, stick with me and I'll make sure your fine. His Lordship," he stated in ridicule, "Can't even open a door unaided, let alone demean anyone with skill, he's fundamentally an old school bully, just like his father."

"Johnathan!" Sir Henry bellowed, as he stood motionless and visibly irritated at the museums door.

"See what I mean?" Johnathan replied with a smirk. "Quick follow me, he doesn't like to be kept waiting," he highlighted.

As her newfound friend dashed up the stairs, Abigail smiled to herself.

"Good, a new way of annoying the precocious schoolboy. I do think that I will have fun today," she announced to herself lightening the atmosphere, as she merrily skipped up the stairs and through the doors that were held courteously open by Jonathan, so that she may enter the Museum unhindered.

Although it was winter, the light from the artificial light illuminated the hallway of the Museum, casting a strong yet comforting light that reflected a warm ambiance off the wood panelling, that was both compelling and embracing. Observing Sir Henry striding at a considerable rate along the corridor, Abigail strove to maintain her proximity to his demanding pace.

"We're going down to the cellar, we have recently had a delivery of two ancient Egyptian sarcophagi, the first allegedly belonging to Mentuhotep from the Eleventh Dynasty, which would be around 2060 B.C." Sir Henry coldly stated as he descended the stone steps that led to the very bowels of the building.

As they walked along the extensive corridor that appeared to stretch the full length of the museum, Abigail marvelled at the myriad of rooms that appeared to be segregated off from the main body of the institution. Approaching a set of strong wooden doors at the far reaches of the corridor, Sir Henry ceased in his march and turned to look at Abigail.

"As I was saying, we have two sarcophagi, one containing what we hope is a pharaoh, or at least one of his descendants, and the other we think may be the high priest. What I require you to do, Lady Cornwall," he said in a condescending tone, "Is to keep your eyes open, and your hands, and your opinions to yourself."

At that moment Johnathan arrived out of breath, following his brisk walk along the corridor, he smiled at Sir Henry and pushed the cellar doors open to allow him access to the extensive chamber beyond. Inside the room there lay the remnants of two packing-crates, beside which, stood two magnificent sarcophagi, each resting upon procured hospital gurneys. Beside each were stood two men, burley in physique and in eager anticipation of any physical work pronounced.

"We shall open both sarcophagi here, and after we have discovered who is held within, I will take the most senior statesman and you shall be left to examine the lesser inhabitant," Sir Henry decreed with a rather snide smirk.

"I've been informed that they have cut through the seal's and were primarily awaiting your presence before they continued," Johnathan respectfully informed Sir Henry.

Without a courteous response, Sir Henry took a deep breath and looked at the labourers.

"Well get on with it, I don't have all day," he discourteously declared.

At this instruction, the men gripped the rope that was attached to the pulley mechanism which was situated above the first Sarcophagus and pulled. The immense weight of each Sarcophagus lid expressed itself upon the faces of the labourers as they endeavoured to winch the stone slabs from their eternal resting place. There was the slight sound of the infusion of air, then a gentle fragrance of spices and embalming fluids escaped into the surrounding atmosphere.

Sir Henry physically gagged, demonstrating his weak constitution. Not wishing to appear physically fragile in front of his audience, he then bellowed at the workmen to raise the second sarcophagus lid. After their endeavours were fulfilled, both Abigail and Jonathan peered pensively at the lesser of the coffins inhabitants. There, before them, lay the almost perfectly preserved remains of an ancient mummy, its desiccated skin evident through the decaying bandages. Abigail smiled to herself, for she marvelled at the artistic endeavours of the ancient embalmers who had strived to preserve this body nearly 3000 years prior. Stepping a little closer she peered further into the sarcophagus, her eyes hungrily searching the remains that lay within, but they returned unrequited for the mummy appeared as though his entombment may have been undertaken in some haste.

"May I examine the body?" she tentatively enquired.

Sir Henry looked over to her and sneered.

"Do what you like with the high priest, I am to take the pharaoh into a private room and undertake my examination. I will leave you with Jonathan, who will support you in your theological endeavours," he stated dismissively.

"May I look at the pharaoh's body before you take him away?" she enquired.

"You may have a minute or two while I gather my thoughts," he pretentiously stated.

"Thank you," she replied as she walked over to the second, larger Sarcophagus.

THE MUMMY

There, she observed a body, meticulously wrapped in the finest linen bandages, the soft undulations of the body beneath its eternal casing were almost fresh in appearance and unnaturally deceiving, for they demonstrated the form of a newly deceased individual.

"Fascinating," she whispered. After a few moments the errors of discrepancy began to glaringly express themselves to her. And so, she turned and look back into the high priest's sarcophagus, an expression of dark curiosity gathering on her face.

"There is something wrong here," she declared.

Sir Henry turned and offered her a disparaging glance.

"In what way?" he sarcastically enquired.

Abigail turned and looked closely at the head of the mummy which rested in the high priests Sarcophagus. Peering up the nasal passage for a few moments, she stepped back and considered her options before stepping closer to the pharaoh's body and undertaking the same action.

"What are you doing you foolish girl?" Sir Henry demanded. "Your first day in my employment and your acting like a bewildered schoolgirl."

Abigail smiled.

"That may be so, but I am a bewildered schoolgirl with a theory," she professed.

A slight air of intrigue captured Sir Henry's interest and he thought for a brief moment before derisively responding.

"Pray tell, what you have surmised?" he enquired, looking to the ceiling, feigning disinterest.

Realising that her actions were being closely scrutinised, she lowered her tone and stood a little closer to Sir Henry, to court conjecture, as if they were together in an illicit confederation.

"If you look closely at the high priest, as I have just undertaken, there are two glaring discrepancies," she stated.

"And what are those?" Sir Henry bullishly enquired.

Realising that she had captured his interest, Abigail stepped a little closer to the smaller Sarcophagus and smiled. Pointing with her left hand she discussed the presenting situation appertaining to its desiccated inhabitant.

"This gentleman appears not to demonstrate any of the wounds inflicted upon a body during the process of embalming. I have looked up his nose and it appears that there is no evidence of a Trans-Nasal Craniotomy. Also if you look on the left side of the abdomen, there are no physical scars or incision which would denote the removal of any bodily organs. However, if we look at specimen number two," she said, while pointing with her right hand. "There is partial evidence of a Trans-Nasal Craniotomy and partial organ removal. Something which can be confirmed by the undertaking of an autopsy."

Sir Henry smirked.

"There will be no autopsy, you're here to observe and to catalogue your findings," he coldly stated. "Anything else?" he enquired rhetorically.

"One more thing," she interjected.

"Yes," he replied disdainfully.

"That is not a pharaoh," she declared, pointing to the inhabitant of the major sarcophagus.

Sir Henry let out a laboured and contemplative breath.

"And what makes you think that?" he coldly enquired.

"Sarcophagus one, belonging to the high priest, that mummy, has his arms situated across his chest, whereas mummy number two has them across his… err private parts, as denoting a high priest," she announced.

"All this from a barely out of university graduate," Sir Henry woefully declared. "God give me strength."

Turning to the porters he bellowed out his instructions.

"Take the primary Sarcophagus to the main examination room," turning to Abigail he sneered. "I'll leave you and the high priest here, to become a little better acquainted. Remember, no autopsy, and only look with your eyes, you may partially unwrap the bandages, but nothing more, and please ensure that you document all of your findings," he firmly instructed in a rather terse juvenile tone before leaving the room.

Johnathan looked at her and smirked.

"He seems a little more agreeable than usual, the arrival of the mummies must have cheered him up," he said sarcastically.

"More like, the only play-friend that he has is a corpse, is probably closer to the truth," Abigail replied flippantly.

"So what do you think of your first professional encounter of Sir Henry?" he enquired.

Reaching into the sarcophagus, Abigail lifted a tiny carved artefact and held it to the light.

"This isn't my first encounter with 'Sir up himself,'" she glibly replied. "He asked my parents for my hand in marriage about 10 years ago," she coldly declared. "Unbeknown to myself, or my parents, his father, Lord Walter had deemed that we were a suitable match and should be considered for marriage. Even though I had never met or heard of his son prior, and I perceive that my dowry was probably more attractive than I was to Lord Karvahill."

"How did he know of you?" he asked.

"I suppose through my father, who had a seat in the House of Lords, he and Walter were, shall we say political acquaintances. And, where my father is comfortable in his endeavours, Lord Walter is somewhat aspirational. Forever forging alliances and cultivating relationships. All in the name of the political and social advancement of his family's name. Whereas my parents, they were what you could define as 'old school.' They were comfortable in their own skin, they just accepted who they were and didn't really aspire to anything. More my father, and after my mother died, he became a little more reclusive and we spent many years together realising the worth of our relationship. All that would have been lost if either my mother or my father thought in a similar way to Lord Walter."

She smiled and looked at Johnathan.

"Don't worry, and I'm not speaking out of turn, but Sir Henry's reputation as a political and social lightweight precedes him. He has neither grace nor poise and has been rejected by over half of the suitable debutants and social butterflies of London. A good education can cover a multitude of sins, but it cannot conceal the discomfort experienced by any individual who is socially uncomfortable no matter how much they desire their aspired environment and yearn for it to become their natural surroundings, thus severing them from the shackles of their own dark history, and allowing them the subtle grace to belong. This form of social resolve could never occur to Sir Henry, for he comes from bad stock, he is driven by his own father's aspirations, and is as capricious and as light as the early morning dew. His own history follows him like a dark tide, which pollutes everyone his presence touches."

Johnathan smirked and looked at her with wide eyes.

"And you let him go?" he said with an air of dark sarcasm. "Just think of how fulfilled your life would have been now, ten years after your marriage?"

Abigail smirked.

"Within six months, he would have been on a mortuary slab, and I would have been swinging from the gallows at Tyburn,"

"You would have given the marriage that long?" Johnathan glibly interjected.

Abigail laughed.

"Keep this type of conversation going, Mr Pringle, and I can see that we may become very firm friends," she announced with a smile. "Now, be a darling and pass me a pair of scissors, I think that there are artefacts concealed below the bandages of our friend here, she stated, pointing into the sarcophagus."

Undertaking this as requested, Johnathan watched as Abigail skilfully transverse the outer layer of bandages and gripped the artefact with the prongs of the scissors, doing so she gently withdrew them into the artificial light of the room.

"Strange," she whispered.

"Why?" Johnathan enquired.

"These type of artefacts are generally secured within the wrappings close to the body with resin, they were intrinsic elements for the transition into the after-world." She held the scarab relic for a moment, before placing it on the edge of the sarcophagus. "This doesn't really make any sense." She said, placing a cautionary finger on her lip, as she contemplated her evidence.

"Please explain," Johnathan requested.

"Sorry, yes," she said with a smile. "Well, here we have a man who proclaims to be a high priest, yet his burial positioning denotes that he is of a higher, possibly royal cast. However, if you read the hieroglyphics that are painted on the inner part of his sarcophagus, they tell the tale of the high priest Nehi." She looked at Johnathan and smiled. "That doesn't really help us, as there were literally thousands of high priests throughout the history of Egypt, many of whom, we don't even have a name for. There was a high priest to Akhenaten who shared the same name, but that was the 18th Dynasty, and he died around 1336 B.C, long before this man was born." She scratched her head in dismay. "The problem is, most of the temples had inner temples, and they too had a specified high priest designated to that temple. So one temple could have twenty or more lesser high priests within its boundaries. And, as we are discovering, the ancient Egyptians worshiped thousands of deities, each one requiring a high priest. Each of these high priests were also regionalised and, so the conundrum unfolds."

"Wasn't this Akhenaten the pharaoh who brought in Mono-thingy-ism?" Jonathan enquired in a rather clumsy manner.

Abigail thought for a brief moment, then realised what he was endeavouring to highlight.

"Monotheism, you mean? The worship of a single deity," she highlighted.

"That's it," he urgently agreed.

"Well, yes and no," she stated. "It was very apparent in his court and those around his palaces, but to the general population of Egypt, they fervently adhered to their old ways. And it must be said, so did many of the high priests. After Akhenaten's death, everything reverted back to the old religion and it has remained that way ever since."

"Until now," he innocently interjected.

Abigail smiled.

"And has remained that way ever since," she reiterated.

Jonathan smirked to himself.

Observing this actions Abigail enquired as to the source of his amusement.

"Mono-thingy-ism," he stated with a smile. "I'm starting to sound like Sir Henry and his haphazard explanation of things."

"A lot of people aspire to be as haphazard as he is one day," Abigail stated.

"Like yourself?" Jonathan enquired, mockingly.

"Hardly," she stated. "I understand that I am newly qualified, but I am extensively read and without sounding overtly arrogant, I do perceive I may have forgotten much more than that buffoon will ever learn."

"Are you religious at all?" he enquired.

Abigail smiled.

"Hardly. To me, religion falls short when you request an answer to two simple words," she stated.

"Which are?" he enquired with a smile.

"Prove it!" she stated. "Modern religion is based upon the subjugation of women, enabled by the words recanted to a bigoted man, by an unseen deity floating on some ethereal cloud. All hokum and conjecture, something that doesn't require proof or foundation."

Looking back at the mummy she let out a long laborious breath, for it appeared that her task ahead was almost unfathomable.

"C'mon, back to work, we have a lot of exciting discoveries to experience," he said encouragingly, nodding to the mummy.

****

It was almost lunch time by the time that she had unwrapped the first superficial layer of bandages from the mummy, revealing an inner, more precise core of very high grate linen wrappings, something in itself which presented her with a conundrum.

'Why would they use such intricate embalming methods upon a high priest?' she thought.

Realising that fatigue was not conducive to an enquiring mind, she looked up at the clock on the cellar wall.

"I think we require a break for refreshments," she announced. "And because of your sterling work, I think we should discover a local tea shop and I will provide lunch, as a thank you."

"Although I don't generally accept invitations to lunch from young women, considering we are living in an age of enlightenment, and this morning your presence has not been anything but a total pleasure, I respectfully accept your delightful invitation. Please allow me to freshen up and wash my hands, and I will be with you in due course," he said as he picked up his jacket and left the cellar.

Looking at the clock on the far wall, Abigail smiled to herself.

'Why do they have a clock in a cellar?' she wondered.

Chapter 3.

Lucy's Tea Rooms were situated a little distance from the museum, there was adequate street signed in order to cultivate the trade from the passing tourists who frequented the attractions nearby. Although the trade was not bristling, it was however, apparent and Abigail and Jonathan partook of a table away from the hustle and bustle of the main throng of visitors. As they patiently waited for the tea and scones to be delivered, Abigail looked inquisitively about the room.

"Even though the museum is closed, this place appears very busy," she stated.

"I often come here," Jonathan stated. "If you get here just before noon and a little after one, you can generally get a seat and the waitress service is usually excellent," he stated with a broad smile.

As the tea and scones arrived, Johnathan sat forward in his chair and poured the tea and offered Abigail the first cup, he then directed her to the scones, and after pouring himself a cup of piping hot tea, he sat back in his chair.

"So, how do you think your first day is going?" he enquired.

"Well, we're only half way through and I must say that it's rather enthralling getting my hands on a real mummy," she said in excitement.

Johnathan smiled.

"Don't get too excited," Johnathan warned. "Sir Henry could be monitoring you. If you don't do exactly as he requests, he may reconsider your contract. What he doesn't tell new employees is that they have a two-month probationary period and if you fall below his desired expectations he would have no qualms in dismissing you without reference or recourse."

"Thank you for warning me," she whispered. "But why didn't you mention this earlier and stop me from getting so carried away unwrapping the mummy?"

Johnathan smiled as he sipped his tea.

"As with all places they have walls, and most walls have ears. Most of the employees within the Museum are indebted to him in some way shape or form, be it financially, emotionally or just plain fear. He is the type of individual who would foster friendship in order to attain information that could be either used against you or a member of your family, thus holding a bond to him far greater than any employment contract could legally undertake."

"And what does he have over you?" she enquired in curiosity.

"My father," Johnathan honestly replied.

Abigail looked at him with an air of confusion. Realising her predicament, he explained his compounding quandary.

"My father was the butler to Lord Karvahill and about three years ago he fell ill, while I was working away in France as an illustrator for a prominent magazine. Upon discovering my father's situation, I dutifully returned to England, and offered my father any support which I could physically or financially muster. Now initially, Lord Karvahill was generous and forthright, but I should have realised that he was a greater mirror image of his despicable son, and as events unfolded and the cost of treatment became compounded by the vast interest that his lordship levied upon the initial loans. My father's predicament grew until it was too much for him to endure and he passed away less than six months after my return. Being an honourable sort I upheld my father's debts to his lordship, knowing full well that he understood my admirable values and he has me working for his son, both day and night at a vastly reduced wage, thus making it almost impossible to clear my father's debts and ensuring that I remain within my own servile bondage."

"How much do you owe him? If it's not too impertinent to enquire?" Abigail sensitively asked.

Johnathan took a deep breath.

"Well, including the medical bills and the cost of the funeral and other outstanding debts that were owning to his lordship, I would say that I now owe him about fifty pounds."

Immediately realising that this amount of money represented very little to herself, she smiled and nodded without comment.

"I have managed to reduce this amount from one hundred Pounds over these past few years and feel that it will be obligation free from Lord Karvahill in about three years or so," he announced with an expression of glee.

"Do you have much more saved?" she enquired.

"I have about fifteen Pounds; I have only managed to amass this because I am living a very frugal life. An elderly relative allows me to remain in their home, without obligation or financial enumeration, for they understand my predicament all to well. I do offer some financial contribution to my upkeep, but generally he declines this with a smile and requests that I purchase a new shirt or tie, so that I may look a little smarter while within my work."

"Isn't it strange," she highlighted. "If I were to take you on face value upon our initial meeting this morning. I would have perceived that you were living in the lap of luxury. Well dressed and travelling in an excellent Rolls Royce motor vehicle."

"All of this belongs to Sir Henry," he said pointing to his suit. "And I fear that I was impressed to wear this to affect yourself."

"Me, in what way?" she asked.

"Sir Henry wanted to impress you and put you in your place. He was nervous about your employment and in reality wanted to distance himself from you. After you informing me of your rejection of marriage all those years ago, I can now understand why," he said.

"But he gave me the job," she stated in dismay.

Johnathan smiled and shook his head.

"Was Sir Henry there at the time of your interview?" he asked.

Recalling those events, Abigail shook her head.

"Come to think of it, no he wasn't," she stated.

"There were three eminent professors and a member of the board for the museum. Those professors were from Oxford, Cambridge and Durham, and they knew of your reputation and how you excelled in your studies. You were the best candidate by far. However, Sir Henry endeavoured to quash your engagement, and it was only through his father's intervention that your position was truly secured, that and the insistence of the interview board."

Johnathan smiled.

"Which is why Sir Henry is so ghastly to you. In his feeble mind he perceived that if he continues with his bitter campaign against you, a meek and feeble woman, you will buckle under his attrition and leave of your own volition, thus justifying his initial misgiving related to your employment."

"Why are you telling me this now?" she cautiously enquired.

"I suppose for selfish reasons," he declared. "I can see that you are a genuine and learned individual who would make a strong ally and friend. Something I could do with at present. I am spending too much time in Sir Henry's viperous company and I feel that he is draining all the humanity from my bones. He even asked me to befriend you and relay any salacious information you may divulge back to him, so that he may amass any scandal against you."

Abigail laughed.

"I only wish that I had some to convey. My life consists of work and home, I have no suitors or interest in that way and I spend my evenings dutifully with my father," she announced.

Placing her cup back onto its bone-china saucer she looked Johnathan directly into the eyes.

"More to the point, why did Lord Walter intervene?"

"Well, after our conversation earlier I can only surmise one thing. As no other woman in London would consider being in his company, let alone become betrothed to him, the only other viable option is yourself. Maybe he feels that a war of attrition between you both will break down the walls of your displeasure and you may become fond of his son's acidic nature," he surmised.

"I think you have more chance of witnessing a man walk on the moon, than observing those events which you have described," she coldly stated. After a short period of consideration, she offered her newfound friend a long purposeful smile.

"What is it?" he enquired.

"Cat and mouse," she replied. "We could play both Sir Henry and his father at their own game," she said with a wicked glint in her eye. "But I'm not saying if I am the cat or the mouse," she stated.

Johnathan laughed.

"Whatever you do, it will only be a fraction of what both he and his father deserve. I have shed enough tears over those people in my time in their employ, to last an eternity."

"I don't understand, has their intervention been that bad?"

"Yes," he replied as his emotions began to rise. "It strange, only the other night, my uncle, in his own simple way, tried to console me against those dark emotions that were rising within, and it is only now that I understand what he was endeavouring to do. He told me a joke that his neighbour's granddaughter told him that morning, and I must say that upon initial hearing it I laughed heartily. He then repeated that very same joke and I laughed again, but not a vehemently. He then repeated the joke and after a while I asked him why he was undertaking such a futile gesture. And, he replied to me 'If you cannot laugh at the same joke over and over again, why do you constantly cry at those people who you know will endeavour to hurt you over and over again? You're expecting that emotional attrition, you understand the damage that it will do, both mentally and emotionally, and you're waiting for their dark justification in relation to their own sinister deeds that deeply bruise your already spent emotions, but still you find their action deplorable and anathema to their previous conduct. Yet, you still allow it to occur, for you are in fear of that which we do not know. You still blame yourself for the malicious actions of another. How many times have you heard the phrase, 'Better the devil you know? In my case, I know that devil only too well."

Taking his father's fob watch from his pocket he smiled and looked at Abigail.

"We have about 30 minutes left to enjoy these cream scones, before we must return to the museum. Sir Henry is a stickler for time keeping."

Lifting a scone from the cake stand before her, Abigail smiled.

"Then we won't disappoint him, will we?" she said, as she thrust the over encumbered scone into her mouth.

Chapter 4.

By the time they had returned to the museum it was almost one p.m. Even though it was early afternoon, the winter skies were already darkening as the clouds gathered overhead foretelling a portent of snow and a dramatic drop in an already chilly temperature.

Abigail and Jonathan crept into the museum's main entrance and made their way cautiously down to the cellar. There, they discovered everything as it should be, undisturbed from the time that they left. Within moments of their arrival the door swung urgently open and Sir Henry briskly stumbled into the room.

"These administrators are the bane of my life, with their penny pinching cut backs and their desire to draw more patrons into the museum," he decreed.

"Is everything alright?" Abigail enquired in a, none committal tone.

"Oh, I don't know why I bother," he blustered on, "I'm endeavouring to bring these Egyptian attractions to the museum, in the wake of Lord Carnarvon's fabulous discoveries, and all those mealy-mouthed pen-pushers can do is scream at me that I have gone way over budget," he declared as he peered into the sarcophagus.

"I'm pleased that you haven't butchered our specimen," he said. "Please, until further notice only catalogue your findings, no more unwrapping. There are whispers that those bureaucratic nincompoops who manage the finances of this Museum are considering returning one of these specimens and have left it to me to decide which one, so the less physical interfering the better."

"That would be a little difficult if we have both begun our investigation," Abigail stated.

Sir Henry shook his head in despair.

"And when would I find time to undertake my investigation? When I have spent all of this morning looking over accounts and invoice slips, and arguing with the uneducated and buffoons of this world."

He allowed his temper to subside and gathered his thoughts.

"No, today has been too much to endure, I will call it a day and meet my father as his club and discuss a possible solution to this presenting issue. You may remain here for as long as you wish," he said looking directly at Abigail. "You may leave when you desire, when you do, ensure that the lid to the sarcophagus is placed back on top to warrant the mummy's safety; if you require support, there are several workers within the building who are to remain here overnight guarding our precious artefacts, and also Pringle will remain with you until you leave," he said looking at Johnathan.

Turning, he quickly exited the cellar without a bye-your-leave, leaving a static atmosphere hanging in his wake.

"Is he always this charming?" Abigail mischievously enquired.

"No there are times when he can be particularly nasty," Johnathan mockingly stated.

Walking over to the Sarcophagus, he looked down at the desiccated remains that lay within.

"Well, it doesn't look like you'll be doing anymore investigations today," he highlighted.

Abigail looked a little pensive, but then after a brief moment an expression denoting devilment swept across her face.

"I wouldn't be so sure," she calmly stated. "As my mother used to say, 'there's more than one way to skin a cat,'" she declared. "The only problem is, and I don't think you're going to like this, I need you to get up close and personal with our friend the mummy," she said looking down at the high priest.

"I don't think I'm going to like what you're about to suggest, but fire away," he said in a rather pensive tone.

"Well, I can't look at the mummy in any great detail, but I can look at what is written within the sarcophagus," she said with a smile.

"Right, well that's a good idea," Johnathan stated innocently.

"The only thing is," she continued, "I need you to stand over the mummy and lift him out while I read the hieroglyphics scribed beneath him."

Johnathan smiled nervously at Abigail, as his mind turned in turmoil.

"Let me get this straight, what you want me to do is, stand over the coffin and lift out the corpse, while you read those scribblings?"

"Yes," she cautiously announced.

"Really? And you don't think that any part of what your requesting is slightly creepy?" he enquired.

Abigail shook her head and smiled submissively.

"No, why would it be? We've been asked to undertake and investigation and that's what we're going to do."

An expression of great distain washed across his face.

"No," he highlighted. "*You're* being asked to undertake an investigation; *I'm* being asked to cuddle a corpse."

"Oh, don't be foolish, he's over three thousand years old," she glibly professed.

"Oh, and tell me, how does a great age make him any less of a corpse?" he asked.

Dismissing his objections, more in fear of his refusal than arrogant supposition, she encouraged him to participate.

"Come on, take that jacket off and put on one of those warehouse aprons, and well get started," she instructed, turning to look back into the sarcophagus, shielding her emotional eyes away from Johnathan's displeasure. After a moment or two she looked over to where Johnathan stood and to her delight he was wearing the aforementioned garb. Smiling, she beckoned for him to move closer.

"What I require from yourself is for you to lean into the sarcophagus and slip your fingers beneath the mummy; as you do so, gently lift him towards yourself, allowing enough purchase for me to observe the hieroglyphics etched beneath," she instructed.

Johnathan shook his head in disbelief.

"How long have we known each other?" he enquired. "And you're already testing our friendship," he stated with a contemplative smirk. "I think both Sir Henry and I have underestimated you, I get the impression that the days are going to be eventful and no two shall be the same."

Abigail smirked.

"Perish the thought, that any day of my life could be construed as mundane?" she stated with smile.

"Can you read these pictures?" he asked, nodding towards the images that were painted on the inner sides of the sarcophagus.

"Fluently," she replied. "I've always had a strong interest in ancient Egyptian archaeology, I got if from my mother. She was a very learned individual, who took an interest in her own education, but also in that of those around them.

"So, what do they say?" he asked.

Peering into the sarcophagus, Abigail allowed her mind a little time to decipher the pictorial language, before she answered.

"Well from what I can read," she began looking back at Johnathan, "because the mummy is concealing a majority of the hieroglyphics, there are several prayers to the god of the dead, Osiris, and also the god of mummification Anubis. Requesting safe passage into the afterlife and also extoling the fact that this was a just and honest man, high priest to the god Sekhmet." She looked up to her companion. "He was the god of destruction. The denotation of a lion's head can be used to describe him." Looking back at the hieroglyphics she paused as an expression of curiosity gathered in her features.

Realising that there was some confusion, Johnathan asked of her displeasure.

"Is there something wrong?"

"Yes, these hieroglyphics were meant to be read in continuity, if there were pieces missing, or they were deliberately defaced, their potency or true meaning was lost," she highlighted.

Johnathan peered into the sarcophagus, his eyes searching the shadows that concealed the edges of the coffin.

"Two seconds," he stated as he released his grip on the side of the casket and walked over to the far corner of the cellar, returning, he demonstrated to Abigail that he was in fact holding a torch. Turning it on, he shone the light into the sarcophagus, illuminating the hieroglyphics.

"There's a small section that's been defaced," he said, as his eyes fell upon the area that appeared to have been deliberately vandalised.

"Why would they do that?" he asked.

Abigail shook her head.

"Either this was not the inhabitant's intended coffin, or it was as a mark of damnation," she explained.

"What do you mean?" he asked.

"Well, the rationale for mummification to the ancient Egyptians is for your body and your name to remain for an eternity, if not, then you are wiped from the pages of history, and time itself," she explained.

Johnathan appeared perplexed for a brief moment.

"Doesn't that equate to what you were endeavouring to highlight to Sir Henry this morning?" he asked.

Realising that he hadn't fully elucidated his premise, he continued.

"When you were saying that this chap," he highlighted, pointing into the sarcophagus, "was in fact, a pharaoh."

"My sentiments exactly," she stated with a smile, "The plot grows thicker and thicker. How utterly intriguing."

Johnathan stepped forward and leant precariously into the coffin, looking at Abigail as he did so.

"So you want me to wrap my arms around this mummy and lift him out of the coffin?" he asked.

"No, not out of the coffin, just about six or so inches above, so that I can read what is written below his body," she instructed.

Johnathan grimaced and lowered his hands around the body.

"You have 30 seconds, that's all, so I suggest you read quickly," he announced.

"A minute, and I'll buy you lunch tomorrow," she said with a churlish smile.

Johnathan bit his bottom lip.

"One minute and I'm counting," he firmly stated, turning his head and looking directly at the minute hand that moved slowly around the face of the cellar clock.

"Go!" he cried, as he embraced the mummy and lifted its decayed frame from the sarcophagus.

THE MUMMY

Immediately, Abigail's lowered her head and shone the torch onto the back of the sarcophagus, her eyes frantically searching the hieroglyphics that were beautifully depicted on the polished wood of the casket. Her lips moved as she read the inscription back to herself over and over again, as a memory aide.

Johnathan could smell the sweet acrid presence of the ancient embalming fluid that was now as hard and as strident as stone. He closed his eyes in disbelief as the mummy's face was only a few mere inches from his own, and its very presence caused him a great deal of personal discomfort. Opening his eyes, he looked back at the cellar clock, a mere 30 seconds had passed. Imbibing a deep breath, he closed his eyes once again, praying for time to accelerate and liberate him from this archaeological injustice.

Abigail shook her head in confusion, although she could fluently read the hieroglyphics before her, she came to a section whose presence brought misunderstanding, for their occurrence was not conducive to the correct justification or structure of the depiction. Touching the surface of the casket, she allowed her fingers to gently glide upon the polished wooden surface, this they undertook freely, until it came into contact with the unnatural inscription. There, they came into contact with a rough peculiarity on the surface that was neither natural nor apparent. She allowed her finger tips to rest for a moment as she contemplated her next action, this was compounded by Johnathan braking the uncomfortable silence with his words.

"You have ten seconds remaining," he whispered uneasily from the side of his mouth.

This caused her to shudder in surprise, as her fingers pressed down upon the surface of the casket. This action, although insignificant, caused a small panel of wood to fall open from the case and reveal a slight inconsequential roll of papyrus, neat and compact in its constitution. Reaching forward, she gathered it in her fingers and withdrew if from the sarcophagus. At that moment the door to the cellar opened and Sir Henry marched uncompromisingly into the room. Observing Johnathan in his necromantic embrace, he bellowed angrily at him.

"What are you doing you foolish imbecile?" he screamed. "Put that body down, it's worth ten years of your wages you inbred moron," he raged.

Johnathan patiently lowered the mummy back into the coffin and stood firmly, staring at Sir Henry.

"I'm sorry," Abigail began, but her words were stemmed by Johnathan's explanation.

"It's my fault Sir Henry, I noticed that there were inscriptions on the back of the inside of the coffin, and I lifted the mummy out without informing Miss Abigail of my intentions, thinking that it would afford her a little time so that she may decipher them."

Sir Henry shook his head in dismay.

"I don't employ you to think," he screamed before turning his attention to Abigail. "I was returning to inform you that they're locking the doors to the museum, so I suggest you both make it an early finish. But after this misconduct, I have half a mind to leave you both in here overnight as penance," he decreed.

Placing her hand discreetly into her pocket, Abigail turned to Sir Henry and smiled.

"How very gallant of you, allowing us to leave so early. My father will be pleased," she stated, knowing full well how Sir Henry's father had endeavoured to ingratiate himself upon her own father's goodwill on a myriad of occasions.

Sir Henry smiled.

"Take your belongings and leave, both of you, but I expect you to be here all the earlier tomorrow, we have plenty of work to do."

Johnathan took off his apron and put on his jacket.

"I'll walk you to the bus stop," he said.

Smiling, Abigail gathered her belongings and took hold of his arm.

"Always the gentleman," she stated, as they both exited the room.

Turning off the light, Sir Henry shook his head in disbelief and walked out of the door, leaving the room to become invaded by the shadows and darkness.

As they stepped from the museum, the winter skies were heavy and foreboding, foretelling of an ill-temperate downpour that was imminently waiting upon the horizon.

Turning to Johnathan, Abigail offered him a warm smile.

"Thank you for covering for me," she said.

Johnathan smirked.

"Don't worry, it's all in a day's work under the employment of Sir Henry. By tomorrow he will be tormented by another catastrophic all-ensuing incident in his insignificant life, and the traumas of yesterday will all be forgotten, only to be replaced with another suffrage that drives his dark ignorance."

"You really don't have that much respect for him do you?" she enquired.

Johnathan smiled.

"More than he deserves. I suppose the only respect I can give him is the freedom he allows me while under his employment. He's so self-absorbed, as is the same with his father, that the mice pretty much run the empire while the cats sit and preen themselves."

"Which is how it has always been within this world," she replied.

"Did you discover anything exciting?" he asked.

Abigail looked at him in confusion.

Realising her dilemma, Johnathan elucidated.

"When you were reading the hieroglyphics?"

Abigail smiled.

"Let's just say, I'll tell you tomorrow."

Leaning over, she placed a deserving gentle kiss upon his cheek and offered him a farewell smile.

"I'm going to meet my father at the Dorchester, now remember what Sir Henry said. He wants us here bright and early tomorrow morning," she mockingly stated. "I'll meet you here, on the steps at about 8a.m.," she highlighted, as she turned and was immediately lost in the throng of pedestrians that littered the streets outside of the museum.

Chapter 5.

Most of the evening had almost fallen by the time Abigail had situated herself in the drawing room of her home. The lamps were already lit and the room was bathed in a soft reassuring glow against the cold air of winter's embrace. Understanding the dark ramifications of her previous larcenous actions, Abigail lifted the small, tightly rolled papyrus from her pocket and placed it gently upon the desk at which she sat. Gently holding the edge, she allowed her finger to push the main body of the papyrus roll, until it gently unfurled, revealing the hieroglyphics scribed masterfully upon the ancient documents surface. Drawing the light of the lamp a little closer, she marvelled, as her eyes searched the writing that befell her anticipatory vision. For there, bathed in the soft artificial light of this modern illumination, rested a spell of incantation that had not been observed in its magnificent splendour for almost three thousand years. Abigail pulled her chair a little closer, gathered herself nearer the desk. Her heart quickening in her chest as the steady rhythm of excitement filled her soul. She took a deep breath, as she began to decipher the illustrations that were presented to her modern eyes. Initially, her senses were confused by their dark connotation. However, as she contemplated their construction reoccurring in her mind, the clarity of their meaning began to dispel the confusion that she initially encountered upon her primary examination.

"What have we here?" she whispered to herself, as she placed an inquisitive finger at the base of the papyrus strip and moved it slowly under each of the denoted hieroglyphs, as she endeavoured to decipher each of their meanings as individual phrases and then decode their meaning in conjunction with their neighbouring provincial axiom.

Taking a silver retractable pencil and a sheet of paper from the draw of the desk, she scribbled a number of possible solutions to the first and initial conundrum that presented itself to her.

"What are you endeavouring to tell me?" she whispered inquisitively to herself. "This looks like Horus, and the symbol for protection. So I would surmise that we are requesting the god of the underworld and the dead to offer us protection," she deduced.

She then shook her head.

"But that doesn't make sense, for the following cartouche gives a name. So are they asking for protections for this person named here?" she asked herself.

She sat back in the chair.

"First of all, before I go any further. Who is this asking protection for? I need to decipher this cartouche and discover the name of the person who this spell is protecting," she said.

Standing from the chair she walked over to the substantial bookcases that sat in the alcoves on either side of the fire surround, the gentle glow of the fire's flames offering a soft colour to her complexion. After a moment she retrieved her desired book and walked back to her chair and sat back at the desk. Flicking through the small volume, she turned to the texts that was appertaining to her desire quest. Studying the pages for a few moments she placed the book onto the desk's surface and returned her attention back to the hieroglyphics.

"So why would a high priest have a spell of protection in his sarcophagus?" she said, mulling over her predicament.

"Has this man done something that angered the spirits or the gods?" she asked herself.

Shaking her head, she returned her attention back to the papyrus.

"Protect me, Anubis!" she whispered.

Taking a deep breath, she contemplated her words.

"Anubis wouldn't offer protection. He was the god of the underworld and of embalming."

She paused and thought a little deeper.

"Where is the name Anubis derived? Well, if I am to understand my studies, it is derived, or have the same root as the word for royal child, which is 'Inpu.' Does this mean that the chap in the casket is a royal child?" She surmised to herself. "That can be so, but the word 'Inp' is related to the meaning of decay, which then attributes it to Anubis. So I'm going in a circle. But once he was adopted by the son of the king, Osiris, his name then became 'Imy-ut,' meaning, 'he who is in the place of embalming.'

"Is that right?" she enquired of herself out loud.

Lifting the pencil and paper she scribbled on it with ferocity, speaking as she undertook these actions.

Anubis was the patron of lost souls, the patron of funeral rites, guarding of the underworld, and measurer of hearts. He was also associated with the Eye of Horus who acted as a guide to the dead and aided Osiris."

She threw the pencil and paper on the desk and buried her head in her hands as confusion gripped her.

"Think! Think," she cried to herself, "It's staring you in the face, find the pattern, the rhythm, once you have discovered that, the rest will flow naturally.

Looking back at the papyrus she smiled to herself and began to read the inscription.

"O' God Anubis protect me?" she paused, as realisation struck her.

"No, that's incorrect. It says 'My God Anubis deliver me'," she whispered as her eyes read the hieroglyphics further, "Bring me back from the darkness of the underworld and allow my mortal form, to once again feel the natural earth below my feet."

Abigail sat back in the chair.

"This isn't a spell of protection, this appears to be a spell of life," she stated to herself.

Allowing her eyes to cast briefly over the papyrus, she continued with her decoding of this ancient enigma.

"So how can I decipher this conundrum?" she enquired of herself, as she endeavoured to read a little further.

"The head of the great bull is severed. Npnw-snake, I say this about you! God-expelling scorpion, I say this about you. You have not gone away dead, but you have gone away alive. Sit on Osiris's chair, with your baton in your arm, and govern the living, and govern those of the remote places."

She continued to read the hieroglyphics until she skilfully concluded the incantation. Sitting back in her chair, she let out a laboured breath and closed her eyes. At that very moment there was an uncomfortable lull in the air and the atmosphere changed to an unnatural hew. Opening her eyes, Abigail looked pensively about the room, as the whisper of a wind began to gather in the ether. The light from the oil lamps began to flicker as their essence was gathered in a gentle bluster of unnatural air. Moments later and unearthly stillness permeated the atmosphere.

Allowing the Papyrus to naturally gather itself into its original position, Abigail lifted it from the desk and placed in gently into her coat pocket, which was hanging over the back of the chair in which she sat. Turning, she looked at the long case clock that stood in the corner of the room, the time it dictated was 9:43. p.m.

"Well if I'm to start early, I should retire to bed and be all the fresher for the morning," she said to herself, as she stood from the chair and walked over to the first lamp, extinguishing the flame she cast the room into partial darkness. Turning to the final lamp, she repeated the task and made her way to her room with aspirations of uneventful slumber.

Chapter 6.

It was almost 7:30 a.m. by the time that Abigail reached the steps of the museum, there she discovered Johnathan waiting in dark anticipation. Recognising the concern etched upon his face she asked him directly of his concerns.

"Is everything alright?" she anxiously enquired.

"There's been a burglary in the museum, it must have occurred last night around about 10p.m. The guards are being questioned by the police and Sir Henry isn't a happy chap. He's been thundering around screaming at everyone. I thought I'd meet you at the door so that you may fortify yourself for the interrogation that is surely about to ensue."

"A burglary," she said, as her hand moved slowly to the pocket that contained the papyrus.

"Yes," he confirmed. "One of the mummies has been stolen."

Abigail looked at him in confusion.

"Who would want to steal a mummy?"

"You'll be amazed," he replied. "Ever since Howard Carter's discovery in 1922, mummy fever has swept across Europe and it shows little sign of abating."

"Do you think that a fellow museum has instigated this theft?" she asked.

"Either that, or a private collector," he speculated.

"What sort of mood is Sir Henry in?" she enquired.

"A little sourer than normal," Johnathan replied.

"I bet he wants to see me, as I was the last person to see the mummy," she stated.

Johnathan shook his head.

"It wasn't that high priest's mummy that was taken, it was the pharaoh's," he said.

"Did they take everything? The sarcophagus can be worth more than the mummy," she highlighted.

"No, that's the strange thing about it. The lid was upended and thrown haphazardly about the room, and there is evidence of the body being dragged across the floor and out through the door, which was shattered in the thief's exit. It was this noise that alerted the caretaker to the incident," he explained.

"I think we should go in, after all, the police will want to question us," she said as she walked slowly up the steps.

"I have already given my statement," Johnathan highlighted.

"Well I have nothing to fear, I was with my father at the Dorchester, and there were plenty of eminent witnesses who would vouch for my presence until 8: 00p.m., and my father and I took a cab home and were ensconced within thirty minutes of leaving," she stated.

Opening the door for Abigail, Johnathan offered her a reassuring smile.

"I think that the police have come to the same conclusion as Sir Henry, it was a gang of thieves sent to procure one of the mummies for a rival museum."

I don't understand," she said, pausing at the entrance. "Why didn't they take the sarcophagus as well?"

Johnathan smiled.

"Surely the sarcophagus can be identified, whereas a mummy is simply a mummy," he surmised.

Abigail offered him a smile.

"Good point of deduction and lateral thinking, you could be a contemporary to Sherlock Holmes, if you continue like this," she jovially stated, as she walked into the dense melancholy atmosphere of the museum's main hallway.

Observing Henry a few yards along the corridor, she turned to Johnathan and winked. Then, without hesitation she rushed over to Sir Henry's side, flustered in her approach.

"Henry, are you alright?" she enquired feigning her concern. "Johnathan has just informed me of the theft, you must be devastated?" she stated, as she gripped onto his arm. "Oh, the thought of someone nefarious coming into the museum after dark scares me. It sends a shiver down my very spine."

THE MUMMY

Unencumbered by her dark sarcasm, Henry placed a comforting arm around Abigail and looked directly at Johnathan.

"I don't want you to leave Lady Cornwall's side, if she goes to lunch I want you to accompany her, when she leaves, you leave. Am I making myself clear?" he sternly enquired.

Stemming his amusement, Johnathan pursed his lips and nodded to Sir Henry.

Turning to Abigail, Sir Henry offered her a rakish smile.

"Do you think that you should be in here today? I won't mind if you go home."

"No, I think if I continue with my work, it will take my mind off these harrowing events, and if Johnathan is with me then I don't think that I'll worry as much, whereas, if I were at home, it would make it more difficult for me to return tomorrow," she modestly stated.

"Maybe you're right," Sir Henry replied. "Ask the porters to move your mummy onto one of the rooms on this level, where there's more natural light and you're closer to me if you require any academic assistance. There's a perfect room at the corner of the building, it has windows on two side, and a line of windows looking into the corridor, that should offer you a little reassurance."

"Thank you," she replied, as she released herself from his gip and walked slowly along the corridor.

Observing her departure, Sir Henry looked at Johnathan and urged him to follow.

As he drew level with Abigail, Johnathan turned and smirked at her.

"That was a good performance," he stated with a smirk.

"Three years in my university's dramatic society, and an outstanding performance as Ophelia, as highlighted in the Cambridge Gazette, 1919," she highlighted, "And this now means that you have my company for the foreseeable future."

"And for that my lady, I am eternally grateful," he replied. "Why did you react to him like that?"

"You catch more flies with sugar than you do vinegar, and I don't think I want to make an enemy of Henry. He's an imbecile, but he's also a dangerous imbecile, and that's the worst kind. He's very much a loose cannon, riding upon his own erratic emotions and making snap decisions without considering the consequences. There's an old axiom, 'keep your friends close, and your enemies even closer.' Henry lives off power, most simple-minded fools do. If he thinks he is in a position of power, he is happy, and probably going to be more compliant. Last thing I want is for him to put me into some other part of the museum cataloguing insects for the next twenty years. This is where I want to be, and I intend to remain here for as long as is safely possible. Or until a better offer comes along," she stated.

"I agree, but I also have a word to the wise. I have known Sir Henry for some considerable time now, and he is not as foolish as others would purvey," Johnathan stated. "Yes, he is childish and headstrong, but he also has many of his father's cunning attributes. He is a reasonable businessman and is able to manipulate a situation to his own devises without consideration or effort. If you are going to play him at his own game, I would suggest that you take into mind that he would be a difficult storm to ride and at the end of it, you may not be in any physical or emotional state to celebrate your victory."

Abigail contemplated his words.

"I understand," she said, "but I will not allow him to walk all over me, I am more of an archaeologist that he will ever be, and I will stand by my principles as long as there is breath in my body," she declared.

"A very amicable consideration, but please be careful, I have seen him in his most tempestuous of rages, and it is not a pretty sight to behold, and those on the receiving end of his dark judgement have been both physically and emotionally scarred by that experience," Johnathan cautioned.

"Thank you, your caution it is taken dually into consideration, and I respect you for your honesty," she replied. "I think we should go into the cellar and direct the porters in their endeavours," she directed.

****

It had taken the porters almost an hour to relocate the sarcophagus into a new, more enlightened room. Admittedly it remained at the rear of the building, but its illumination was blessed with natural uncomplicated light that flooded in from the large majestic windows that ran the full length of the outer wall that faced the streets of

THE MUMMY

London. In that time, the police interviewed Abigail for a mere ten minutes before they continued with their hunt for the missing mummy, leaving her to return to her own investigations.

As Johnathan busied himself at the far end of the room Abigail looked pensively at the mummy that rested majestically in the casket before her, her mind turned over Johnathan's previous words.

"May I ask you a question?" she enquired of her friend.

Johnathan turned and offered her a broad smile.

"Anything you like," he replied.

"When we were talking previously and you highlighted that Henry could express dark judgements, were you hinting that he was physically abusive towards his previous fiancée?" she thoughtfully enquired.

Johnathan took a deep and purposeful breath before he replied.

"Let's just say that Sir Henry has been engaged so many times, Garrard's had a designated goldsmith in permanent employment to furnish his proposal requirements. His relationships do not last long and are becoming more infrequent as his dark history follows him like a bad odour rising up from the Thames. The problem is, he doesn't take into consideration that his social circles, although vast in his eyes, are quite élite, and so gossip, among other things, spreads like wildfire. You above all others should realise this, for you are higher born than even any of Sir Henry's aspirations."

Abigail smiled.

"Unfortunately, not so. After my mother's passing, I was no longer enthralled by the glamor and glitter of being a socialite. I perceived those who were enticed by its glare as being vacuous, shimmering butterflies that were too delicate to be touched, but too conspicuous to be ignored, and that was not a true reflection of who I was." She laughed lightly to herself. "My father used to say to me that the gas lamps used to go out more than I did, and I suppose he was right. Then my studies took over and I realised that the only way that I could discover myself, was by myself and not as part of someone else's needs."

"And, have you discovered yourself?" he enquired.

"As best as could be expected, and a little more than desired," she stated.

Turning, she looked directly at Johnathan.

"And what about you?" she asked.

Johnathan churlishly smirked as the pallor of his face darkened.

"Me!" he stated, as he let out a long arduous breath, as he endeavoured to conceal his embarrassment.

"Now there lies a dark tale," he began. "I was married and had a child, she was less than three years old when the good Lord decided to take her, and in doing so, compelled my wife to take her own life in order to join her. Which is why I returned to my father, all those years ago, and I have had little experience of the fairer sex since. I concur with you in relation to the complexities of others. Managing their emotions when you can barely manage your own. Although the single life is not of my wanting, it is practical, and suits me for the time, I feel that after I have paid back Sir Henry's father, my own father's debt, then I will be able to view the world with less cynical eyes."

"Do you have any idea where you will go?" she asked.

"As far away from London and the Karvahill family as I can physically get," he firmly replied.

Abigail smiled.

"I think that by the time I have finish the investigation into this mummy, I too will probably feel the same way," she declared.

Turning, she looked out of the windows and could feel her darkening mood immediately lift.

"Oh, look! It's snowing, how I love the snow," she stated. "Most people love the spring and summer when all of the flowers and buds come to life, but I prefer the autumn and winter, because you truly feel alive. The dark night's closing in and the lamps on in the drawing room, with the curtains drawn. Cosy and tranquil."

"You must be a big fan of Christmas," Johnathan surmised.

"Not particularly," she replied. "I think this Dickensian view of Christmas is neither endearing nor socially aware. This time of year can conceal some of the most difficult and emotionally enduring times, and for some people a true unending financial encumbrance. Some families never break the bond of the previous festive financial commitment and compound their burden tenfold, just to ensure that their families have festivities that people like myself could take for granted."

"What do you do at Christmas time? How do you celebrate?" he asked.

"Together," she replied. "That to me is one of lives most precious of gifts. After losing my mother, it forced me to realise the value of our mortal existence. Up until that point, I had never lost a single person in my life. By the time I was born some of my grandparents were already dead, so I did not know of their love, but to me, my life was comfortable, and I did not mix in the lower echelons of London's society."

"So how did you attain your highly apparent social conscience?" he enquired.

Abigail smiled.

"Once again, my mother," she stated. "I think I was going through that stage of becoming a precocious brat at around the age of thirteen. Demanding new dresses and to be taken to the most prestigious of social gatherings. When one day, out of the blue, my mother announced that I wasn't going to attend school and I was going to support her in a few errands. The thought of missing a day's school filled me with glee, an emotion that soon left me for some considerable time. The memories of that trip which we undertook haunt me to this very day. I didn't understand much of my mother's life, as a child I just viewed her as an extension of myself. Someone who was there when I woke in the morning and someone who was there when I closed my eyes at night." She paused for a moment as her emotions began to rise. "You can understand how difficult that emotion is when it is no longer being comforted by that all too mundane, yet beautiful sight? How we take our lives for granted. These precious fleeting moments that culminate in our brief existence, terminating in the memories of others."

"Losing your mother must have been one of the most difficult things for you to endure," Johnathan sympathetically stated.

"It was, but I also feel blessed, for I knew her company, her grace and her fortitude. She had all of those attributes that I aspire to attain," she said.

"I think she'd be very proud of you," he said with an air of genuine compassion.

"Thank you," she whispered.

As her emotions welled, Abigail, lifted the back of her hand to her mouth to quell their rising before she continued.

"My mother was more than a mother; she was a social saint. Unbeknown to myself, or my father, she would work in the poorest parts of London, helping the hungry and the needy. She has a considerable income, which was bequeathed to her by her own parents following their death. And she utilised this to facilitate education and food distribution to the penurious of this affluent city. She had a true heart of gold. And when she took me, on that fateful day, to visit the rundown slums and workhouses, and the makeshift hospitals and schools, she changed my life eternally. For not only did she give me focus, but she also gave me an understanding of my own social position. She made me realise, through actions, rather than words, that every society has an underclass and if you ever perceive yourself as living in that underclass you are deluding yourself, for mark-my-words, there will always be someone worse off than yourself, that you can take as a guarantee. Look at Henry, arrogance is a blinding attribute to hold so close to your heart. Many of those people I have encountered on that day and subsequently, were noble and honourable people, fettered by the chains of social injustice and lowly birth. They were driven by one desire, to rise above their fateful contradiction and attain a standing of honour and pride in this life. Attributes which were bestowed by mere birth upon Henry, yet he frittered and denounced them as surely as he denounced his own heart. I realised a long time ago, as I have encountered many Sir Henrys in my time at university, that beneath that strong arrogant exterior, is a weak and broken man, who, when times are tough, runs back to the stalwart foundation from which he was honed, his father, another arrogant individual, who perceives himself as being better than his fellow man. Where in fact his fingers are bleeding and his knees are scrapped to the bone, from all of his social climbing; however, he is too ignorant to realise that if he were to look down, he would understand that in all of his years as a social interloper, he has in fact, risen only a breath above his initial preliminary position."

She laughed lightly.

THE MUMMY

"Nothing can be as cruel as your own imperfections."

"It's strange how much influence our parents have upon us," Johnathan highlighted, "When my daughter was born, my fatherly experiences were completely different depending upon whose company I was in, be it my mother's or my father's. I had always had an excellent relationship with my father and his influence was always calming, so I was able to make good decisions. But my mother was a completely different creature, she criticised everything that I did, so eventually I overthought the whole situation and I would end up making mistakes. It confused both my wife and myself to such a degree, that we ended up basing all of our decisions upon how we felt my mother would respond. Which is ridiculous, but we are taught to conform from the earliest of ages, to respect our parents, even when we know they're making a selfish, or a completely erroneous decision. We become passive observers rather than primary instigators in our own child's life, and allow the veil of inexperience to cover our own eyes. Maybe, this is what is occurring with Sir Henry, maybe he is emotionally castrated by his father's intervention, so much so, that he seeks its restitution at every turn. After all, our parents are not infallible, and his creating a dependency within his own son, may fulfil a selfish desire within himself."

Maybe you're right," she replied. "I can associate with that sentiment. After visiting those downtrodden people in the less salubrious parts of London, I had an overwhelming urge to unfetter myself from all worldly chattels and to offer my services wholeheartedly to the poor."

"What happened?" he innocently enquired.

"Nothing," she replied "But a large dose of common sense from my mother. She understood that the heightened fires of one such as my age burn brighter than most and so directed me in my endeavours until experience dampened my ardour and I felt that my social duties were somewhat appeased. Even during my time as a student I would support the sick and the needy. The difference between Henry and myself is that I understand that I was born to privilege, whereas he does not. He is driven by the desire for all of those things that he does not have, whereas I am contented with my lot in life and I understand that equality is a greater demon to conquer than poverty."

Johnathan smiled.

"What?" Abigail enquired, returning his smile.

"I think that your mother would be very proud of you," he respectfully stated.

Abigail returned his smile and lowered her head.

Realising that he may have caused a slight tinge of emotional embarrassment, Johnathan turned to the mummy.

"Why don't we get started on our friend here and see if we can unravel some of the mysteries that he presents," he said, refocusing the direction of the conversation.

"Good idea," Abigail stated.

Chapter 7.

For the remainder of the day, Abigail, supported by Johnathan, busied themselves with cataloguing the artefacts that they discovered directly below the initial layer of the mummy's bandages. By the time they were set to finish, the natural light that permeated the room from the world outside had faded and was replaced by a deep crimson red of the late afternoon sky, that was punctuated by the now heavy drifts of winter snow that gathered in its torment, proclaiming the forthcoming winter downpour.

Johnathan watched as the snowfall gathered, its presence bringing back memories of his idyllic childhood, running in the snow with his father, and building snowmen taller than himself, memories he treasured, but lost, for his own experiences were cruelly taken from him, at the passing of his beloved father. Taking his pocket-watch from the breast pocket of his waistcoat, he flipped open the silver protective frontage.

"My God, it's almost 5 p.m.," he stated in amazement. "I'm supposed to be collecting some groceries for my uncle and if I don't hurry the corner shop will be closed, it will only be open till six, and Mr Twivey, the grocer, is very punctual," he declared.

"I'll see you tomorrow," Abigail innocently replied.

"But I have to stay with you," he firmly stated. "Those were Sir Henry's instructions."

Abigail rolled her eyes.

"Forget what Henry said, I'll be following you out of the door, all I have to do is tidy away a few of my instruments and I'll lock up the room and be safe at home by the time you're collecting your uncle's groceries," she stated with a smile.

"You don't mind then, if I go?" he awkwardly enquired.

"Of course not," she protested. "I'll only be a matter of moments myself, get yourself away and undertake your uncle's errands and I'll see you in the morning."

Taking his coat from the stand, Johnathan removed the work apron and slipped on his coat. Looking out of the window he smiled.

"I should have brought my overcoat, but I didn't expect the weather to turn so nasty," he stated.

"Be careful, if Sir Henry sees you, he might dock your wages if he observes that you have caught a cold from not wearing enough outer garments," she stated, a weak pastiche of her employer's previous comments made upon their initial meeting, on the museum's steps.

Johnathan shook his head and opened the door; turning to Abigail he smiled.

"Thank you, and don't forget to turn off the lamps," he said, as he closed the door and made his way out of the museum and into the cold winter night.

Turning to look at the artefacts, Abigail smirked to herself as she continued in her studies.

Behind her, there was a shuddering in the sarcophagus, as if the mummy were being rocked by unseen hands. There was no noise emitted from these actions, so no requirement for Abigail to investigate the preternatural events which were unfolding behind her. Picking up one of the scarab amulets, she held it in front of the table lamp and close to her eyes, reading the minute inscriptions aloud as she turned it in the light.

The mummy had ceased in its movement, and lay motionless in its casket. As time progressed the bandages appeared to flex as the sinew and muscle within began to expand and exert pressure upon the antediluvian bindings. The creature slowly rose from its eternal rest and sat up in silence. Slowly it turned to Abigail, who was oblivious to its actions, and held its position there for a few brief moments, observing her industrious activities.

Placing the scarab back onto the desk, she lifted another artefact and studied its inscription closely.

The mummy was now standing outside of the casket and facing Abigail. All about there fell an unnatural and hallow silence that was gripped with both apprehension and anticipation entwined.

"I don't understand," she whispered to herself. These are the usual type of artefacts that are buried with mummies. There's something distinctly different about them, but I just can't put my finger on it."

The mummy remained in its position, observing Abigail's every movement. Its presence was somehow sinister, yet intriguing.

"Oh c'mon, Abigail, think! You're missing something, a connection that's so obvious a first year under grad student could get it," she said, scolding herself. The gas lamp that sat on the far table offered a sympathetic glow from its open flame. After a few brief moments, the conflagration began to dance and flow as an ethereal breeze kissed its kind light, sending dancing shadows across the room.

Without consideration, Abigail dismissed this portent of darkening events and looked down upon the examination table, there she noticed a larger scarab artefact, with an impressive lapis-lazuli shell. She made to reach for it, just as an imposing shadow fell across her own and a linen wrapped hand also reached towards the artefact.

Turning quickly, Abigail, made to scream, however, instead of observing a mummy wrapped corpse, there standing before her, was a semi naked and impressively powerful chested Egyptian, who denoted magnificence, as well as nobility.

He stared at her with his dark brown eyes and smiled.

"I am blessed that you have awoken me," he stated in his ancient soft tone.

Abigail nervously smiled, as unconsciousness consumed her, and she fell onto the examination room floor.

****

Her senses were stirred back to life and Abigail could feel the presence of strong hands beneath her head, supporting her as consciousness returned.

"Are you alright?" a sympathetic voice enquired.

Opening her eyes, Abigail looked urgently around the room, her eyes searching the dark shadows that huddled in each and every corner.

"What's the matter?" the voice enquired.

Looking up, Abigail was pleased to see Johnathan's features being framed by the light of the overhead lamp, and offered him a cautious smile.

"What happened," she enquired.

"I was going to ask you the same thing," he replied.

"I thought you were going to undertake some errands for your uncle," she enquired as she endeavoured to right herself. Supporting her, Johnathan replied to her question.

"As I was leaving I encountered Sir Henry, and he informed me that the stolen mummy had been discovered, abandoned in one of the alleyways, not far from the museum. The talk of theft, has now turned to that of festive high-jinx, and the police feel that the mummy may have been taken by students as a dare. I thought I would return and inform you, so that you were less scared of remaining in the museum after hours."

Turning to the sarcophagus, Abigail was confused, for there lay the undisturbed remains of the high priest. A pensive look of deep anxiety, tinged with a whisper of pure horror, etched itself firmly upon her features. Observing this, Johnathan physically manoeuvred her to a comfortable leather chair.

"Are you alright?" he gently enquired. "Do you require a drink of water?"

"No, I'm fine," she insisted. "I must have been working too long, my senses have become a little addled."

Taking the small piece of papyrus from her pocket she smiled at Johnathan.

"Before we go, maybe I should return this to its rightful owner," she stated, nodding at the mummy. "Help me lift him up and I'll put this back," she said, as she stood from her chair and walked over to the sarcophagus.

Johnathan rolled his eyes to the ceiling, but supported Abigail in her endeavours. After they were concluded, he shook his head and offered her a wry smile.

"Maybe you should go home now, it will all be here in the morning," he stated looking at the ancient artefacts.

"Maybe you're right," she agreed. After retrieving her hat and coat, she linked her arm into Johnathan's.

"You can walk me to the cab, and I'll take you to your errands. I would be grateful for the company," she nervously highlighted.

"Is everything alright?" he asked, as he could feel her arm physically shaking as it tightened into his own.

"I'm fine," she whispered as she looked back at the mummy, her eyes catching a slight glimpse of dark mortal naked flesh that rested beneath the bandages. It was then that she realised that her encounter was all too real.

Chapter 8.

After a light supper and a rather stilted conversation with her father, Abigail made her way to bed. Her mind was racing with the dark images that confronted her previously that day. The image of the foreign stranger who stood majestically before her in his muscled magnificence, pursued her every thought. His presence was not only disturbing, but also beguiling, she was enthralled by his magical presence.

Abigail stood next to her dressing table, her mind in sensual turmoil as the images of her encounter haunted her every thought. Outside, there was a gentle ambiance that hung in the air, a calm that was not only serene but endearing. The snow was falling in perfect fragmentation and drifting in tides across the ground in magical mantle, that appeared to envelope the world in its soft and tender touch. The streetlights offered a yellowing warm ambiance to the comforting image that befell her tired eyes. For she knew that life had changed in that encounter, and her fervent imagination had well and truly overstepped its obligation, or, fantasy had stepped into this realm of reality. And all that she had perceived as being natural, including death, was now a myth and the order of the world was torn asunder, and the history of mankind was being rewritten before her very eyes in hieroglyphics upon ancient papyrus.

Looking down upon this world, Abigail smiled to herself as she reached up to draw the curtain, it was then that the shadow of a stranger caught her sight and she ceased in her trials, her eyes searching the shadows of the street below. Turning in her confusion, and without consideration for her own welfare, she rushed out of her room and down the stairs to the front door of her home. There she hesitated for a brief moment before she urgently undid the locks and cast the door viciously open, exposing her home to the bitter winter delights that consumed the world without.

Rushing into the street the naked skin of her arms and neck began to tingle as the light smattering of snow enticed her warm flesh with its cold kiss. Abigail eyes searched up and down the street but returned with no avail. She examined the fresh snow that covered the ground before her and observed only one set of footprints, her own. Closing her eyes in despondency, she turned to return to the safety of her home, but ceased in her endeavours, for she felt the strong and powerful presence of a stranger.

"Your skin is as soft and as pure as alabaster," he whispered.

Abigail opened her eyes and was confronted by her handsome stranger, a nervous smile broke across her lips as her eyes looked past him and into the safety of her own home. The light from within, illuminated the deserted street and offered her a little solace to her presenting dilemma.

"Who are you?" she asked. But the stranger looked at her in confusion. Realising that she was conversing in her native tongue, Abigail repeated her question in her own form of broken ancient Egyptian.

The stranger smiled at her linguistic endeavours and bowed slightly.

"My name is Siamun, son of Amon," he stated.

"I'm Abigail," she coyly replied.

She took a slight pensive step away from him and smiled nervously.

"I don't understand; how can you be here?" she asked.

Siamun smiled.

"It was your prayer. It was a blessing from the high priests, a command to the gods to allow me to breathe life once again," he stated.

"You're a high priest?" she whispered.

Siamun slowly smiled.

"I am no high priest, I am the son of a Pharaoh, admittedly not the first born," he stated with a smirk, "but born of nobility none-the-less."

"But you're here, with me in 1928, London. Am I dreaming this? Have I gone mad?" she enquired, whispering these words to herself.

"You are not mad, and I am here with you now, in this London," he declared.

Siamun looked up and smiled as the delicate flakes of snow drifted from the heavens and fell lightly onto his naked flesh.

"What delights are these?" he enquired as he returned his gaze to Abigail.

"Snow," she abstractly replied.

"Snow," he repeated. "A new and pleasant delight."

Abigail waved her hand confusingly in front of her companion.

"This can't be true, this can't be happening, I must be in my bed dreaming this," she stated.

Siamun smiled and reached out, gently taking hold of her hand. Softly guiding it to his muscular chest, he placed it close to his heart and offered her a coy smirk.

"You have started this beating again; you have brought me to life. You have granted me purpose and fortuitous time to fulfil my dark destiny," he stated.

Abigail could feel her heart swoon in her own chest as its beat began to rise as her flesh began to tingle. Her emotions were in turmoil, as her mind cascaded downwards, against the stringent empirical teachings of her advanced education.

There was a high pitched peel as a whistle was sounded in the distance, its presence shattering the dream that was weaving itself between these souls that stood in innocence on this virginal night.

There then came a cry, that filled Abigail's heart with terror.

"Murder!"

She turned to look at Siamun, but all she could observe was her own hand reaching out before her, and an accusing void where he once stood.

Chapter 9.

There was a heavy pounding of a demanding authority demonstrated upon the Cornwall's front door which brought both Abigail and her father rushing to answer it at 8 a.m. that following morning. As he opened the door, her father was greeted by the austere expression of a plain clothed detective, who was accompanied by a uniformed constable who stood a respective distance behind his senior officer.

"I'm sorry to disturb you on such a bleak morning," the officer stated in a dour voice, as the snow continued to fall in its winter delight. "We're here to investigate an incident which occurred at the address of Lord and Lady Aster Could you tell me if you or your daughter heard anything which could have presented as a concern at around 9.00 p.m., last night?"

Lord Cornwall, offered the officer a perplexed look.

"After my daughter and I had supper, she retired at about 9 p.m. and I remained in the library until about 10p.m., I recall looking at the grandfather clock as I walked into the hallway, as I noticed that the temperature had dropped considerably, and it was only then I noticed it had begun to snow heavily," he explained.

"Would it be possible for us to come in and discuss the situation with you a little further, as we are led to believe that you are an acquaintance of his lordship?" the officer stated in a slightly accusing tone.

"Of course," Lord Cornwall stated, opening the door wider, indicating that both gentlemen were free to enter his home.

After a few moments all parties were situated comfortably in the drawing room, bathed in the warm glow from the open fire.

"So, how can I help you?" Lord Cornwall enquired.

"I don't wish to bring alarm to yourself or your daughter," the officer began, "But there has been a tragedy at the Aster household." He stated, looking at Abigail with an expression of concern. "I don't wish to distress you, young lady, but were you acquainted with their daughter, Miss Elizabeth Aster?"

Abigail smiled.

"Of a fashion," she replied. "We met on the social scene and at a few gatherings; I would say that we would pass company generally once or twice a month. However, I haven't seen her of late, as I have only just returned from my studies at Cambridge."

"How long ago was that?" he asked.

Abigail took a deep breath and thought about her answer.

"Well, I finished my dictation in May and returned home in September of this year after I have concluded all of my affairs in Cambridge. So, I guess I have been home for about 10 weeks or so."

"And have you seen Miss Elizabeth in that time?" he enquired.

Abigail shook her head.

"No, I can't say that I have. I haven't really participated in the social scene since my return and it wasn't a past time that I was considered rekindling. I have just begun my work as an archaeologist at the British Museum and I've been concentrating my activities upon that," she highlighted.

"Archaeologist," the officer stated in a rather flippant tone, "how admirable."

"Can you tell me what has occurred, so that you feel free to enter our home on such a morning and question us without recourse?" Lord Cornwall enquired in a rather harsh, commanding tone.

Realising his positon, the officer offered him a respectful smile.

"Unfortunately, Milord, there appears to have been a tragedy which occurred at the Astor household. Miss Elizabeth was found dead, more to the point strangled, at around 9 p.m. last night, and I was just wondering if either yourself or your daughter observed anything out of the ordinary?"

"Elizabeth!" Abigail exclaimed. "Who would do such a terrible thing?" she asked.

"That's what we're endeavouring to discover, Ma'am," the officer replied.

"But she was such a gentle soul, one of the kindest people I know," Abigail highlighted.

"Do you know if she had any enemies, anyone she had fallen out with? Socially slighted? A disgruntled suitor?" the officer enquired.

"As I say, I haven't seen her in some considerable time," Abigail stated. "As for a suiter, Elizabeth wasn't like that, I can't recall the last time she was seen out on the town with a young gentleman."

"We're undertaking house-to-house investigations, but we came to your residence first as Lord Aster informed me that he was one of your firmest friends," the officer stated, looking at Lord Cornwall.

"Yes," he replied. "We were both attendees at the House of Lords, and we would meet in the members' lounge after sessions. I stopped attending on such a regular basis after my wife died. It all seemed a bit preposterous, all pomp and hot air. Death has a way of focusing your values." Lord Cornwall looked down and shook his head. "To lose a wife is devastating, but to lose one of your children, that must be soul destroying," he stated as he looked up at Abigail, tears of compassion welling in his eyes.

Standing, the officer reached out his hand to Lord Cornwall.

"Thank you for your time, I'm sorry if the news has caused you distress, as that was not my intention." He turned to Abigail and offered her a respectful smile.

"I would be grateful, if you can keep this news to yourselves, we understand that gossip can spread like wildfire, but even an hour of confidentiality could bring us a little closer to apprehending Miss Elizabeth's killer."

"Poor Wilfred and Catherine, they must be devastated," Lord Cornwall stated, as he ushered the officer to the front door. Turning, the detective looked to Lord Cornwall and offered him his card.

"If you hear of anything, please don't hesitate in calling me," he said, as he placed his bowler hat upon his head and opened the front door.

Docking the brim of his cap to Abigail, he stepped out into the torrential blizzard, closely followed by the hapless constable.

"Elizabeth, dead! I can't believe it," Abigail declared. She took a deep breath as the pain of her loss welled up from within. "I can't even comprehend how her parents must feel," she said.

Lord Cornwall offered her a weak smile and embraced her, holding her for what appeared a lifetime, kissing the top of her head, and expressing his undying love to his most precious of possessions. Breaking the embrace, he looked deep into her eyes.

"I know I don't tell you this enough, but I love you with all of my heart and soul."

Abigail smiled.

"And when you don't tell me, I already know."

Looking at the Grandfather clock, Abigail stepped back in surprise.

"It's nearly 8:30," she exclaimed. "Father, can you call me a cab, otherwise I will be late for work."

"You surely can't be considering going into work after hearing this news?" he asked.

"Father, it is my third day of employment and, as we both know, Sir Henry isn't the most agreeable of employers. And if I start with excuses within my first week of engagement, he would feel either aggrieved or downright annoyed and terminate my positon forthwith," she stated.

"But you don't have to work, you have your mother's wealth and soon you will have mine. You can become a lady of leisure, a social butterfly," he said.

Kissing him gently upon the forehead she laughed lightly.

"And we both know that would kill me, a trapped bird in a gilded cage. Nothing could be more repugnant," she declared as she rushed urgently up the stairs and into her room to gather her belongings.

Lord Cornwall smiled.

"You can tell that you're your mother's daughter."

Chapter 10.

By the time Abigail had reached the museum and made her way to the examination room, the building was already bustling with life. As she briskly walked along the long dark corridor she realised that the atmosphere has somehow changed, it appeared lifted, brighter and less melancholy. As she reached the door to the examination room she observed two shadows conversing within. Realising that one belonged to Johnathan she paused for a moment, endeavouring to discover the identity of the second. It was only after a short while did she discover that it was, in fact, Sir Henry. Without appearing to eavesdrop, she turned her head in order to offer herself the maximum opportunity to hear the private conversation which was being pervade within.

"Are you sure when you visited the museum last night that this mummy was missing?" Sir Henry enquired.

"Yes sir," Johnathan replied. "I did as you asked, I returned to the museum to collect your papers and when I came into this room the sarcophagus was empty."

"Yet, the mummy is here and all is as it should be," Sir Henry stated.

"Should I tell Miss Abigail of the incident?" Johnathan enquired.

"No," Sir Henry insisted. "We don't want to alarm anyone unduly."

Abigail was about to place her hand on the door's handle but the conversation continued, its contents causing her to pause in her actions.

"Have you managed to glean any information from your friendship with Miss Cornwall?" Sir Henry enquired.

"Nothing of any importance," he replied. "It's really just mundane information."

"Remember, information is power, and I require as much as I can attain," Sir Henry coldly stated.

Suspicion crept into her mind as she pursed her lips in defiance and turned the handle and pushed the door firmly open.

Turning, Sir Henry offered her a broad smile.

"Good morning, how nice of you to join us," he sarcastically stated.

"I'm sorry Henry, but I can't be bothered with your childish emotional games this morning," she cuttingly retorted.

"Get out of the wrong side of the bed?" he childishly replied.

Abigail looked at him with distaste, but held her composure.

"Were you ever acquainted with Elizabeth Aster?" she enquired.

Sir Henry thought for a moment.

"Tall thin girl, very protective parents, American I think, lots of money, very little breeding or class."

Abigail offered him an icy stare.

"She was murdered last night," Abigail coldly stated. "The police were questioning my father as he had a close professional relationship with Lord Aster, which is why I'm a little late. If you wish to garnish my wages, please feel free, but there are things in life which mean more than a social position, and I felt that supporting my father during these difficult times was one of those."

"I'm sorry, I didn't mean to be so flippant," Sir Henry quickly interjected. "How is your father?" he asked, feigning interest.

"As well as can be expected," she replied in an emotionless tone.

Taking off her jacket, she placed it upon the coat-stand and walked over to the sarcophagus, briefly peered in at the mummy. Looking up she smiled unemotionally in Johnathan's direction.

"I don't think I'll require your services today," she coldly remarked. "I'm going to decipher some of the hieroglyphics and spend most of my time studying. I find it better to undertake this alone, and in silence." she said, looking from Johnathan to Sir Henry.

Sir Henry stood quietly for a moment until the realisation that he was being dismissed dawned upon him.

"Very well, I have a hundred and one tasks that I must complete before this day is over, and now that I have Johnathan's company, these may be achievable. We'll bid you adjure and if possible I may drop in at lunchtime and offer to take you out for some light refreshments?" he pensively enquired.

"I would prefer to be alone," she stated as she turned her back upon her companions and sat at the desk, feigning the interest in her studies.

Whereas, her mind screamed for salvation, for she was terrified of being left alone with the mummy.

As Sir Henry and Johnathan left the room, Abigail felt disgust, but also disappointment at the thought that her trust, which she had offered in true friendship, was being manipulated by both Henry and Johnathan alike. She shook her head, as she questioned her own integrity. 'Should she return to her home and spend her time in the company of her father in his remaining years?' she thought to herself. After all, she was a considerably wealthy woman in her own right, and employment was not a governing factor in relation to her life. However, self-value was. And she felt somehow complete, undertaking the mundane rigours of the day. Employment was a major factor in retaining her own personal identity, and she felt as though she belonged, rather than existed in this world. She felt part of a wider community rather than a member of the social elite.

Lifting the pencil from the desk she placed the tip between her teeth, the acrid wooden taste bite deep into her senses but, instead of repelling her these bitter sensitivities were somehow alluring, urging her to continue with her studies. It brought back the memories of Cambridge, of times spent in deep contemplation in the libraries, urgently scribbling as the deadline for assignment completion loomed angrily upon the edifying horizon, a horizon peppered with male chauvinists and bigoted fools.

"I'm worth more than this," she whispered to herself in her ancient broken language.

"You most certainly are," came the distinct ancient masculine tone.

Turning slowly, Abigail stared coldly at Siamun.

"Where did you go last night?" she fervently enquired.

Siamun smiled, but looked cautiously down to the ground.

"I fear that there is danger in your life, and there is also a murder upon the horizon," he stated.

"I know, you killed one of my oldest friends," Abigail stated.

Siamun smiled and shook his head.

"It is not I who have undertaken such a dark deed, but Nehi."

Abigail looked at Siamun in confusion.

"Who?" she enquired.

"Nehi is the high priest who accompanied me into the afterlife. He was buried with me, as me," he explained.

"What do you mean?" she asked.

Turning, Siamun looked at the door, observing the bolt, he walked over and gently pushed it into place, in order to attain both privacy and security.

"I would rather not be disturbed as I recant to you my sad story. Please, feel free to ask me to stop and I will return to the sarcophagus, you are not my prisoner, but my saviour. However, I do think that you require an explanation as to why both Nehi and myself have fallen into your life."

"I'm intrigued," Abigail said, as she sat back down onto the office chair. "I could do with a little honesty at the moment," she stated.

Siamun looked at her in confusion.

Realising his dilemma, Abigail dismissed his concern with a wave of her hand.

"Pay no attention to me, I just feel that I have lost a little of my confidence recently."

"Are you attributing this concern to your friend Johnathan?" Siamun enquired.

"It would appear that he is not a friend of mine," she coldly stated.

Siamun smiled.

"You have no justification in this statement," he said. "You are doing your loyal friend a disservice, he was replying with diffused answers to this Sir Henry, whenever he enquired about anything of a personal nature appertaining to yourself. He would not offer or release any information and coldly stated that he was unaware of your intentions or actions. I only know this for I have closely observed the undulations of your open conversations during my time in your presence, and it is apparent that this recent conversation between employer and employee was both closed and guarded."

Abigail offered Siamun a nervous look.

THE MUMMY

"The problem which you have experienced is that you were only privy to one side of a conversation, whereas I, I was enlightened by both. Please feel reassured that your friend Johnathan is, as I have just described him, your friend."

Walking over to the sarcophagus, Siamun allowed his hand to gently stroke the edge of the surface.

"You attribute too much to other people's words. It is their actions that should be measured," he smiled to himself as he contemplated his next contribution to this conversation. "I realise that as time has passed, human expectation and emotions remain as they have always been, we all strive to achieve greater things in life, to be more accomplished than our forefathers; however, you cannot become enlightened when you are blind to the truth. The more that people talk the less they hear, all they are doing is repeating information which they have personally gathered or has been indoctrinated into them by others who perceived themselves as being more enlightened that they are, when in fact all they are doing is merely repeating information that somebody else already knows and has purveyed it back to them; maybe we should all learn to listen, then we may discover something new, something that could enlighten and enrich all of our lives." He looked down into the sarcophagus and pondered his presenting situation before he turned and smiled at Abigail. "My time is limited, and I feel that I owe you an explanation as to why I presented myself to you on that cold winter's night."

Chapter 11.

"Even though I was born of royal blood, my life within the palace was subject to favour and the goodwill of the pharaoh. My father had brief periods of kindness, but he ruled his house as he did his country with a hand of iron. I was his fourth son, tenth in the line of his children. I knew that I would never be Pharaoh, but I was also passed by in relation to all other aspects of the royal lifestyle. My mother, the fourth wife of the Pharaoh, was a beautiful and blessed woman born of temperament and grace. She had neither malice nor ambition and her most disarming feature was her lust for life and ability to live for the moment. When the years had not passed thirty, she was taken from me and I was brought up by a nursemaid. A woman that was neither nurturing nor my mother. To the outside world my life was blessed, but living within that palace, were the bonds of royal rigor and servitude to my father, and the god incumbent here on this earthly realm."

Siamun smiled as the dark memories of his past raged to the forefront of his mind.

"As you can surmise, love was my downfall," he said as he sat on the chair next to the sarcophagus. "Nehi and I were the same age, he was born to the priesthoods and I was born into royalty. We met when we were aged 6 and from that moment on we were as thick as thieves and bonded by a blood that was stronger than anything experienced by a brother of this earthy realm. As time passed it was highlighted that we grew accustomed to one another in both looks and demeanour, that even my father experienced difficulty in relation to telling us apart. Even after he entered the priesthood and was chosen by my father to be his high priest within the palace, our friendship continued. My father undertook this action, for he knew that this bond could not be broken, even by his dark royal decree. My father may have been Pharaoh, but he was also unkind, and felt that the way to strengthen a child's character was to deny him the yearnings of the human soul. He knew that if he took my friend and confidant away from me, then the only person I could turn to would be himself."

Siamun smirked nervously, as a wave of embarrassment washed over him as his memories drifted into his mind.

"However, there was another. Her name was Amunet, and she was as beautiful as the morning sun. But as is with a royal life, my pathway was already dictated and I was betrothed to my own sister, for my father was a fervent follower of tradition, and if you were to deviate from his decree, you would feel the full task of his wrath. And, because of my own selfish actions, this occurred to both Nehi and myself."

"Why was Nehi brought into it?" Abigail asked.

"Because he would do as any other brother would do, and stood to defend me against the pharaoh. My father's anger was both swift and damning, a force unquestioned in the royal court."

"I don't understand," she said.

"Nehi lied to my father and informed him that he was meeting Amunet at these observed clandestine meetings to save me from his wrath. Something that I deeply regret occurring to this day," he said.

"Why," she asked.

"Because my father knew that he was lying and as punishment for this, he bestowed unspeakable torments upon his mortal flesh. And, because I was held responsible for both of our actions. My father was to have me slain and Nehi buried alive without the funeral rites bestowed upon a high priest," he stated.

"Your father did that to you? But why?" she asked.

"To us both," he stated as he lowered his head in shame. "Nehi was like a brother, I loved him as I loved life itself, and he committed one final act of selfishness, to save my immortal soul from eternal damnation. His priests commanded a considerable influence over all those associated with death, the afterlife and embalming. Understanding the dark situation, and with pure selflessness, Nehi instructed his priests, unbeknown to all others, including Pharaoh himself, to switched our bodies and poor Nehi befell my abhorrent fate. Whereas I, only suffered the eternal darkness, was buried alive, without ceremony or religious endorsement. Unsanctioned by the touch of the master embalmer, I was wrapped in linen, covered in embalmers resin, and sealed alive in the casket intended for poor Nehi."

A single tear ran down his cheek.

"However, before this, I was subject to the eternal aberration that haunts my mind for eternity I remained buried, for I understand that these actions were intended for myself. I observed them cut out Nehi's tongue, gouge out his right eye, and when he struggled in terror, they broke his jaw and other bones. But more terror was to come, for as I lay there in my own casket, blind to the revulsions of this world, I could hear Nehi's muffled cries as they undertook the embalming ritual upon his living form, as was degreed by my father."

"My God, your father sounds like a monster," she cried.

Siamun smiled and lowered his head.

"My father wasn't a monster, he was just a man who had lived with power for too long. Power corrupts and attracts corrupt people." He took a deep breath. "I suppose the only saving grace, was the fact that the priests placed a spell in the sarcophagus that could bring our souls back, for a short period of time."

"But why?" Abigail innocently enquired.

"Hope," he replied glibly. "So that we may confront my father after he recanted his decision, and recognised the error of his ways." He turned and looked emotionally upwards, stemming the tears that were building within. "But this was not so, for I have lay there, in the darkness, for several long millennia, listening to the world as it turned. Forgotten to all those who loved me."

"So that's how you came back to life," she declared. "The papyrus?"

Siamun smiled.

"Yes, it was intended to offer me retribution against the rigours of the after-world. It was not intended to give me immortality, but justice. And, your recantation of that prayer, has brought both Nehi and myself back to this mortal world. And, in some strange way, we are now all connected, for your presence holds influence over both of use," he stated.

"What do you mean?" she asked.

"You are the master of our fate: each sarcophagus contained a different prayer, they could be used individually or collectively. Mine was intended for Nehi, and his in turn was intended for myself, for surely if I were to be resurrected then so would my brother," he explained.

"So are you saying that it was Nehi who murdered my friend Elizabeth?" Abigail tentatively asked.

"It appears so," he answered.

"But how? You returned as you were in your previous life," she stated.

"I agree," he replied, "But I was not embalmed, and with that, subject to the rituals associated with that process. My father wanted me obliterated from history and the afterlife. His anger demonstrated no boundaries," he highlighted.

"So how come you weren't resurrected in your own time?" she asked.

Siamun smiled.

"My father had spies all over the kingdom and when they discovered the plot to resurrect me, he had the locality of my body's final resting place changed and instructed the embalmers to destroy any written evidence of both mine and Nehi's identity," he said.

"Why didn't he just cremate your body?" she asked.

Siamun looked at Abigail.

"Not even my father would anger the gods with such blasphemy," he stated. "For he had his own eternal soul to consider."

"How do you know your father was at the foundation of your downfall?" she asked.

"The chief embalmer was a man who was always in league with the highest bidder, he had the eyes of a snake and the morals of a jackal, and he informed my father of my assignation with Amunet, and he was handsomely paid for his betrayal. And, it was into his hands that both my and Nehi's fate was placed. However, because of the skilled intervention of my brother's followers, he believed that Nehi was myself and I was Nehi, so I had to endure both my brother's screams as the embalmer informing him of my father's decree. I can only surmise that my father instructed him to undertake these actions to intensify my eternal suffering."

Abigail shook her head in disbelief.

"What happened to Amunet," she asked.

"Because she was not of noble blood, she was executed and her body burned so that she would never know eternal rest. I heard the sword fall upon her flesh, and her screams die, as they ushered me away to my own demise."

A single tear of empathy ran down Abigail's cheek.

"I wish you were back in your sarcophagus so that I didn't have to hear such a torrid tale," she innocently stated.

Turning, she observed Siamun as he walked over to the sarcophagus.

Confusion consumed her.

"What are you doing?" she asked.

"As you have instructed," he replied.

"No I didn't mean it like that," she replied in a rather perplexed tone.

Siamun stopped in his trials and smiled at her.

"You forget, fair one, as I have stated I am at your command. The prayer denotes this," he explained with a smile. "You can command me how you desire, but I cannot undertake any actions that could harm another living soul," he highlighted.

Abigail smiled.

"I would state that the last thing that you need in your life is someone controlling you. I would say that you have experienced a lifetime of this sort of treatment, back in ancient Egypt."

Siamun smiled and looked up at the lamp that hung from the ceiling.

"The wonders of your world are masterful and intriguing," he whispered. "True enlightenment from the gods."

Abigail smirked.

"It's called electricity, and the men who devised it, although they would love to be denoted as gods, are far from that, and I can reassure you that they are only mortal men. The world has technologically advanced since your time, a wonder which would give me a great deal of pleasure to demonstrate to you," she highlighted.

Siamun eyes lit up in excitement.

"Would you show me your world?" he tentatively enquired.

"With pleasure," she stated. "But we must firstly find you suitable attire, as not to draw attention to yourself, and secondly. You should not, and will not speak. If you require anything, seek privacy and ask me directly, preferably when we are alone," she instructed. "You will remain here and I will collect you just before the museum closes, but you must return before dawn.

Siamun smiled.

"Agreed."

Chapter 12.

Her father's clothes appeared to fit Siamun reasonably well, he did require a few personal adjustments and clarification on the use of buttons and other accoutrements appertaining to the style of that era, but nevertheless, he presented well and looked like a visiting dignitary that would turn heads in relation to his dashingly good looks rather than his preternatural presence.

"Your father's clothing is very appealing. Conducive to this cold climate," Siamun stated.

Abigail smiled.

"I don't think my father would miss them. I think he hid them in the back of the wardrobe in the hope that one day he would lose a little weight and would be able to wear them again, a longing of a time long forgotten," she explained.

"Your clothing is very apparent for the temperate climate you experience here," he stated. "May I enquire of something?" he asked, looking at here with bemused eyes.

Abigail nodded.

"Last night, when we were in the street. How did the clouds descend from the heavens?"

Abigail looked at him in confusion, until realisation dawned upon her.

"Snow!" she exclaimed. "That was snow."

Siamun looked at her with a blank expressing upon his features.

"You know rain?" she asked.

Siamun nodded.

"Well it's a frozen version of rain," she explained.

Siamun nervously smiled.

"What is frozen?" he asked.

Abigail sat back in her desk chair, realising the dilemma of her predicament.

"I don't know the ancient Egyptian for snow. I don't even know if you have ever encountered it." She looked at him and enquired. "Did you ever leave Egypt?"

Siamun shook his head.

"No, I have never been to any other city other than that which I was born into," he explained.

Abigail smirked.

"Then you won't know what snow is. All I can say is its cold, but it won't harm you," she said, offering him a respectful smile.

Standing, she walked over to the door and opened it. The museum was bathed in dark shadows and silence. Turning back to Siamun she winked.

"Are you ready for your adventure?" she enquired.

Siamun smiled.

"Lead the way," he said as he walked over to her side.

As they stepped out into the night air, a fresh flurry of snow began to gather and fall, the flakes turning in their perfect delight, illuminating the night against the winter darkness.

"It's almost magical," Abigail said.

"It is a true wonder," Siamun stated with a smile.

"Where should we go first? Abigail asked rhetorically, her heart pounding in her chest in excited anticipation. Turning to Siamun she giggled in exhilaration, her face fully animated by her enthusiasm.

"I think that if this is going to be your first journey into this modern world, we should make it brief and eventful, without making it too exiting as it may be too much for you to handle, emotionally," she said.

At that precise moment a motor vehicle turned the corner and sounded its horn at a pedestrian who was crossing the road in a rather lackadaisical fashion. Siamun physically jumped and made to rush back into the museum. Gripping his arm, Abigail urged him to remain where he stood.

"It's alright, it's only a car," she explained, while endeavouring to conceal her amusement. "Surely you saw one last night when you made your way to my home?" she asked.

Siamun shook his head.

"I saw no such creature," he stated, his limbs shaking in fright.

"It's just a mode of transportation, a bit like you using a chariot," she explained.

Siamun turned and looked at her in amazement.

"That is no chariot. Where are the horses to propel it? And from what I could see, it had eaten the rider," he stated.

"I'm sorry, but it is alright. It's just a piece of modern machinery, that's all." She highlighted, endeavouring to calm his nerves.

"Look. As long as you're with me, you'll be safe" she said reassuringly.

"This modern world, although magnificent is also perilous. Full of horseless chariots and bright light. I don't know if I can endure such wonders. Maybe we should return to the museum, I feel a little more comfortable there," he said.

"Alright, I have a suggestion. Why don't we walk a little further along the road, you can see a little more of this modern world's delights; and as soon as you desire, we can return to the safety of the museum," she stated.

Siamun nervously smiled.

"I am brave, I am a prince of Egypt," he muttered under his breath as he took a tentative step down the museum's steps and out into this wonderful, dangerous world.

Although it was only early evening the night skies were dark apart from the shimmers of show that drifted lightly down from the heavens and onto the ground at their feet as they walked briskly along the almost pedestrian unoccupied streets adjacent to the museum.

"I think we're in luck tonight," Abigail stated. "I think the cold of the night air has encouraged a lot of people to remain indoors and in the warmth."

Siamun smiled.

"I find this cold invigorating, it makes me feel truly alive," he said.

"I'll remind you of that in a few hours' time when your frozen to the core and want to return to the warmth of the museum," she said.

Siamun stopped walking and turned to Abigail.

"I would like to thank you for this opportunity, for giving me a chance, for accepting me briefly into your life," he said. Realising that Abigail's attention was not focused upon himself but upon the marks in the snow that stretched far away from them and into the distance.

"What is that?" she enquired.

Siamun turned and looked at the drag marks that were made in the fresh snow before him. His eyes searching for the illusive answer.

"I don't know," he replied, as he lowered himself to his knees so that he could inspect the disturbance a little further.

"It looks like someone has been dragged through the snow," Abigail surmised.

Siamun Slowly rose to his feet.

"Or *'something'* was being dragged through the snow," he stated cautiously.

"What do you mean?" Abigail began to enquire, however, no sooner had the words escaped her mouth, when an unholy scream echoed in the street around them. Turning so Siamun, she urged him to return to the museum, however, the noble heart that beat within his chest declined this invitation and commended him forward to discover the source of such torment.

"We must discover what is wrong," he cried, as he rushed into the dark back-allies of the city.

"Stay close," she commanded as he accompanied her into the shadows.

Following the disturbance in the snow, they eventually came across an elderly lady who was cowering in a doorway.

"What is wrong?" he enquired.

Horror etched upon the woman's face she screamed at his questioning.

"What the bleeding hell are you saying?" she shrieked.

Realising that his words were foreign to her, Siamun smiled and stepped back and allowed Abigail to reach where he stood before he continued.

"Ask her what happened," he urged.

Casting him a disparaging glance Abigail knelt next to the old lady.

"Are you alright?" she enquired.

"No, I'm bloody not, not with that horrible creature dragging itself out of the shadows, all wrapped in bandages with that evil expression on its face, it's enough to give me nightmares," she declared.

"What was it doing?" Abigail asked.

"It was walking along the alleyway, looking for something," she replied.

"Do you know what?" Abigail asked.

"How the bloody hell would I know? It's not as if I'm going to stop him and ask, now am I?" she churlishly decreed. "All I can tell you is he was after something, or someone, and I'd hate to be there when he finds them."

Turning to Siamun, she offered him a nervous smile.

"Nehi?" she nervously asked.

Siamun nodded.

As they hurried along the alleyways and through the deserted streets, Abigail could sense her heart beating urgently in her chest as a feeling of belonging consumed her. For this felt like an adventure, a reason for being, a rationale for life. Not the presenting dangerous situation, or the possible trauma of what they may discover, but the very aspect of the event that lacked the mundane, and the expected. In that moment she had transcended the apex of her own existence and moved from upper-class, well-educated debutante, to a detective, problem solver and pinnacle of society. How she felt alive, how invigorating these moments were with this dark stranger, how mundane her life prior to their meeting appeared in her rose-tinted eyes.

Stopping, Siamun observed the tracks in the snow ceasing at the rear doorway of an impressive townhouse. Looking tentatively at Abigail, he held a finger to his lips, requesting her silence.

THE MUMMY

Gently placing his hand upon the wooden garden door that led into the back of the property, Siamun pushed forward, the door offered little resistance and as it swung open it revealed a garden dressed in moonlight and shadows. He turned and looked at Abigail, an expression of dark concern washing across his features, for he understood that the atmosphere had changed, it had turned to that of a darker shade of death.

Chapter 13.

As the creature moved slowly through the dimly lit house it met little resistance as it continued its blind meandering journey. It was as if the night had cast its dark shadow across this domain and all were in slumber. The sound of the hall clock chiming sent an eerie peal of unwelcome resonance into the air, and yet Nehi ignored its unsolicited presence and continued on his fateful journey. The sound of his dragging feet upon the course carpet sent an eerie shiver into the night air as the darkness appeared to conspire in its mournful assignation of evil. The mummy made his way up the back stairs of the property and out into the hallway that led to the family bedrooms. In the library below, there were voices and laughter, as it was evident that a select social gathering was ensuing, and not all desired parties were present.

As Nehi moved mechanically along the dimly lit corridor, his right leg dragging clumsily behind him, his mind concordant with a single unyielding compelling desire. As he approached the room he intended to enter, he could hear the muffled sound of playful voices conversing from within. Pausing at the doorway, he listened for several moments, eavesdropping upon the conversation that was unravelling.

"Rosie, do you think Lord Bingham's son will attend?" she asked.

"I do hope so my lady," the maid replied.

"I've waited for such a long time to see him again, we were betrothed almost six months ago, and in that time, I've only set eyes upon him on two occasions and they were from an unsafe distance. Why did I fall for a military man?" she rhetorically enquired.

"It wouldn't have anything to do with his dashing good looks, would it milady?" the maid enquired.

There was the brief sound of light jovial laughter before the conversation continued.

"Is everyone here Rosie?" she enquired.

"Well we were expecting Lord Bingham and company, just as I came to help you dress milady. I've been here about 15 minutes, so I would assume that he has already arrived," Rosie said.

"I do hope so, but I didn't hear the door bell," she said. "Will you go downstairs and look," she nervously enquired.

THE MUMMY

"Of course," Rosie stated.

Nehi could hear the approaching footsteps grow in volume as the maid advanced to the door, looking down, he could see the door's hand turn and he smirked in his deathly anticipation.

As the door swung open, the dark hallway was bathed in bright illuminating light that seeped and raged from the room and out into the cold dank corridor. The maid, looking down at the shawl that she had over her arm, slowly allowed her eyes to rise from their safe position until she looked fully into the crimson eye of the mummified horror that stood before her. A scream endeavoured to seek release from her throat, but was thwarted before it could be initiated, as the creature brought its hand brutally down upon the maid's head, breaking her neck in its vicious descent.

Ignoring the commotion that ensued in the corridors, the bedroom's occupant continued in her endeavours, blissfully unaware of the tragedy that was unfurling around her. As she primped and preened her hair, she became aware of the shadows that flickered and danced across the far wall of the room, these appearingly insignificant actions caught her imagination, and ceased her infernal preening.

"Rosie, is that you?" she enquired as she slowly turned in her chair to face the open bedroom door. However, instead of discovering her maid, there stood the decayed remains of her dark deliverer. He who would take her soul into the underworld to be consumed by the Great Ammut.

The sound of the air escaping from her throat as she endeavoured to scream, brought a singular delight to mummy's fractured mind, and a sinister smile broke across his fractured features. Entering the room, he moved mechanically towards his intended pray, his right arm outstretched in anticipation.

Standing from her chair, the victim moved closer to the window, as her eyes searched for a means of escape from this abhorrent monster that presented itself before her. She could feel her senses cascade in on themselves as her mind began to shut-down in the sheer terror of this vision consumed her. Closing her eyes, she prayed for one last spark of invigorating energy as she opened her mouth and screamed.

Chapter 14.

It was the sound of shattering glass that brought both Abigail's and Siamun attention to the horrors that were unfurling before them. Realising their predicament, Abigail stepped backwards and held out her arm to prevent Siamun from entering the garden.

"We can't go into the house, otherwise the authorities will consider us to be a part of these dark events. You must wait here," she commanded. "And I'll go to the front of the house and knock on the door. Stay in the shadows and don't draw attention to yourself." As these words escaped from her mouth, Abigail realised the absurdity of her request. Shaking her head, she rushed urgently along the alleyway and out into the open street.

Undertaking his instruction, Siamun concealed himself in the darkness and fervently observed the shadows that swathed the house and its grounds in unnatural darkness, his eyes searching for any activity of life, be they of mortal or immortal in origin.

As she approached the front entrance of the property Abigail could feel her throat tighten as it dried to a point where it appeared almost impossible for her to converse. Swallowing severally times, she lubricated her throat enough to initiate a conversation to highlight her concern. Holding the brass door knocker in her hands, she held it motionless for a moment, before she cast it down, sending a loud and urgent echo into the hallway and beyond. Within moments the door was opened, revealing the commotion that consumed the household within.

"Is everything alright?" she enquired of the butler who stood before her.

"Yes ma'am, I can assure you of that," he coldly stated as he endeavoured to close the door.

"Who is it?" a masterful voice commanded.

"Lord Hawthorn?" Abigail enquired.

"Yes," he replied.

"It's me Abigail Cornwall," she highlighted.

"Simpson, don't be a buffoon, and let Lady Abigail in, the night is perishing," he commanded.

Entering the house, Abigail was consumed by the sheer tumult that consumed everyone within. Her eyes darting back and forth from servant to guest.

"Is everything alright?" she asked.

"I don't know, we heard a scream and the footman had gone upstairs to investigate," he said.

"At that moment, his daughter, Lady Margaret ran down the stairs and into the hallway, her body shaking in terror. Realising that her father was present she rushed over to his side and embraced him, tears streaming down her cheeks.

"It was ghastly, father, ghastly. It killed Rosie and then wanted to kill me," she screamed.

"What did?" he enquired, in a calm and rational tone, endeavouring to placate the heightening situation.

"There was a creature, wrapped in bandages, it tried to kill me," she sobbed.

Turning to his wife he nodded for her to take their daughter into the safety of the drawing-room, while he investigated her claims. Recalling Abigail's presence, he turned to his daughter

"Margaret, look who's here," he said, pointing to Abigail.

"I was passing, doing a little late night shopping, looking for Christmas presents for my father, when I heard the commotion," she incoherently babbled. "Realising that it was your address, I just wanted to ensure that you were all alright."

The butler moved silently over to his lordship's side and whispered.

"The police have been called and will be here forthwith," he said.

Realising her predicament and that of Siamun, Abigail quickly made her excuses and endeavoured to leave.

"I realise that this is a difficult time, I should not have encroached," she mumbled.

"Don't be foolish," Lady Hawthorn stated as she walked over to Abigail's side and placed a commanding hand into the small of her back and ushered her into the drawing room.

"Your company is most welcome on such a horrendous night. While we wait for the police to arrive you can tell me how your lovely father is doing, we don't see him much in our social gatherings anymore," she wittered.

Lord Hawthorn closed his eyes and shook his head, exacerbated at his wife's puerile response to her daughter's dilemma. Turning he looked to his butler and rolled his eyes. Who in turn offered him a cautious smile.

As she entered the drawing room, Abigail turned and looked out into the hallway, her eyes searching for the return of the footman who was sent out to discover the whereabouts of the creature.

"So, how is your father?" Lady Hawthorn enquired.

"My father is fine," Abigail replied, "But I am more concerned about Lady Margaret," she firmly stated.

"Of course, we all are," Lady Hawthorn stated, rubbing her daughters with the palm of her hand, feebly endeavouring to offer her daughter a little comfort and reassurance.

"What did you see?" one of the dinner guests enquired.

"It was a horrible thing, all dressed in bandages, just like something described by Howard Carter in his newspaper interviews," she stated.

"Are you saying you saw someone dressed as a mummy?" Lady Hawthorn cautiously enquired, her tone holding a smattering of ridicule.

"No mother, what I saw 'was' a mummy, it killed Rosie, don't you understand?" she cried.

"Oh God," Lady Hawthorn exclaimed. "Poor Rosie, where am I going to find another maid as good as her?" she asked rhetorically.

"Mother!" her daughter cried.

"What? Lady Hawthorn said in amazement. "I'm just saying it's very difficult to find good staff, that's all."

At that point Lord Hawthorn entered the room, flanked by a plain clothed police officer.

THE MUMMY

"Well, they can't find anything. There's plenty of evidence, disturbed snow and a broken window, but there is no sign of this man in bandages that you say came into your room," he stated.

Margaret shook her head.

"And am I imagining Rosie's death?" she angrily protested.

Abigail stood and walked over to Lord Hawthorn's side.

"May I leave, my father will be worried," she said.

"Of course," he replied. "I'll ask one of the chauffeurs to drive you home."

"There's no need," she said. "I'll be fine, after all, with all of these police officers about I should be perfectly safe."

"We may need to question you," the police officer stated.

"It's alright," Lord Hawthorn said. "She wasn't here when the incident occurred. She arrived just after, and if you need to speak to her, then I can give you Lord Cornwall's address and you can talk to her at a suitable time."

"Yes milord," the officer agreed.

"Thank you," Abigail said as she slipped from the drawing room, along the hallway, out of the front door, and into the welcoming world of winter.

"Are you alright?" Siamun enquired as he stepped from the shadows of the doorway opposite.

"I was scared that they might discover you, and arrest you," she said.

"I followed Nehi when he left the building. I tried to reason with him but something has changed," he stated. "It was as if he didn't recognise me, our history as brothers had been wiped from, his mind."

"What do you mean?" Abigail nervously asked.

Realising that the streets were beginning to fill with pedestrians and onlookers alike, Siamun placed his hand into the small of Abigail's back and urged her away from the gathering crowd.

"All I can surmise is that there are two prayers. The one you discovered in my sarcophagus, which brought me back to life, and there must be a second. A controlling prayer that merely animates the corpse, so that it will undertake its master's bidding." Siamun smiled a reticent smile. "That was intended for myself, as it was placed in my proposed casket. This demonstrates how much my father hated me."

Abigail offered him a compassionate smile and linked her arm into his as they walked down the snow covered street.

"It's either that, or there is someone controlling Nehi, someone who has a greater power over the dark arts, greater than anything you or I could ever comprehend," she said. "And, you must also take into consideration the fact that Nehi has experienced a partial mummification. Those rituals were generally performed upon a freshly deceased corpse, but were in fact undertaken on someone who was very much alive."

"I had not considered that," he stated. "There is also another concern, and it is a lot worse than I previously considered. It would appear that my father had in fact instructed the embalmers to inflict a great deal more injuries upon Nehi's form, than initially perceiving by myself.

"Why would your father do that?" she asked in disgusted.

"So that in the afterlife, I would not tell the God's of the underworld of his misconduct or see my desired pathway to the ancestors resolved. We Egyptians believe that our forefathers watch our every mortal move and judge us in relation to our actions," he highlighted.

"Our world is a little different. I suppose with the advancements in science we're all a little more sceptical in relation to the beliefs that were previously held by other cultures," she said.

Siamun stopped, and turned to look directly at Abigail.

"So, you don't believe in anything?"

Abigail thought for a while before replying.

"We have the church, and we have other faiths, but in relation to abject beliefs, such as the ones which you are describing, no, very few people now believe in the existence of a God."

Siamun smiled.

"So what do you believe in?"

"I believe in science; I believe in what I can see. I believe in knowledge and understanding. I believe that we are all equal and there should be no differentiation between men and woman," she stated.

Siamun laughed.

"You wouldn't have survived long in my father's court. He saw women as possessions and in relation to faith, he was the singular God that you should worship."

Abigail smiled, not warm and compassionately, but uneasily.

"Do I get the impression that you didn't believe in your father's belief system?" she asked.

Siamun sighed as his ancient memories flooded back.

"All my father gave to me was a distrust in men and a dark anger that consumes me to this very day. Fathers are supposed to empower their children, uphold them to the light, ensure that they become a productive and valued member of their society. However, my father, as did his father, ruled with hatred and instilled fear into all those who came into contact with them." Siamun shook his head and smiled. "The only true affection and feeling of love that I ever felt, apart from that bestowed upon me by my beloved mother, was that which I felt from my surrogate brother, Nehi. A free thinking and somewhat innocent soul."

Siamun looked momentarily to the skies as a fresh deluge of snow fell lightly from the heavens.

"And look what has happened to him now," he stated, looking directly at Abigail. "My father's contemptuous touch reaches down through the millennia and festers our lives, even to this day."

"Were there no compassionate times with your father?" she asked.

Siamun nodded.

"Before my mother died, but they were very infrequent. And, after she passed over to the next life, my life was filled with scorn and derisory encounters with my so called beloved father."

"Did your brothers and sisters realise?" she asked.

Siamun laughed.

"Of course they did, and they manipulated each and every situation. Fuelling the fire of his mistrust. It was how the royal court survived. Each scorpion riding upon the back of another until a stronger beast presented itself and the previous host was disposed of to maintain their silence and the sanctity of the secrets which they held."

Abigail smirked.

"I hate to tell you this, but not much has changed. Life repeats itself through the centuries, and we all fall foul of the same mistakes. I suppose it's human nature, we all want to strive for something better," she said.

"And are you like that, Miss Abigail Cornwall?" he firmly enquired.

Feeling her embarrassment rise, more because of the close proximity of his body, rather than the question proposed. Abigail took a slight step back and pulled her coat about her.

"I have no need to seek the favour of another, I am content in my situation in life. I neither want or desire anything else. For these urges are what propel us into darkness."

"An innocence I reflect, however, it was this innocence which brought my downfall," he stated.

"We are similar you and I," she said. "Both lost of a mother's love," she whispered.

"And your father?" he enquired.

Abigail smiled.

"A man who is as gentle and as kind as I could ever dream for."

"Then you are blessed," Siamun stated with a smile.

"I do believe I am," she replied, as she turned and linked her arm into his, and walked further into the blizzard that was rising all around.

As the turned the corner that led to the museum, Siamun smirked to himself, observing his emotion, Abigail stopped and enquired to the foundation of his amassment.

"This world," he replied.

"What do you mean?" she asked.

"Here I am, a prince of Egypt, who should have naturally perished several millennia ago, and I'm walking around in this modern day foreign city with a beautiful woman on my arm, and it feels as though I don't have a care in the world."

Abigail smiled.

"Apart from your adoptive brother causing havoc and reeking mayhem across London."

Siamun raised his eyebrows and pursed his lips.

"We must discover his whereabouts and put a stop to his dark actions. For my time is precious and somewhat limited," he announced.

Looking at him in curiosity, Abigail nervously smiled.

"What do you mean?" she asked.

Siamun allowed his arm to fall free from hers and he stepped a little forward before turning to face Abigail.

"I know of the spell that was placed upon myself and was initially intended for Nehi, my brother, who was a wise and benevolent man, had taught me the basic ways of the high priest, and ensured that I understood in the invocations of the Gods. The spell that has enlightened my soul has but a few days in which it can invigorate my form, after that moment I am obligated to return to the underworld and my body must therefore return to dust," he coldly stated, his voice unemotional.

"Does the prospect of no longer existing scare you?" she passionately enquired.

Siamun laughed lightly.

"I have known death, and he does not scare me. Am I not living proof that it is not the end?"

"What will you do in the meantime?" she asked.

"In what way?" he asked.

"Well, you're a living breathing man, here now, before me. Where will you go?" she queried.

He laughed.

"Back to the museum, where I will rest in my casket."

"But you may be discovered," she highlighted.

"I will be there, in full sight, for any who choose to observe my decayed mortal remains. However, in rest, I may still observe the world but to those who observe me, I appear as my deceased self," he stated.

"Can you hear our conversation?" she pensively enquired.

Siamun smiled.

"As clear as I hear you now," he stated.

Abigail smiled, as a tinge of embarrassment washed over her cheeks.

"May I enquire of you, how you gained this interest in my people and country?" he asked.

Abigail thought for a brief moment before replying.

"I don't really know, I was taught about ancient civilisations as a child and that sparked my interest. I always loved the idea of those dusty and evocative lands, filled with mystery and dark passion. However, it was only when I was eighteen years of age, and just after my mother had died, when I realised that I wanted to undertake a course of employment that was both fulfilling and educational. My mother instilled in me a strong feeling of self-worth, I understand that I am living in an enlightened civilisation where woman have the vote and are now emancipated against the rigors of male ownership."

Siamun smirked.

"In my society, women have the same equal rights as a man, be they unmarried, divorced or widowed. The only differentiation was the position they held within our society, be it through birth, marriage or employment. Admittedly, most of them held the title, 'mistress of the house,' but this was not a demeaning title, but an honourable one. However, in a legal sense, both men and women were perceived as equal. Unlike the Greeks," he quipped. "However, we were all bound by the laws of my father, and I am sad to say, he was not a fervent follower of his own decrees." Siamun looked up the deserted road, as the snow gathered in its intensity. "I would be grateful if we could continue both of our social education at a more suitable time," he stated, as the shadow of oncoming pedestrian's invaded they're intermit rendezvous.

Looking down at her watch, Abigail observed the time.

"Gracious, it's almost 10 p.m.," she declared. "We must get you back to the museum."

"I thank you for your kindness, but I am more than capable of undertaking these actions without your support. I would bid you goodnight and hope your journey home is a pleasant one," he said, offering her a polite bow.

The church clock struck 10, and announced to the world that night had long since fallen. Abigail looked skyward and observed the gentle drifts of snow as they fell in their delicate flurry. Turning back to Siamun, she was surprised to find an empty space where he once stood, leaving only an unearthly atmosphere in his wake. She smiled to herself, as her heart turned in its confusion. Looking directly at the ground, she observed that it bore little witness to her companion's presence and those tracks that proceeded her were singular and alone. It was as if he were a ghost of her imagination, a wandering soul, lost on this winter's night.

"What am I to do?" she whispered, as she turned to walk the short distance to where the cabs congregated. As she did so, she walked impolitely into a wandering pedestrian. Standing back, she offered him her heartfelt apologies.

"It's me," the stranger stated. "Johnathan. I've been sent to the museum by Sir Henry to collect some of his paperwork," he announced, presenting the aforementioned documents to her. "You undertake too much for that man," she stated in chastisement.

"I know I do, but hopefully it won't be for much longer," he stated with a smile.

"Before you go," she said, ceasing Johnathan in his tracks. "I do believe I owe you an apology," she stated.

Looking at her in confusion, Johnathan enquired as to why.

"I was rude and abrupt to you this morning and that is unpardonable," she stated.

Johnathan smiled.

"To tell you the truth, I've been bombarded with such verbal detritus from Sir Henry for all of these years, I no longer hear it," he stated with a smile. "May I enquire as to what brings you out on a night such as this?" he asked with genuine concern.

Abigail looked to the heavens.

"The snow, it always reminds me of Christmas, and my mother, a time I haven't enjoyed since she passed. However, they are two things that I now hold dear to my heart," she said, offering Johnathan a broad and warm smiled. "My mother would always make such a fuss at this time of year. She understood how precious a child's memories were and endeavoured to make mine as cherished as she possibly could."

"I don't wish to be a chauvinist, but I do think it's time that you get yourself home, there's news that Lord and Lady Hawthorn's daughter was attacked by a madman and her maid was murdered. That appears to be the second assault in as many days. It's not safe," he declared.

"I understand," she replied. "Would you do me the honour of escorting me to the cabs, and then you can be reassured of my safe journey home."

"It would be my pleasure," he stated, offering her his arm.

"And I will see you bright and early in the morning, so we can study Sia…" she paused and quickly corrected herself. "…the mummy once again."

"I'll see you at eight, sharp," he said as they reached the roadside and the waiting cab.

Stepping into the rear of the cab, she gave the driver her address and sat back into the seat and allowed her mind to wander. Her eyes watched the snow as it drifted in vast swaths across the road, covering the world with its innocent presence.

Realising that his patron desired silence, the driver smiled to himself and honoured her unspoken request as he diligently made his way through the deserted streets of London.

Chapter 15.

Abigail sat on the edge of her bed, her youthful features were bathed in the soft lamplight that smoothed away the rigours of this tempestuous world, as she wistfully contemplating the events of the evening that she spent with her exotic prince. She smiled illusorily to herself, as the image of his forthright features presented themselves to her innocent mind. How she had longed for love, but how she had feared its presence. Life was simple and the complexities of another's yearning were almost too much for her mind to endure. Understanding her dilemma, she stood and walked over to the dressing table; there, she began to decant her modest, yet tasteful jewellery, a predominate amount of which previously belonged to her beloved mother and held a great deal of sentimental value, into the designated receptacles that sat on the dressing table

There was a gentle knocking on the door, and Abigail turned and smiled.

"Yes," she said.

"Are you decent? May I come in?" her father tenderly enquired.

"Of course father," she replied with a smile.

The door slowly open and Lord Cornwall stepped into the soft light of the room.

"How are you my dear?" he asked.

"I'm fine, just a little tired," she replied.

"You were out late tonight, you're normally tucked up indoors by 8 o'clock," he stated.

"I know, I was captivated by the snow, and I lost all track of time," she said, her lie biting deep into her heart.

Lord Cornwall smiled and shook his head.

"You're still my innocent child," he whispered, as he leaned forward and kissed her tenderly upon the forehead.

"Why do you ask?" she enquired.

"It would appear that there has been a second attack, however the intended victim remains unhurt, but her maid died in the assault," he said.

"Lord and Lady Hawthorn's daughter," she announced, surprising her father with this accurate information.

"How do you know?" he asked. "This hasn't been made public knowledge by the police or the press. It only came to my attention because the postman, who delivered the evening post, discovered the incident from one of Lord Hawthorn's footmen."

"Unfortunately father, my experience was a little closer. I was in fact passing Lord Hawthorn's residence when I heard the shattering of glass and suspected a burglary, I knocked on the door and was confronted by the trauma of what had occurred," she stated.

"Please tell me that Lord Hawthorn accompanied you home?" he enquired in exacerbation.

"No, Father, Johnathan, my work colleague, accompanied me to a cab. I wasn't in any danger," she stated, her partial lie assaulting her innocent mind.

Lord Cornwall shook his head in dismay.

"I understand that I have no jurisdiction over you and you are way past the age of consent, but I do wish that you wouldn't be so flagrant with your own safety. You may be innocent my dear, but the rest of society is not, and anything could have happened to you tonight."

"I understand your concerns, Father," she replied. "But, as a working woman, I am required to keep salaried hours, and if that means I must stay out after dark, then so be it. I cannot be wrapped in cotton-wool. I understand that you would like me to remain within the safety of these four walls, but nothing could be further from my own desires. Mother empowered me to reach out and experience life, as she did, and in doing so I feel that I am keeping both her wishes and her spirit alive."

"And her obstinacy and belligerence," he said with a smirk.

"Two of my best character traits," she coyly replied.

"I know that I can't hold you to me forever and some handsome man will whisk you off your feet, but until that time comes, I will endeavour to maintain your safety to the best of my venerable abilities," he declared.

"And for that father, I can only love you all the more," she said, returning the kiss to his forehead.

Turning, he made to leave, pausing for a moment he looked back at Abigail.

"Is there anything else?" he enquired.

"No," she lied, shaking her head.

"Very well, I'm making a fresh pot of tea, will you join me in the parlour?" he queried.

Abigail smiled.

"I'll be down in five minutes," she said as she turned back to the dressing table and placed her mother's engagement ring into a silver ring tray. Hearing the door close, she looked pensively out of the window, watching the snow as it fell in broad drifts across the buildings that littered this affluent part of the city.

****

By the time that she had made her way to the parlour, her father had stoked the fire and an impressive blaze was roaring in the hearth, sending out its warm and welcoming embrace on this bitterly cold winter's night. Observing his daughter entering the room, he offered her a smile.

"Come, sit next to the fire, I have fresh tea and shortbread," she said.

Abigail smiled.

"Mother's favourites."

"And mine," he interjected.

"And now mine," she said, as she sat in the old comfortable wing chair, the blaze of the fire warming her ankles and shoulder. "How I love winter," she mused. "I love the dark nights and the embrace of the quiet."

"You always were peculiar," her father stated in jest.

She laughed.

"I like to think of myself as original."

"You certainly are that," he playfully retorted.

Abigail allowed her attention to be drawn to the fire, her mind wandering in contemplation.

"What happens to us after we die?" she innocently enquired of her father.

"That's a rather unusual question to be asking. What has brought this on?" he enquired.

"I suppose on hearing of the death of one of Lord Hawthorn maids, and also the death of Lord and Lady Aster's daughter. That sort of news make you re-evaluate your life. It sort of reflects back to you your own mortality," she stated.

Lord Cornwall sat in the chair opposite, a cup of fresh tea in his hand.

"I don't really know," he replied. "Your mother had her beliefs, but didn't really have any firm ideologies in relation to the matter."

"Do you ever feel that she's close?" Abigail enquired.

"Who, your mother?" he affirmed.

Abigail nodded.

"Sometimes, but I don't know if it's an ethereal presence, or just my overactive imagination. I know that your mother embraced all of these newfound ideas, after all, it was following the Great War, and every household in England encountered a loss. As a nation we had never experienced such a bloodied and protracted conflict, nothing so vicious or demeaning." He laughed lightly to himself. "I know that the politicians highlighted their joy at our eventual deliverance from the savage Hun, but there were no winners, only victims," he stated. "And, the only way to comprehend the loss was to embrace the grief, something which we did as a nation."

"I suppose it was the first war that disseminated this nation indiscriminately, from Lord to vagrant," she declared.

"And you, you were also terrified by war's presence," Lord Cornwall stated.

Abigail looked at him in confusion.

"Maybe you were too young to remember," he said. "But when the Zeppelin's first floated over London, you thought the devil himself had taken to the skies. The destruction they expelled was incomprehensible, and it was this singular event, which endorsed both your mother and my opinion that we should relocate to the safety of the countryside for the duration of the conflict."

"What age was I then?" she enquired.

"I don't know, about fourteen, maybe fifteen," he replied.

"I don't recall these events," she highlighted.

"Maybe your mind has blotted out the memories, after all, I can only recall some of the events of that night as clearly as if it were yesterday, and I am no stranger to the horrors of war, but I don't mind telling you, I too was afraid. This was the first time that war could be inflicted upon the innocent. Previously, war was an event which occurred in a far off lands, and those fighting were reassured that their beloved were left behind in the safety of their own homes." Lord Cornwall ceased in his recantation and stared blindly into the fire, his mind awash with the images of destruction. "Society was never really the same after that, everything changed. We lost an innocence, a feeling of superiority. We were no longer the pivotal power on the world's stage. Others could rise up and challenge our decree, and that was something this Empire had never previously encountered." He looked down retrospectively into the swirling steam that rose from his cup, his mind adrift upon its light emissions. "We may have won the war, but we experienced more than a bloodied nose. I can only hope that we never encounter such human atrocities ever again in my lifetime."

"Let's just hope that we have learnt our lesson," she replied.

"I doubt it," he stated.

It was the sound of the front doorbell ringing that brought Lord Cornwall out of his dismay, looking at the mantle clock he shrugged his shoulders in confusion.

"Who would be calling at such an ungodly hour?" he asked rhetorically, as he stood and made his way out of the parlour.

"Maybe if you invested in a house keeper, then you wouldn't have to answer the door yourself," Abigail stated.

As he walked out of the room and into the hallway, Lord Cornwall turned to his daughter, who was also venturing into the cold hallway.

"And if I grew wings I could be a butterfly," he stated sarcastically.

Abigail smiled and rolled her eyes to the heavens.

"Go back to the parlour, there's no need in us both getting cold," he insisted.

Abigail turned and made her way back to the parlour, compliant with her father's wishes, leaving him alone in the hallway.

As Lord Cornwall opened the front door a strong blast of cold winter winds brought into the main reception a thin drift of the seasons embrace. The stranger stood motionless at the door's entrance, his black top hat covered in a slight peppering of winter.

Looking up, he glared in his hosts direction.

"Cornwall," he stated coldly, as he stepped over the threshold uninvited, and offered his host his hat and cane in a conceited manner.

"Walter. What brings you here at such an ungodly hour?" Lord Cornwall enquired as he closed the door and cast his guests belonging onto an orphaned chair that sat unloved next to where he stood.

"I was talking to Lord Aster and it appears that there has been another incident, when I heard that your Abigail was involved, I thought I'd undertake an obligatory visit and ascertain as to her wellbeing," he arrogantly stated.

"Please, come into the parlour," Lord Cornwall requested, "Abigail is in there and has come to no harm."

"Without further invitation, Lord Karvahill urgently rushed into the parlour, observing Abigail seated next to the fire, he stemmed his ardour, and walked more congenially towards the fireplace.

"You appear to be well," he enquired of Lord Cornwall's daughter.

"From your tone, you sound a little disappointed," she retorted.

Without understanding her wit, Lord Karvahill continued.

"Nothing could be further from the truth," he stated. "After discovering the tragic events which occurred at Lord Hawthorn's home tonight and those other events which occurred at Lord Aster's home, one can't help but feel that there is something dark encircling our social group."

Abigail looked at him in confusion.

"I don't understand, what do you mean?" she enquired.

"Well, I don't think it's a coincidence that these mummies are brought into the British Museum and soon afterwards there are two murders. I think that we're confronted by the same sort of curse that Lord Carnarvon encountered in 1922," he declared.

Abigail smirked.

"Do you think that one of these mummies has come to life and tried to kill people?" she stated in a derisory tone.

Lord Karvahill looked at her with displeasure.

"No, I'm not stating that, what I am saying is that there is a possibility that there could be a faction, a group of people who are displeased with some articles of antiquity being relocated to another continent for study. Under the guise of a possible curse, they may have sought to discourage others from investing in financially or offering patronage into something which could be classed as dangerous."

"What brings you to this conclusion?" Lord Cornwall asked.

"My son informs me that one of the mummies was stolen from the museum, and later discovered abandoned in an alleyway behind the building. It was initially thought that this act was undertaken by a rival museum, then later, possibly student high jinks, however, following these dark events, my suspicions are rising as to the possible source of our dilemma," Lord Karvahill declared.

"May I offer you a cup of tea?" Abigail dismissively enquired of their guest as she rose from her chair and walked over to the table where the refreshments lay. "May I point out to you that Lord Carnarvon died of a well-publicised insect bite, he was already of weak constitution, and this infection hastened his demise. There is no such curse placed upon a tomb and if that were, then the tombs initial invader, Howard Carter would surely be the first victim of this aforementioned curse. However, I can reassure you that he is in, what could be described as, very rude and prosperous health."

"I am only demonstrating concern," Lord Karvahill continued. "After all, you were present when both sarcophagi were opened."

Abigail smiled and walked slowly back to her chair and sat down.

"As was your son," she highlighted.

"I understand that, this is why I have such a fear of what could ensue from these actions," he stated.

"Was it not your interest in archaeology that compelled your son to undertake his studies in this highly academic field?" Abigail enquired.

Lord Karvahill thought for a brief moment before replying, he experienced difficulty in understanding if her words were accusing or merely attributory.

"Yes I have an interest in archaeology, especially in the area associated with ancient Egypt. Sometimes I think that this may have been unwise to encourage my son in relation to the purchasing of two highly expensive mummies which appear to be presenting him with nothing but contention ever since they metaphorically set foot onto British soil," he stated.

"I understand your concern, but I don't think that the presence of two, several-thousand-year-old corpses are going to affect either your son's or my own welfare. I thank you for your concern, but as far as I am concerned, everything shall be business as usual," she announced.

"And I can't dissuade you from your decision?" Lord Karvahill asked.

"No," she replied, shaking her head.

"You are as stubborn as my son," he stated. Looking to Lord Cornwall he smirked. "I think their union would have been well matched," he said as he turned and left the room to gather his belongings.

Abigail smirked and looked at her father in dismay.

"I think you should see your guest out," she stated sarcastically as she turned and looked welcomingly into the fire's heart.

"Maybe he's right," her father stated in jest.

Abigail turned and threw a cushion at her father and laughed.

"Over my dead body," she shouted.

Lord Cornwall smirked mischievously at his daughter.

Chapter 16.

That following day the snow had abated its torrential downpour, leaving the world covered in a soft blanket of innocence. The time was just past 7.30 a.m., as Abigail washed, dressed and made her way down to the dining room. As she stood outside of the door she could hear voices, muttering in light tones, and an innocent curiosity filled her thoughts. For a moment she waited pensively outside, endeavouring to catch a whisper of the conversation's content. Realising that her endeavours were to no avail, she gently pushed the door open and entered the room, there she discovered the detective who had called that previous day.

"Hello," she innocently stated as she walked over to the tea pot and poured herself an ample cup of tea.

Standing, endeavouring to uphold the protocol of polite society, the officer offered Abigail a slight bow of respect.

"I'm sorry to intrude again, but I'm still undertaking my enquiries," he stated with a nervous smile.

"I understand," she replied as she sat in her chair by the fire. "I was expecting your visit, in relation to what occurred at Lord Hawthorn's residence last night."

The officer sat back down on the sofa.

"Not primarily," he replied.

This caused Abigail a tentative amount of concern, but she sipped her tea while holding her emotions close to her chest.

"May I ask you a question directly, Lord Cornwall?" he asked, returning to his enquiries.

Lord Cornwall nodded, but did not reply.

"No doubt you will be aware of the discovery of the tomb of Tutankhamun in late 1922?" he asked.

Lord Cornwall nodded.

"Can you tell me, have you ever patronised this or any other expedition?" the officer asked.

Lord Cornwall offered the police officer an unemotional yet innocently perplexed expression.

"I don't understand, what has this got to do with the issues which have recently occurred in relation to my friends?" he asked.

"It could mean a considerable amount," the officer continued. "You see, after my initial investigation, I was endeavouring to discover who would undertake such barbaric action upon Lord Aster's daughter. However, now that there has been a second occurrence, I now need to discover the link between Lord Aster and Lord Hawthorn, and there lies the dilemma. For it would appear that, apart from social gatherings, they were pretty much strangers. However, after further enquiry, it transpired that there was a possible tenuous link that connected all parties. It would appear that both Lord Aster and Lord Hawthorn had connections with Lord Carnarvon, as were several other predominant peers, whose affairs are now under investigation."

Abigail looked at her father in amazement.

Not waiting for encouragement, the officer continued.

"It would appear that some of the finances which were procured to fund the archaeological dig in the Valley of the Kings, undertaken by Howard Carter, which subsequently discovered the tomb of the boy king, were provided by both Lord Aster and Lord Hawthorn."

"I didn't know that," Abigail stated.

"As were some of the funds from Lord Karvahill. However, there is a darker side to this financial union. It has been alluded that the discovery of the tomb in 1922 was staged and in fact it had been discovered several months prior to the original press announcement, and the reason for its finding being delayed has been attributed to Lord Carnarvon and Mr Carter's perceived nefarious affairs," he stated.

"I don't understand," Lord Cornwall said.

"It has been speculated that several priceless artefacts were shipped back to England, in the desire to be sold on the black-market with the aspiration of using these funds to finance further expeditions. We are looking into the financial matters of both gentlemen, as it would appear that around this time, both of their finances increased considerably, demonstrating themselves by the purchase of several properties in predominant parts of the city. However, that is mere speculation," he stated with a smile.

"How does this have a bearing upon recent events?" Abigail enquired.

THE MUMMY

The officer smiled, not in jest, but in concern.

"It would appear that there are those who would desire to see the ancient antiquities returned to their rightful country of origin. Those who observe archaeology as the theft of their heritage. It has been surmised that these people, who could be described as fundamentalists, who would not stop at anything to deter people such as yourselves from funding any future excavations in their country," he said.

Realising that the officer's assumptions were either empirically or socially constructed, Abigail pondered his perceivably implausible supposition. She understood the truth, but this recantation of fabricated events intrigued her to such a degree that it fettered her otherwise enquiring mind. She remained silent, yet observant.

Standing, the officer reached into his breast pocket and withdrew a card and offered it to Lord Cornwall.

"If you can think of anything else, please don't hesitate in calling me," he said. "Don't worry, I'll see myself out," the officer said as he bowed politely to Abigail and left the room. Waiting to hear the front door close before she continued her conversation, Abigail sharply, yet respectfully turned to her father.

"Did you ever fund any of these expeditions? she asked.

Lord Cornwall smiled.

"No, I despised Lord Carnarvon, I recall discussing with him your future desires and impending examinations that could have eventually procured you a placement at a predominant university and I asked him for a, 'letter of recommendation,' which he declined, stating that 'a woman's place was in the home, not out in the field of archaeology.' Also, it was only a year or two following your dear mother's demise, and I had pretty much turned against the world and offered it very little interest. At that time, I was in a dark place, and your aunt Mordred looked after my affairs until I was comfortable enough to re-enter this circus called polite society. Lord Carnarvon's rejection of my request was simply another emotional blow endured in life."

"Why didn't you get on with Lord Carnarvon?" she asked. "Was it purely because of his attitude?"

Lord Cornwall scratched the top of his head and he smiled with pride at his daughter.

"I'm so pleased that you have retained your innocence," he stated. "But, no, I disliked him for a number of reasons, the primary of those being the way that he treated others, especially those who he perceived as being socially inferior than himself."

"What do you mean?" she asked.

"I lied to the officer, I was approached by Lord Carnarvon, and it was enquired of myself if I would loan him a substantial amount of money to fund his expedition," he explained.

"I hope you didn't," she stated.

"I most certainly did not. You see I had already been bitten by that misguided action once before. You see the problem with Lord Carnarvon was that he perceived my kindness as a weakness, but didn't take into consideration that the hand that fed him could also strike him down," he explained.

"I don't understand," she said.

"I had previously entered a financial partnership with Lord Carnarvon several years prior, and I was appalled at the way he distributed the wealth of others, primarily myself, and those as fortunate as myself, yet, those who he employed, were paid less than a subsistence wage and were held with brutal managerial force below the breadline," he stated.

"Did you ever see your investment returned? she further enquired.

"Yes, but at what price? From the second that the funds were returned to myself, some full two years overdue, I had the distinct impression that it could be perceived as no more than blood money. The suffering that my financial sustenance enabled, was beyond reproach. I was appalled at the injustice procured in my name. Workers were treated as less than third class citizens, their wages were cut as interest increased in the archaeological world and Carnarvon knew that with this interest brought intrigue, and with that workers, who would undercut their rivals and work for a less than honourable wage. Carnarvon wasn't just a capitalist; he was a master capitalist. He wasn't interested in the archaeology or the discoveries that could be found, all he wanted to do was capitalise upon the findings and self-perpetuate the interest in both himself and his endeavours."

Lord Cornwall shook his head and looked directly at his daughter.

THE MUMMY

"Can you recall all of the hullaballoo that was reported in the papers in relation to the discovery of the tomb of the boy king Tutankhamun?"

"About what?" she asked.

"The curse," he replied.

"Yes, I recall that, it was all over the broadsheets," she replied.

"Hogwash," Lord Cornwall replied with a smirk.

"It was all invented by Lord Carnarvon, long before he even ventured to Egypt. I overheard him discussion the probabilities with Howard Carter, when they met in the club several years prior to that expedition even being considered. Carter kept on stating that he was convinced that there was a lost tomb in the Valley of the Kings, and he convinced Carnarvon to fund his initial expedition. There was a problem however, Carnarvon had a rambling country estate, which devoured money without exception, and he highlighted to Carter that he could only afford to fund a maximum of two digs. It was then that I overheard both parties contrive the tale of a curse, which they knew would ignite the public's interest. He didn't realise to what degree their envisaged imagining would ignite the world's press."

"Little did he realise that he would in fact become part of that actual story, a form of rough justice if you like," she stated.

"Yes, indeed. He had little inclination that as his financial worries were about to come to an end, he himself would become embroiled in this nefarious pantomime and become a prime player in this masquerade of cat and mouse," he said.

"I don't think he even considered that he could have died and become part of the folk-lore that has risen around this discovery," she highlighted.

"There is a form of divine justice in this world," Lord Cornwall said, "It's just a pity that all of those poor people he stepped upon to reach his dark desires weren't around to savour their deserved retribution."

"At least your hands are clean," Abigail stated.

"Yes, but, Lord Aster, Lord Karvahill and many others are not. Greed is a traitorous monster, who will turn upon you when you least expect it," he stated. "In the affairs of commerce, I am not innocent, but I did learn from my mistakes, and only offered what I could afford to lose, in relation to these such ventures."

Abigail looked at him in confusion.

"Why do you think Lord Carnarvon did not announce the discovery of the tomb until many months after its original finding?" he enquired rhetorically. "So that he could secrete away many of the priceless artefacts into his own private collection and return them to these shores, where they were sold to the highest bidder on both the American and English market's. He could ask whatever price he wanted, it was a licence to print money. These stolen artefacts saved many of those aristocrats involved in these scandalous proceedings from financial ruin, none so much as your Lord Karvahill."

"At least you had the morality to remain steadfast to your principles," she said.

"I did, but then again I had the luxury of a considerable fortune and the only two people I had to worry about where you and I. It doesn't take much to corrupt someone, and after it has occurred that state of consciousness appears as a normality, and it is everyone else who appears abnormal. Which is why you cannot reason with people such as Lord Karvahill. And, as sure as the apple does not fall far from the tree, I would beg your diligence in relation to his wanton son, for I feel assured that he is sculpted from the same block of cold granite that his father was impressed from," he highlighted.

Looking at the mantle clock, Abigail returned her smile to her father.

"Time is getting on, and I must get into work. Please father, be assured that I am innocent in many areas of my life, as I understand that it has been both sheltered and privileged. But, in relation to Sir Henry and his father, I have no delusions in relation to their integrity. They are both nefarious in their intentions and thrive on their moral ambiguity. While I am working, I am a little protected, for I have the company of my friend Johnathan, who despises Lord Karvahill almost as much as you appear too."

"I don't hate him, because that would take interest and effort. What I do hate is the fact that his presence can have influence upon a member of my family," he stated.

"And, as you have highlighted previously, if I were so encumbered by their presence, I have enough financial stature, I could cease my employment, consider my options, and undertake a similar, less eminent positon, for another less prestigious museum. After all, I understand that I have to be practical, but I'm not going to let some over-inflated windbag, oust me from an employment position which I enjoy. Now if you will bid me farewell, I'll gather my belongings and make my way to work," she stated in a glib fashion, as she rose from her chair and made her way out of the dining room.

Chapter 17.

By the time Abigail had reached the museum, it was almost 9:30 a.m. All about the hustle and bustle of life was rising, bringing with it a plethora of human emotions. As she walked up the steps, Abigail notice that Johnathan was waiting patiently at the top of the stairs. Offering him a smile she made to walked into the museum, but was stopped in her endeavours by her friend's polite intervention.

"May I have a private word with you?" he enquired.

Without demonstrating any emotional concern, Abigail stepped to one side and looked at Johnathan with open and honest eyes.

"Of course, is there a problem?" she asked.

"Please, walk with me and I'll discuss the matter with you when I am certain that there are no eavesdroppers," he said, gathering her arm into his own.

"You have me intrigued," she stated as they walked down the steps and away from the museum.

"I am a little concerned," he began. "As is becoming a matter of course, Sir Henry asked me to return to the museum early this morning, it was past 6:00 a.m. by the time I left, however, during my time in the dark building, I encountered something which disturbed me to such a degree that I felt that I should converse with you and highlight my deep concerns."

"What was it?" Abigail asked.

"I don't know, but it sounded like the ancient Egyptian language was being spoken, I recognised the cadence from your own expression of the ancient dialect," he said.

"Did you recognise any of the words?" she asked.

"It sounded like the word Nehi," he stated.

Without expression Abigail continued.

"What do you think it means?" she enquired.

"I don't know, I thought that you might know," he said.

"Didn't you ask Henry?" she asked.

THE MUMMY

"He's not in a good mood, I was late last night with his documents and he's looking through them as we speak. He asked me to inform you that he was not entering the museum today, as he had a lot of other, more pressing work to undertake," Johnathan explained.

"We could go to the library and look through some of the reference books and discover the meaning of this word 'Nehi'," she innocently stated. "However, before we continue, can you explain to me where you heard this word being spoken?"

Johnathan stopped and turned to face Abigail, his eyes bright but deceptive.

"It was in Sir Henry's examination room," he explained.

"Did you enter and discover the provider of these words?" she asked.

Embarrassment washed over Johnathan's features, as a bright flush of crimson flashed across his cheeks.

"No, I was a little afraid. It's not nice being in that building during the hours of darkness," he said, nodding in the direction of the museum.

"I must admit, you wouldn't get me in there alone, even during the daytime, it scares me," she stated falsely, for Abigail had never been afraid of the dark. Realising that her false declaration had brightened her friend's demeanour, she enquired of his duties ahead.

"What does Sir Henry have in store for you today?" she enquired.

"Nothing, he asked me to accompany you in your endeavours and assist you where possible," he replied.

Abigail took a deep breath.

"That's good, let's start the day with a cup of tea and a cream cake. I'll make the tea, if you visit Lucy's Tea Rooms and purchase two of the largest cream cakes you can find," offering him a smile, she turned to make her way back to the museum. "I'll meet you in the examination room in 15 minutes," she called as she hurried along the pavement.

Inside the museum, she rushed along the dark uninhabited corridors until she came to her own examination room. Inside, everything appeared as it had that previous night. Walking over to the sarcophagus, she observed Siamun's desiccated remains. Offering him a smile, she lowered her head and whispered into the casket, close to his ear.

"Have you been wandering around the museum in the early hours of the morning?" she enquired.

The air was silent, yet oppressive, realising that the situation was not as it should be, Abigail silently rose to a standing position and slowly turned and looked about the room. There in the corner, dressed in shadows, stood the figure of a sole silent individual. Observing her every action.

"Can I help you?" Abigail stuttered.

The figure remained silent.

"I'm not afraid of you," she stated, as a representing level of terror represented itself in her voice.

With her back to the door, she walked away from the sarcophagus and stepped closer to the doorway.

Realising that his silence was attributing to her fear, the stranger spoke.

"There is no need to be afraid," he said as he stepped from the shadows. "I was only visiting the museum to inspect my investment," Lord Karvahill stated as he walked silently towards Abigail, smiling menacingly as he approached. "It would appear that you have a greater affinity for the dead rather than the living, whispering sweet nothings into the ear of a several-thousand-year-old mummy."

Regaining her composure, Abigail offered Lord Karvahill a pensive smile.

"Actually, I was talking to myself, contemplating what next action I was to undertake in relation to discovering more about the mummy of this high priest," she stated.

"And what have you surmised?" he asked.

"That, I haven't yet decided," she said, as she turned to exit the room. "I'm going to make Johnathan and myself a cup of tea. Could I interest yourself in one?" she innocently enquired.

"I don't drink the muck," he sharply declared. "For me, it's a single malt whisky and nothing else, undiluted of course," he blustered, and he rushed past Abigail and out into the corridor.

"Is there anything that you want me to do specifically in relation to the mummy?" she shouted down the corridor to Lord Karvahill.

"Continue as you were," he replied without looking back.

"How very strange," she whispered to herself.

"Stranger than you think," Siamun whispered from the doorway.

Turning, she offered him a smile before she apprehensively looked back along the corridor.

"Get back into your casket, Johnathan is returning forthwith and I don't want him to discover you," she whispered, ushering Siamun back into the room and closing the door behind herself.

"Were you wandering around the museum this morning?" she asked.

As he rested back into the sarcophagus Siamun offered her a smile.

"I went to see Nehi, to reason with him. But he would not talk to me, it was as if he were truly dead."

"Well you were observed," she stated as she turned on him. "Johnathan was in the museum this morning, at about 6 a.m."

Siamun smiled.

Abigail looked at him with concern.

"What?" she asked.

"As was your Lord Karvahill," he replied.

"What do you mean?" she asked.

"He came into this room and stood where you found him, staring at me. Willing me to rise," he slowly stated.

"But why?" she asked.

"I don't know, he didn't move, but remained there, in the corner, demonstrating no emotion or ability to interact," Siamun replied. "After a while, life left me, as is apparent, if not, an immortal soul like mine would feel the passing of each and every grain of mortal sand, and this eternal persecution would be intolerable, but when I awoke, he remained where he stood, a statue, dead to this world."

"This is all getting a little too cryptic for my liking," she declared. "Mummies coming back from the dead I can deal with, but the living skulking in corners, now that's something that creeps me out."

Siamun lay in his casket, watching Abigail as she slowly walked around the room, verbally contemplating Lord Karvahill's actions.

"Does he know that there is an ancient mummy alive here in London in 1928, or is he simply protecting his investment, as my father has previously highlighted? Lord Karvahill, among others, has invested and lost a considerable amount of money in relation to funding these financially risk-orientated endeavours." She paused for a moment and turned to face Siamun. "Could it be that there are some rebel factions from Egypt's political quarter who are trying to stop any further excavations in their land, by deterring those people who are the heart of their perceived dilemma, from investing any further finances into future expeditions?" she asked rhetorically.

Siamun offered her an expression of confusion. Realising his dilemma, she smirked and waved her hand in dismissal.

"I don't understand what you are saying," he stated. "You keep changing from your version of my native tongue to a language that appears to have no rhythm or rhyme to its construction."

"I'm sorry," she said. "This is my own native language, it's called English. I am told that it is one of the most difficult languages to learn," she stated with a smile.

"Maybe you could teach me one day," Siamun enquired. "After listening to you for the short time I have had the pleasure of your company, I have learnt to understand the emotional content of its expression."

"One day," she replied, passively dismissing his request, for she understood that his time upon this earthly realm was both limited and restricted.

"May I asked you a question?" he enquired.

"Of course," she replied.

"Your world, although wondrous and inspiring, is also dark and soulless. How do you live without the guidance of your gods?" he innocently enquired.

Abigail looked out of the window at the dark skyline that offered a malevolent horizon to the sky and smiled unemotionally to herself.

"I suppose as a nation we have turned a historical corner, following the Great War, we were left with what could be described as a dystopian society, which allowed the cut throat and dark opportunists and social climbing ne'er-do-wells, like Lord Karvahill and his son, to claw their carnivorous way up the soft under-belly of the sacred echelons of this regal land, and are in fact, a true reflection of the pure brutality into which this society has descended. Everything which you observed yesterday was a thin veneer, an unrealistic reflection of this life, and the only glimpse of truth was the pure impact of your friend Nehi's actions, upon a cosseted and socially blind collection of privileged vagabonds."

She turned and looked at Siamun.

"And the irony is, Nehi's dark actions, although intended for another, were invoked upon an innocent, as is so apparent in this world."

"Do those of a higher social standing not fight in this Great War, do they not use their power and influence, to uplift those below them?" he innocently enquired.

Abigail took a deep breath and contemplated her answer for a few brief moments.

"As I am sure it was as relevant in your world as it has been in mine, it is all too apparent that those people who are perceived as having a greater intelligence generally use that intelligence as a weapon to beat down those who they perceive as being less intellectual than themselves, rather than using that talent to uplift another person's soul. Yes, many of the great households of this nation scarified their first-born to the guns of war, but it was an expectation, a forgone conclusion, rather than a designated choice. The society, into which I was born, is driven by the false ideologies of a lost generation. As was apparent with yourself and your father," she highlighted, looking directly at Siamun, "The expectation of the parent far outreaches their child's natural ability, and so it is inevitable that their desired objective will fall short of their carnivorous aspirations and leave nothing but regret and disappointment, cause a schism within the family unit."

Siamun looked at her in confusion.

Realising the necessity for clarity, she elucidated her views.

"Your father may have fought many battles and tasted a number of glorious victories, however, those victories were made many generations prior to your own experiences, and, as with all societies, their ability to kill one another, advances and becomes more prolific in its dark integrity, unrecognised by your father, for his experiences were no longer relevant and became outdated and obsolete. But, because he holds a position of ultimate power, he had the ability to damn your soul, ultimately, because of what he perceived as non-compliant, or non-committal indifference on your part. As is apparent of someone your age."

"Our parents do not understand the constant and compounding affect that their selfish actions have upon our lives, and it is only after their death, when we are allocated the luxury that time affords to truly reflect upon their narcissistic interventions, and only then do we fully understand how manipulated and negatively directed we have all been by their covert influence. We are congregated as if cattle, innocent of commerce, blind to parental dark guidance, captivated within a world where love withers upon the vine of life, as surely as the infant takes its first breath," he declared.

Abigail smiled to herself and looked pensively towards the floor.

"You, above all others, truly understand that situation. I, on the other hand, have been very lucky," she whispered. "All I have ever known is love, and the pure terror at the loss of that love. Both measures of the same emotion," she said.

Looking up, she noticed the shadow of Johnathan's return as he walked briskly, almost militarily along the passageway, his actions reflected along the large glass wall that faced the corridor, Abigail turned to Siamun to warn him of her assistant's impending arrival, only to observe his desiccated corpse staring back at her. She smiled to herself, so she felt safe with her secrets. Turning she offered Johnathan a broad smile as he entered the room.

"Tea, I was going to make tea," she announced in a bombastic tone. "You make yourself comfortable, and I'll be back in a jiffy, hot tea in hand."

Johnathan offered her a perplexed expression as she left the room, walking over to the coat stand he placed the cakes on the desk opposite and took off his outer coat, folding it over his arm he looked over to the sarcophagus. Contemplating his thoughts, he slowly walked over to the casket and stared at the mummy who lay within, and offered him a wry smile.

"If only you could talk, I bet you could tell us all a tale or two," he whispered, before he turned and placed his coat onto one of the pegs of the coat stand. At that moment Abigail returned and walked directly over to the sarcophagus.

"I think we'll do a little more investigation today, looking into deciphering those hieroglyphics written on the side of the casket," she stated, without looking in Johnathan's direction.

"Sounds like a good plan to me," he replied.

"Well we must adhere to Sir Henry's wishes, and not unwrap our friend anymore," she stated, nodding in Siamun's direction.

"I wonder what he was called?" Johnathan asked.

"Siamun," she quickly replied without consideration.

Realising her misdemeanour, she turned and smiled at her colleague.

"It's written on the side of the sarcophagus, it appears Sir Henry was correct, he was a high priest," she lied, as she returned her gaze to the mummy and offered him an embarrassed smirk.

"It must take a great talent to be able to read those pictures," Johnathan passively stated.

"I suppose it's a bit like learning a new language, after a while you get used to it. If it hadn't of been for Champollion deciphering the Rosetta Stone over a hundred years ago, I would have been as linguistically lost as you are," she highlighted.

"How did he manage to do that?" Johnathan genuinely enquired.

"The stone had more than one language carved on its sides. Apart from ancient Egyptian, it also contained Demotic and Greek script. All Champollion did was decipher the basics, and later, following his death, other scholars undertook the almost insurmountable task of discovering the meaning of the stones lost inscriptions," she laughed to herself. "It was only discovered by pure accident," she highlighted. "There was a group of soldiers during the Napoleonic campaign in Egypt in 1798, who were strengthening the defences of Fort Julien, a couple of miles North East from the Egyptian port city of Rosetta, when a Lieutenant Bouchard spotted the stone precariously poking out of the sands, that stone had been previously earmarked to be used for fortification, however, Bouchard immediately recognised its historical significance and informed the incumbent general of this historical discovery, and the news of its unearthing quickly spread and it was subsequently relocated to the Cairo Museum. As time passed, and with a considerable amount of political wrangling, the stone was made ward of the British Crown, and it was eventually relocated to the British Museum, where it remains to this day."

"What, it's here in this museum?" he enquired.

"Yes," she stated. "It's only a few hundred yards away, down the corridor. You pass it each day you enter the museum, it resides in the King's Library," she highlighted, with a smile.

Johnathan shook his head.

"I will make time today, after lunch, and visit this artefact, if only to quell my ignorance and broaden my own insignificant education," he ashamedly stated.

Abigail smiled.

"You're not the only person who should hold this shame. As a little girl, I virtually haunted this museum every weekend. I recall that I would beg my father to bring me here, pestering him for days, selfishly requesting him to relinquish his precious time with my mother and his domestic responsibilities, so that I could visit the stone and appease my almost religious fervour for knowledge. Yet now," she coldly stated, her shoulders falling in self-imposed shame. "I barely offer it a second glace as I stride through these magnificent corridors, consumed by the labours of my own work's decree. I suppose as we grow older, we're consumed by what we feel is paramount in our lives, forsaking what truly enriches our existence. Knowledge and love," she quantified, with a smile.

"And tea," Johnathan glibly interjected.

Abigail offered him a confused expression, before realising the joviality of his reply.

"Oh my, the kettle will be boiled dry," she exclaimed, as she rushed out of the room and into the makeshift kitchen.

Johnathan laughed as he shook his head.

THE MUMMY

"Highly intelligent, but also lost to the world of common sense, which is always apparent," he mumbled, in a patronising, yet none-condescending tone.

A non-committal moan emanated from the sarcophagus, capturing Johnathan's attention. He stared tentatively at the mummy within, as his imagination ran rampant around his mind, before it returned with a form of clarity and self-regulation.

The door to the make-shift examination room opened and Abigail entered holding an old teapot and several workman coffee mugs.

"Sorry, but it's the best I could salvage at such short notice," she declared as she looked at Johnathan's perplexed expression. Realising his dilemma, she slowly enquired of his predicament. What's wrong?" she enquired.

"Nothing, "he stated, "but I could have sworn I heard a noise coming from that sarcophagus."

Thinking quickly, she turned to the casket and observed the heating radiator on the far wall behind.

"It's probably some blocked air in the ancient cast-iron heating ventilation system, nothing to be jumpy about," she glibly stated as she stepped forward and placed the teapot and mugs onto the desk and turned briskly to her colleague and offered him a warm smile.

"Right let's get this tea drunk before it gets cold," she said, purposefully redirecting the conversation away from Siamun.

Chapter 18.

Lord Karvahill sat silently in his library as the detective sat quietly opposite, staring patiently into Lord Karvahill's eyes.

"Can you tell me your whereabouts on the evening of Wednesday the 12th December, between the hours of nine and ten p.m.?" he asked again.

Lord Karvahill took a long and purposeful inhalation from his cigar, before he allowed the acrid smoke to be released from his lungs and drift in dense clouds through the air of the library, his apparent arrogant stance annoying the detective further.

"It's simple," he coldly replied. "I was here with my son, you can verify those details with him, I'm sure he'll vouch for me."

Wishing to redirect the conversation, the detective changed his line of questioning.

"I understand that both your son and yourself have a keen interest in archaeology, primarily of the Egyptian variety?"

"Yes, what of it?" Lord Karvahill snapped.

The detective took a sharp breath.

"Can you tell me, were you acquainted with Lord Carnarvon?" he enquired.

Lord Karvahill looked at him sharply.

"You know full well that I was, one of your officers asked me that very same question yesterday," he coldy stated.

Curtailing the conversation, the detective retorted in the same blunt tone that he had subjected to.

"As I wasn't present yesterday, I am just reiterating the questions proposed and confirming my hypothesis," he firmly stated.

"Which is?" Lord Karvahill snapped.

The detective sat forward in his chair, offering Lord Karvahill the firm evidence that he was not intimidated by neither his presence nor his title.

"I am here to ascertain whether there could be a connection between those individuals who have committed these murders and the possibility that either yourself, or your son, could be placed into any form of danger because of your recent purchase of two Egyptian mummies, and your previous financial wrangling with the late Lord Carnarvon," he firmly highlighted.

Their eyes locked for several seconds before Lord Karvahill acquiesced and looked away. Realising that he had achieved a slight triumph, the detective continued with his investigation.

"Getting back to the late Lord Carnarvon, can you tell me how your financial partnership came about?"

Lord Karvahill turned in his chair and lifted the whisky decanter which was situated on a small table next to him, and poured himself an ample drink before returning his attention back to the detective, without offering his unwelcome guest a fortifying drink, exacerbating the appearance of his cold inhospitality.

"I had known Lord Carnarvon for about five years prior to his death, he was introduced to me by Lord Cornwall," he stated, knowing full well that this information was an outright lie. "It appeared that Lord Carnarvon's finances were in dispute and he requires sponsorship to undertake a final expedition to the Valley of the Kings, in Egypt. He had commissioned Howard Carter to head the group, and was spurred on by Carter's claims that he was close to discovering, 'something magnificent.'"

"Did you invest any money into this expedition?" the detective enquired.

Lord Karvahill looked at him with a rather sheepish expression before he answered in a quiet submissive tone.

"Around twenty thousand Pounds."

The detective took in a sharp breath.

"That is a considerable fortune," he stated.

"When investing money, one must speculate to accumulate," Lord Karvahill replied glibly.

"And from all accounts, that speculation almost went wrong," the detective highlighted.

"But it didn't, and my finances were returned, with interest, and so, there was no issue," Lord Karvahill snapped.

The detective sat comfortably back into his chair and smiled at Lord Karvahill.

"And how was this interest calculated?" he asked.

Narrowing his eyes, Lord Karvahill looked intensely at his unwanted guest.

"What do you mean?"

"Well, you're a keen business man, Lord Karvahill, I'm sure that you undertake business transactions on a daily basis and each and every one of those dealings has some form of contract," he asked, more than stated.

"Yes," his lordship replied.

"And did you have a contract with Lord Carnarvon?" he queried.

"Lord Carnarvon was a gentleman and a friend, and there is honour among gentlemen," he retorted.

"As there is amongst thieves," the detective replied with a smile.

"What are you insinuating?" Lord Karvahill bellowed.

"I'm not insinuating anything. Why, what do you think that I'm insinuating?" he tantalisingly enquired.

Lord Karvahill pursed his lips and took a large gulp of whisky before hitting the glass harshly off the table's surface, demonstrating his displeasure, as a cold silence filled the room.

"I can return at another more congenial time, if you require," the detective stated, demonstrating his recognition of Lord Karvahill's apparent displeasure.

"Get this over and done with," Lord Karvahill hissed.

"As you please," he replied. "How were you repaid by Lord Carnarvon?" he asked in a slow and deliberate manner.

"He gave me back my original amount and that was all, there was no interest, no preceding incentive, only an interest in archaeology and my willingness to help a friend," Lord Karvahill declared in a shallow, defensive tone.

Recognising the deceit, the detective smiled.

"Well, that changes the direction of the investigation, for you have previously highlighted that there was an interest incurred by Lord Carnarvon, and from my preceding investigations, it would appear that Lord Carnarvon had several investors, and if each investor procured the funds similar to yourself, it would appear that Lord Carnarvon may not have risked any of his own money in relation to these archaeological endeavours, and he could have amassed that small fortune to furnish his interests with little financial risk to himself," he stated.

The realisation of his aforementioned predicament began to dawn upon Lord Karvahill and he looked coldly at the detective, silent in his recourse.

Appreciating that his words had achieved their desired impact, the detective stood and reached into his breast pocket. Withdrawing his card, he stepped forward and placed it upon the table next to Lord Karvahill.

"If you can think of anything else, please call me on that number, I'll see myself out," he said, as he departed, leaving Lord Karvahill to evaluate the unsurmountable edifice of his own invidious arrogance.

Chapter 19.

The day had continued and the events which unfolded were mundane and predictable, however, Abigail could not take her eyes from the sarcophagus and its patient inhabitant. Even his deathly presence filled her with an anticipation that consumed her with both caution and girlish delight. How she longed for the evening to fall and to be alone with her ancient friend. Even their conversations took her mind away upon the wings of fantasy, and allowed her the escape which she so longingly desired, from this tedious and mundane world that was governed by one whom she despised. Looking over to Johnathan, she offered him a friendly smile, as he worked meticulously organising the artefacts retrieved from the casket and arranging them in historical order, as denoted by Abigail herself. As he had previously demonstrated an aptitude relating to art, she requested that he catalogue the relics and memorialise their historical presence.

"You can leave a little early if you wish," she said, encouraging Johnathan to finish his artistic endeavours.

Looking up from his illustrations he offered Abigail a broad smile.

"Thank you, I might just take you up on that offer, I have a few errands that I must undertake for Sir Henry, and time is a little precious at present, so any recompense would be most welcome," he declared.

Lifting his pocket watch from his waistcoat, he opened the case and smiled.

"I'll remain for another twenty minutes, which will take the time to 4:00 p.m., and then I'll clear my things and leave you to your devices," he explained.

Looking back at Siamun, she offered him a smile.

"That sounds like a good plan, I don't want anyone wandering these city streets after dark, especially after what has been occurring," she stated.

Johnathan turned to Abigail and offered her an expression denoting disorderly thoughts. Realising his confusion, she clarified her concerns.

"The attacks of the two women which the police are investigating," she stated.

"Oh yes, that," he replied. "The police were with Lord Karvahill early this morning, I noticed their arrival as I departed with Sir Henry, just prior to meeting you outside of the museum."

"Controversy appears to court your employer, as surely as it lingers with those unfortunate enough to sell themselves upon these cold streets at night," she stated.

Johnathan laughed.

"Yes, but I feel that their reputation is not as tarnished as those of Lord Karvahill or his son," he replied with a broad smirk.

Abigail laughed, and lifted a protective finger to her lips.

"Be careful what you say, for I fear that these walls may have ears, and trouble, along with misery, loves company."

"How very prudent of you," he replied. "And respectfully cautious."

"I'm not one for idle gossip, nor conjecture, yet there are some people who inhabit this world who are plagued by misfortune and disrepute. Some can cast this impediment aside without recourse or inference, whereas, others are plagued by its stench like a stray black dog, searching for its next meal. Unfortunately, Lord Karvahill and his son appear to be tarnished by that indignity, and it festers within their very essence and deters others from venturing to undertake a respectful acquaintance," she stated.

"Or, it could just be that they have repellent personalities, that only a mother could endure," Johnathan glibly retorted.

"Mr Pringle!" she mockingly retorted, while shaking her head.

"What?" he replied. "It's not as if they both don't deserve it, neither of them are going to win any popularity competitions, now are they?"

"I suppose when you're that rich, being popular doesn't really bother you," she replied.

"Not that I'd ever know," he stated.

"Believe me, money doesn't buy you popularity," she then contemplated her thoughts before she continued. "Well it does, but not with the type of people you would really want to be popular with."

"It's not something that I would ever encounter, especially as I only have about £15 to my name," he stated.

Abigail smiled.

"And to some people, £15 is a fortune."

He contemplated her words for a few moments before offering her an understanding smile. Collecting his paint brushes, and pencils, he placed them in a neat pile upon the desk and took his jacket from the coat stand.

"Do you have any plans for tonight?" she innocuously enquired of her friend.

Johnathan's expression took on the tessiture of a condemned man.

"My uncle has specifically requested that I attend dinner with him this evening, I fear that he has observed the change in my generally pleasant demeanour and attributed this to my time in employment of Lord Karvahill." He half-heartedly smiled, as a sombre atmosphere descended over him. "Please don't work too late Miss Abigail. No job is worth wasting your life for, no matter how much you love it," he said, as he walked out of the room and made his way through the museum and out into the cold winter world that was consuming London.

Abigail took a deep breath and looked pensively to the floor.

"I suppose that will be me, I'll look back on my life when I'm ninety, and say, 'well that didn't turn out how I planned it," she stated to herself in her broken ancient language.

"I suppose what confused us all even more, is the fact that we have an idealistic view in our thoughts on what we perceive that our lives should have been," Siamun replied, as he sat up in the sarcophagus and smiled at Abigail.

"You're a regular 'Jack-in-the-box,'" she stated, offering him a warm smile.

"What is a 'Jack-in-the-box'? he enquired.

Abigail smiled and shook her head.

"Never mind."

Stepping from the sarcophagus, Siamun stretched out his arms and flexed his muscles. Turning modestly away, Abigail, allowed her eyes to linger for a brief moment upon his muscular torso.

"Is there a problem?" he asked.

"With what?" she coquettishly enquired.

"The demonstration of mortal flesh?" he asked.

Abigail smirked.

"It's just that it is not so flagrantly demonstrated in polite society," she stated.

Siamun thought for a moment.

"Am I not polite?" he asked.

Abigail smiled.

"No, it's not meant like that, what I mean is," she appeared a little flustered in her explanation. "Never mind," she said, changing the subject. "You can put on some of the clothing that you wore when you visited the city last night," she stated.

"Are we going to venture out again?" he innocently asked.

"No I just thought that you might feel a little cold," she stated.

Siamun looked at her in confusion.

"How can I feel cold, I am dead," he declared.

"I understand that, but you have been brought back to life, so you must feel something," she stated.

Siamun shook his head.

"No, I am dead. What you observe, is an image of your desires."

"I don't understand," she said, "but I can see you, and you look like a normal healthy young man."

"What you are observing is a true representation of who I was, but the decayed remains which rest in this box are a true representation of what I have become. Granted, the god's have afforded me life, but that is limited and with its own rigid specifications," he highlighted.

"What do you mean?" she cautiously enquired.

"As I informed you previously, my time is restricted, and my actions are intertwined with those of Nehi. The darker he descends down the path of destruction, the darker my own actions will appear to be," he said.

"But how? I don't understand," she professed.

"Nehi and I are blood brothers, bonded by more than emotion, he was my Ka. Because he saved my life, I have forfeited my own, and the debt that I owe him must be repaid. And, if it is so, I must embrace his sins so that he will enter the afterlife a pure cleansed soul," he explained.

"When would this metaphorical transfer of guilt begin?" she asked.

"At the conclusion of each dark action," he said.

Abigail scratched her forehead.

"Then we have a problem," she stated.

"Do we?" he enquired.

Walking over to the desk she pulled out the chair and sat down, facing Siamun.

"How do you feel?" she queried.

Siamun smiled.

"I feel fine."

Abigail raised her eyebrows.

"And that's the problem."

"I don't understand," he said.

She placed a finger momentarily upon her lips as she thought.

"If Nehi had murdered an innocent last night, then surely you would be feeling some of that negative force entering your body by now," she highlighted.

Siamun scratched his chin as he contemplated her hypothesis.

"Granted, I do not feel any different. My actions feel as though they are my own to command, and my emotions are as bright and as vibrant as they have always been," he detailed.

"Then maybe you're wrong, maybe you're not as connected as you initially perceived that you were," she stated in conjecture.

Siamun took a deep breath.

"This is possible, or maybe I don't understand the ramifications of the incantation placed upon us both just after we were mummified," he surmised.

"Can I ask," she enquired. "Were your eyes concealed by the bandages during the time of these incantations?"

"Yes," he replied. "I was already in my casket at the time that the priest was damning my soul."

"So you didn't see anything?" she enquired further.

"Well, no, but who else would they have been invoking the spell of resurrection to?" he asked.

There was a cold silence that remained hanging in the air as Abigail contemplated his question.

"Please, tell me, and do not leave out any information that could help us in our endeavours. What was the last thing that you recall just prior to the priests wrapping you in bandages and placing you in your sarcophagus?"

Siamun looked at her with caution, yet continued to indulge her in her endeavours.

"Apart from those actions which I cannot repeat, which were inflicted upon my brother, I recall being dragged by the guards from the gardens next to the royal chambers to my father's sacred temple, there I was beaten and taken into the preparation chamber along with Nehi. I was bandaged, without anointation, and the only issue of mortal flesh that was not concealed, were my eyes."

"And Nehi?" she enquired.

"He remained as he did in life, held by the guards and forced to watch the injustice that was justified against me. It was only after they completed my wrapping and placed me securely in my earthly prison, did they then inflict a thousand more injustices upon my brother. I can hear his screams ringing in my ears as if they occurred only a moment ago," he explained.

Abigail stood from the chair and slowly walked over to Siamun's side.

"And there is the conundrum" she stated.

"I don't understand," he replied.

"How do you know that the mummy which we observed outside of Lord Hawthorn's home, was in fact your brother Nehi?"

Siamun looked at her in dismay.

"Then who else could it be?" he whispered.

"I don't know, but now, I must ask you something," she said directing her question to Siamun.

"The spell which I inadvertently used to bring you back to life, could that be used on any mummy, or has it been specifically constructed with you in mind?" she enquired.

"I don't know," he replied. "As far as I was concerned, a spell was simply a spell. Yes, they could be attributed to an individual, but the essence of their power remains the same."

Abigail thought for a moment.

"So, if I were to use that incantation upon any of the other mummies within the museum, could it bring them back to life?" she asked.

Siamun shrugged his shoulders.

"Hypothetically, yes," he replied.

"Then shouldn't we try?" she asked.

Siamun offered her a nervous smile.

"Don't you think that this could be dangerous, after all, we don't know what the outcome would be. You could have a whole army of mummies running around this city and have no means of stopping them in their rampage."

Turning, he looked back into the sarcophagus.

"Where is the incantation?" he enquired, as he returned his attentions back to Abigail.

"Don't worry, I put it back, it's perfectly safe. After all, you've been lying on it for a majority of the time," she glibly stated.

Siamun smiled and reached into the casket and using his finger nail, flicked open the secret chamber. The smile fell from his features, as an expression of dark concern consumed him.

"It's empty," he stated returning his attention to Abigail.

Realising that he was not eliciting a joke, her expression turned to that of great concern and she rushed over to his side.

"That's impossible, I returned the parchment myself. The day after I recanted its words, I returned it the following morning," she urgently highlighted.

Siamun shook his head in dismay.

"If that parchment has fallen into the hands of anyone who had an inkling as to the power it possesses, and they then choose to use it for evil, I do not envy your city if what dark enmity could be potentially awoken or disturbed by the spell that is etched upon the surface of that insignificant document. For the entire underworld could be manifested in the name of darkness."

****

The dark stranger stood in silence in the main viewing room of the chamber of mummies, that was secreted in the hallowed area of the museum. They stood purposefully, with their hands raised as if in prayer, their eyes closed to the dust that was falling to the world without. Their lips moved in an urgent chatter as the inaudible words escaped in their deceit and mischief, drifting upon the winds of malevolence until they descended upon the deathly ears of the humbly departed. Their investiture took only a brief moment to complete, but the impact of their intention would last a life-time.

****

Siamun's eyes snapped in the direction of the corridor. His immortal heart pounding in his chest.

"There's something wrong," he declared as he returned his attention to Abigail.

"What do you mean?" she urgently enquired.

"I don't know, but there feels as if there is a disturbance in the balance of life. It's as if something unnatural is occurring," he stated.

Abigail looked nervously at the door to the examination room.

"You're scaring me now," she highlighted.

"That is not my intention. My only wish is to inform you of the truth," he stated.

"Why, what is it?" she asked.

"I don't know, it's as if I have received an infusion of life," he said.

"Could it be Nehi?" she enquired.

Siamun's eyes sharpened.

"It's the spell, someone has recanted the spell," he cried as he rushed out of the examination room and into the main body of the museum.

Chapter 20.

As they entered the Egyptian exhibit an eerie silence haunted the air, all about there hung a dark anticipation, cold and foreboding. Abigail looked nervously at Siamun, her heart pounding in her chest, as small beads of sweat began to form on her forehead.

"What is it? What's wrong?" she tensely enquired.

Siamun shook his head.

"I don't know, there is something different, something just not right. It was as if there was a vibration that swept across the natural tide of life. You know when you're a child and you throw a stone into a pond and the ripples disturb the water?" he asked, looking at Abigail. "It's like that, only darker."

"There doesn't seem to be anything now, everything seems quiet," she said.

Siamun looked around the exhibition area, his eyes narrow and inquisitive.

"I know, too quiet," he stated.

Abigail stepped back and turned to look down the corridor, her eyes sharply meeting the shadowed stranger who stood in the hallway. Slowly, she stepped back to Siamun's side.

"We're not alone," she whispered.

Siamun turned, but only observed shadows, vague and sinister.

"Who are you?" he enquired in his native tongue, his voice echoing in the darkness.

Behind, there came a sound of dragging, almost inaudible at first, but gathering in volume as the creature drew closer. Abigail turned and was horrified to observe a decaying mummified creature moving menacingly towards her.

"Where have these come from?" she cried at Siamun.

Searching, he nodded towards one of the museum's own display cases. Inside, the lid of a sarcophagus began to open, revealing the animated corpse within.

"I would have said that this modern world's dark fascination with my culture may be our own downfall."

"Isn't there anything we can do?" she screamed.

"If we leave this building, we will inflict this immortal danger upon the people of your city. However, remaining here, although prudent in relation to others, may be fatal regarding ourselves," he stated.

"What do you suggest?" Abigail cried.

"My father was a warrior, as am I. I will not shy away from my responsibilities, and so, I shall fight until there is only one victor."

He turned and looked at Abigail and smiled.

"Do not leave my side, move as I move, and we may get out of this alive."

"What are you going to do?" she asked.

"I am going to get you to your freedom, so that you may live to recant this tale," he stated as he took a deep breath, and pushed out his chest."

Abigail contemplated their situation, her mind urgent and cascading.

"If you can get me close to the examination room, I think I can help," she stated.

"Why, what will you do?" he enquired.

"These mummies are skin and bone, decayed by the centuries, wrapped in old resin rich bandages," she highlighted.

"Yes," he replied.

"Well, there is a makeshift kitchen next to the examination room. In there, is an old stove, which is gas powered," she said.

Siamun shook his head.

"Gas can be ignited, as can cloth, especially ancient resin infused cloth," she detailed with a smile.

Siamun slowly nodded and turned to look down the corridor towards their desired destination. Where the stranger once stood, now only remained shadows, and this brought a little reassurance to both their hearts.

"Hurry, make your way to this, 'kitchen,' and undertake your magical devises, then return forthwith. I shall endeavour to fight off these demons of hell until you return."

He turned back to the advancing mummy, only to observe the second mummy, concealed in the glass case, stepping from its casket. Turning to his left, he observed a display cabinet exhibiting items from his own time, there, in broad delightful sight, lay a short handled sword, decayed but remaining defensive. Taking his fist, he closed his eyes and muttered a prayer to Anubis, before him, he observed his own arm return to that of its original decayed form. Smiling he sent it crashing through the glass and he retrieved the aforementioned sword. Smiling, he held the weapon high, as his flesh returned to that of mortality, as he stepped forward, defiantly towards the advancing creature.

Narrowing his eyes, he spoke slowly yet coherently in his ancient native tongue.

"I have no disagreement with you my friend. You should be savouring the delights of the after-world and not plaguing these mortals with your unnatural presence," he said.

The creature advanced without consideration or importunity, blind to the world without, focused upon its only desire, Siamun.

"Stand," he cried, "otherwise I will defeat you," Siamun demanded.

With these words the creature screamed an unearthly cry as it raised its arms and lunged for him.

Turning the sword inwards, he sent its handle defiantly into the face of the oncoming creature, sending its head unnaturally backwards. The sound of breaking bone filled the empty air above. The mummy stopped abruptly in its tracks and wavered slightly, a sense of ambient motion echoing through its body as it rocked silently on its heels. As it did so, the mummy's head righted itself and stared defiantly at Siamun, as sense of pure rage filling its decayed eyes.

Lunging forward, Siamun brought the sword swiftly down towards the mummy, realising the impending danger, the mummy quickly lifted its arm and gripped Siamun's hand, preventing him from concluding his actions. Siamun pushed his whole body forward until his face were mere inches away from that of the decayed face of his assailant.

"Do not defy me, tormented one," he hissed. "I am your prince, and you shall bow before me," he instructed.

The mummy smirked as its grip tightened upon Siamun's wrist, eliciting dark mortal pain through to his weak corporeal senses, highlighting to him his new mortal frailty. Pushing the creature away, Siamun turned the sword several times in his hand as he stood defiantly before this anathema to this modern world.

"To the death," he whispered as he focused all of his mortal attention upon the creature before him.

Abigail had already fashioned a makeshift torch from her petticoat and the handle of an old mop and was now searching the kitchen for the matches to ignite the stove, so that she could fully undertake her designated task. She had turned on the stove gas, only slightly, allowing enough fuel to expel from its dangerous housing. The sharp smell of vapour filling the air and was now growing in its thick velour.

"Come on!" she cried to herself, as she searched the draws, where she perceived that she had returned the matches from her limited culinary adventures that very afternoon.

"I'm sure I put them in here," she cried, as she slammed the small drawers closed on the makeshift kitchen cabinet.

It was the sound that captured her imagination, the sound of the matches being rattling in their box as the veiled stranger, who stood in the doorway, waved the it tantalisingly in their hand. Abigail turned and glared at the shadow that stood defiantly before her.

"You don't scare me, you bastard," she cried, as she lunged forward and pushed the stranger to the floor. To her amazement, the assailant was no stronger than herself, which bolstered her stamina, that filled her with newfound vigour and righteous fortitude.

"Either you give me those matches, otherwise I will take them from your dying carcass," she stated defiantly. Her voice did not betray the pounding petrified heart that raged in her chest.

The stranger stood, reflecting Abigail's defiance stance, before she cast the matches to one side, leaving herself between Abigail and her desired goal.

Abigail smiled.

THE MUMMY

"Playing hard to get?" she whispered. "I must warn you, I was captain of the women's hockey team three years in a row, and we didn't take any prisoners," she stated.

The stranger remain defiant.

"So be it," she stated, before she lowered her body and rushed forward toward the figure, knocking them both succinctly to the ground. The intruder fought defiantly and hit Abigail defensively in her face, before she herself raised her legs, placing her foot onto the intruders' stomach, and cast them over herself and into the corridor outside of the kitchen.

Righting herself, Abigail quickly reached down and picked up the box of matches that rested on the floor beside her. Turning to the intruder, she glared at the stranger with a dark hate, that almost consumed her every emotion.

"So, you want to play 'hard-ball' do you?" Abigail turned her neck slightly, demonstrating her defiance. "Bring it on," she cried as she rushed forward, lowering the upperpart of her body as she did so, contacting the intruder in the midriff, and sending them heartily backwards and into the kitchen, their head hitting the cast iron surround of the stove.

The intruder raised their arm, and as they did so, they revealed the naked flesh of their neck, and a dark realisation, although not fully justified, revealed itself to Abigail.

As the intruder made to stand, Abigail held out the box and took out a single match, nodding to the oven as she did so.

The trespassers eyes narrowed in confusion.

Realising the confusion expressed by the stranger, Abigail raised her hand and opened the fingers rapidly, silent whispering the words onomatopoeia and mouthing the sound.

"Boom!"

Realising the danger, the stranger stood, righted themselves and rushed past Abigail, leaving her bewildered and perplexed and alone in the kitchen. Recognising that the danger had passed, Abigail sank to her knees and turned off the gas supply before letting out a laboured and reassured breath.

Siamun brought the sword down upon the mummies shoulder, slicing deeply into the decayed flesh. The mummy cried as agony consumed him, sending a dust filled scream into the air. Removing the sword, he drew it behind himself to expel the full strength of his abilities. Realising his intent, the mummy fell forward, endeavouring to hinder Siamun in his defiant action. However, these cumbersome attempts were fashion far too late, and the sword swung from the side, cleavering the mummy's head free from its shoulders. Siamun watched in his exhausted plight, as the body fell motionless to the floor. He let out an exhausted breath as a smile of relief broke across his lips. Turning, to view the corridor through which Abigail had previously retreated, he was rest assured of her safety by the silence that confronted his endeavours.

At that precise moment, the glass to the display cabinet shattered, sending shards of glass in all directions. Siamun closed his eyes and slowly turned his head toward the mummy that stepped out of the case and stood defiantly before him.

Opening his eyes, he let out a laboured distasteful breath, as he raised the sword in recognition of the battle before him. Confirming his stance, he lowered his head until his eyes met those of his aggressor. Allowing the gravity of the situation to seep into his emotions, he strengthened himself against the rigors ahead as he fortified his thoughts and expelled all sentiment from his mind. Here, before him, stood a native of his own land, a clansman, a brother, but he must strike him down in order to maintain his own destiny in this modern chaotic world. The eyes that returned his stare were opaque and dead, lost of sentiment or emotion. There was no governance or decree to guide this ancient soul, only darkness, and a desire for death.

Siamun stepped forward and swung the sword high into the air, sending it crashing down upon the outstretched arm of the mummy, a great cry emanating from the dust choked throat of his undead foe, as the blade of the sword bit deep into its perished sinew. Tearing the sword from the decayed flesh, Siamun raised it for a second time and brought it swiftly down upon the creature's shoulder, sending clouds of dust spiralling into the air. As rage filled the mummy, it turned and growled at its enemy, revealing its decayed and rancorous teeth, framed by its bloodless lips. Before Siamun could compose himself the creature stepped forward, his hand outstretched, knocking the sword from his grip and sending it scuttling across the stone floor and into the darkness of the corridor beyond.

Realising that his advantage was now spent, Siamun stepped cautiously away from the mummy who appeared to revel in its newfound advantage. Cautiously, he edged his way towards the darkness of the corridor and his only pathway to safety, however, before he could calculate his next cautious action, there was the sound of rippling in the atmosphere as Abigail stepped defiantly into the chamber, brandishing her naked torch, the flames hungrily licking at the virginal air.

Immediately the mummy ceased in its endeavours, an expression of fear spreading like cancer across its features as the realisation of its scorching predicament fell upon its decayed mind. Stepping aside, Siamun allowed Abigail to advance, his sense of chivalry had long since departed, for he understood that the women of this century were both forthright and commanding.

Realising that she must fulfil her duty, Abigail swung the flaming torch from right to left, bringing it into deathly contact with the mummy's ancient apparel, immediately the conflagration devoured the linen, sending hungry wisps of sanctifying flames deep into the creature's tinder body. Immediately the mummy stood as if petrified, as the hunger devoured him from within, consuming his mortal flesh. Siamun closed his eyes and turned away, as the anger of the flames rage growing exponentially as the seconds angrily passed, and great towers of black acrid smoke rose from the creatures tortured remains, as it crumpled into an unrecognisable mound upon the chamber's floor before them.

Siamun smiled and turned to Abigail.

"You took some time," he jovially stated.

Abigail laughed lightly.

"I was otherwise indisposed by someone dressed from head to foot in black, I could only make out their eyes."

Siamun looked at her as a sense of deep concern compelled him.

"Was this person from your country?" he asked.

"I don't know, I didn't try and reason with him, I assumed that he was the person I saw in the corridor earlier," she explained.

Siamun tentatively contemplated her words.

"Was this stranger a warrior, armed with a rounded dagger by their side?" he asked.

"Yes," she replied without deeper consideration.

Siamun allowed his eyes to wander, as they focused upon middle distance, as his mind recalled an image from several millennia ago.

"Medjai!" he stated, as he turned and looked cautiously at Abigail, who in turn shook her head in confusion.

"My father's bodyguards," he stated.

"That's impossible," Abigail stated. "How could they be here? In this time?"

"I think that is a quandary we have to unravel at a more convenient time," he stated, as he walked over to the pile of human dust that rested in an unholy mound upon the floor of the chamber. "What should we do about this?" he enquired.

"We can clean as much up as possible, and leave the rest until morning. With all of the recent events which have occurred, this will just be seen as another weird occurrence and there will be no suspicion cast upon myself," Abagail highlighted. Turning, she looked cautiously up the dark corridor, her eyes searching the shadows for any evidence of the concealed stranger. An uneasiness began to rise within her soul, for Abigail knew for certain that she would be confronted by the stranger for a second time, but then, the outcome may not be to her advantage.

Chapter 21.

After almost an hour of constant diligent labour, Abigail and Siamun had managed to return the exhibition hall back to some form of what could be described as respectable order. The broken glass of the display cases remained destroyed, but the area around them was clutter-free and demonstrated little reference to the events which had recently occurred. Abigail looked at her watch and was shocked to observe that time has so irreverently slipped by as it was almost 8:30 p.m. Looking over to Siamun, she offered him a relived smile.

"What do you consider a fitting conclusion to tonight's events?" she enquired.

Siamun offered her a confused expression.

Abigail smirked.

"How should we conclude this day? Do you wish to remain here in the museum or would you like to see some more of the sites of London?" she asked.

Siamun smiled, but this demonstration of emotion was half-hearted and somewhat distant in its expression.

"What's wrong?" Abigail enquired.

"The stranger you stated you observed in the corridor and the possible encounter with the Medjai does not offer me anything but caution and confusion. I do not understand how or why there could be someone from my father's court here and now in your time," he stated.

Abigail smiled and shook her head reassuringly.

"It's alright, there are no ancient Medjai wandering around London. What I do perceive is that these people could be fundamentalists, opposed to any further excavations being undertaken in your home country. Since the discovery of the tomb of Tutankhamun five years ago, and the subsequent global interest in anything archaeological, this has placed a considerable amount of strain upon your country's resources, as well as placing a rather ethical dilemma into the hands of both your politicians and country folk alike. Investigations bring prosperity and employment and the residual effects of any discovery bring with this a longevity to these proceedings. Tourism, social interest, financial gain, all of which would benefit your country's economy. However, others could perceive this as a negative invasion of another society's ideology, and some of your people are quite happy for the designated sites of immense archaeological interest to remain buried in the sands or abandoned in the fields. Which is where you have these Medjai, who are possibly exerting their influence upon us at this moment. I truly understand the dilemma, although I am an archaeologist, I am also sympathetic. I understand the global pressure placed upon your people. Do they rape and pillage their own history for the benefit of their present society, or do they turn their back upon the world and miss a possible opportunity to enlighten others with their grace and antiquity, while benefiting those who live in the very different and presenting modern world?"

Recognising that Siamun was demonstrating very little interest, she paused and allowed her words to filter into his mind. Realising that the silence was now compounding, he looked at Abigail and nervously smiled.

"Are you not interested in what happens to your country's treasures?" she asked.

Siamun smiled.

"You are confused. You are speaking of things which are equated in the past-tense. Whereas, everything which you have described to me is within my own living memory. How can I become emotionally involved in a people who were not born to me? I had long since perished before they were even a consideration in their great-grandparents thoughts." He smiled and walked over to Abigail's side. "All I have are the memories of my ancient life and the time I was awoke and heard your voice in the cellar of this great building. Other than that, all I have are the dark clouds of memories from the underworld. Something cogent, yet unfathomed. I have the images of spectres and nether-beings, the undead and the restless souls drifting constantly through my thoughts, and the thought of my impending return to that dark place, alone, fills me with an eternal dread."

"Was it disturbing, death?" she sensitively enquired.

Siamun smiled.

"It was not as I had expected, but more than I could have anticipated. It was an adventure," he whispered.

Realising that he was not going to elucidate upon his explanation, Abigail made to walk back to the examination room, as she turned, she observed a long shadow being cast down the corridor that led to the exhibit room in which they stood. Quickly turning to Siamun, she whispered for him to conceal his presence, however all she encountered were shadows and mystery. Turning, she observed Sir Henry briskly walking towards her gesticulating as he approached.

"What are you still doing here?" he demanded. Without the courtesy of allowing her to answer, Sir Henry continued. "The security guards informed me about 30 minutes ago that there was a disturbance in the museum, and because of what has recently occurred, I requested them to remain at their posts and not to investigate." He shook his head in dismay as he placed his arm around Abigail's shoulder. "Do you realise that there are half a dozen police officers outside?" he rhetorically enquired.

"More for your protection than mine," she retorted.

Dismissing her quip, he continued.

"What's been going on?"

"I don't know," she lied. "I was in my examination room and I heard a loud crash and when I arrived here, one of the display cases had been destroyed."

Sir Henry walked tentatively over to the highlighted case, peering in, he sneered at the damage he observed.

"This is either students, fundamentalists, or another jealous museum," he declared.

"I've spent the last half an hour cleaning up the mess," Abigail stated, concealing her true understanding of the situation.

"Something which is possibly more apt to your talents," he impertinently retorted.

"Touché," Abigail whispered under her breath, as she offered Henry a reassuring smirk.

Turning to her, he smiled unemotionally.

"Don't you think it's time that you returned to your home?" he stated, rather than requested.

Abigail looked nervously around the room, searching for signs of Siamun, however, none were forthcoming.

"I'll just gather my belongings from the examination room and leave," she said.

"Please, take my carriage, the driver will escort you to your home safely," Sir Henry commanded.

"As you wish," she stated passively, not wanting to enflame the darkening situation.

With that, Abigail hurried from the exhibition room and along the corridor towards the examination room, her heart pounding in her chest as fear gripped her mind.

"Please be there, please be there," she muttered to herself as she gripped the handle of the door and entered the room. Her eyes searched the dark corner until they eventually fell upon the empty sarcophagus and her heart sank with fear. "Oh, no!" she whispered.

At that moment Siamun appeared from behind the open door.

"Is everything alright?" he whispered.

Abigail made to cry in surprise, but held her tension. Turning to Siamun she grimaced, her eyes wide in anger and she hit him firmly across his broad chest. Stepping fully into the room she closed the door behind herself, she turned upon her friend.

"You had me terrified, I thought that Sir Henry was sure to find you," she whispered urgently, endeavouring to control her shaking voice.

Siamun smiled.

"Sir Henry is of both slow stature, and intelligence. He is reliant upon his presence and social standing to offer him prominence, as sure as a jackal uses its cunning to ensure its own safety on a daily basis. He is no more my equal as is a beggar boy to a king," he proudly stated.

"A simple, 'I'm too quick for him', would have sufficed," she replied with a glib smile.

"And allow him to stem my ardour, where is the pleasure in that?" he enquired.

Abigail shook her head in dismay.

"Men, with all of your posturing and provenance. Why can't you be direct and come straight to the point?"

Siamun smirked.

"Just like you women. You are all as deceitful and as malevolent as any man. You only undertake things in a differing way," he said.

"What do you mean?" she enquired.

"Men are direct," he stated, "whereas women are underhand."

"We most certainly are not," Abigail objected.

Siamun smirked.

"Women will poison, whereas men will kill. The responsibility will be owned," he stated.

"Poppycock!" she declared.

Siamun looked at her in bemusement, realising his dilemma, she offered him an explanation.

"Rubbish, stupidity, it's not true," she said.

Siamun looked down to the floor, the smirk on his lips widening.

"You're teasing me!" she exclaimed with surprise.

"You're allowing it," he retorted.

Realising her social and also her sexual position, Abigail stepped back and used the palms of her hands to flatten her dress, as she regained her composure.

"You are naughty," she declared.

"I do try," he whispered.

Abigail blushed.

Realising that his words were having an imperious effect upon his hosts emotions, Siamun tactfully changed the direction of the conversation.

"Are you to undertake any actions tonight? Are we to explore this city once again, or do you wish me to remain here in this chamber until you return upon the dawn?" he enquired.

"In light of what has occurred, I think it would be prudent if we do not undertake any adventures this evening," she decreed.

Siamun smiled.

"I understand, however, I cannot promise that I will not undertake such an adventure myself, for I have a hunger for knowledge, and a thirst for the truth. Please, be reassured that I will be safe and present upon your return this following morning, but I feel compelled to discover the source of this mystery that has befallen us."

Abigail walked slowly over to the coat stand and retried her belongings, turning, she offered Siamun a cautious smile.

"All I can ask of you is to be safe, and discreet in your tribulations," she requested, as she walked past him and out into the corridor.

Chapter 22.

Siamun had travelled some considerable distance, wandering through the dark streets and alleyways of London, the snow had been perpetually falling since he began his private expedition, and in all that time its presence was neither cumbersome nor daunting. He had marvelled at the edifices that reached up to the snow-filled heavens, denoting this magnificent race of seafaring warriors, who had conquered the world and brought to heel many an empire, creating a nation both strong and patriotic. He smiled at the jingoistic epitaphs that littered the streets and parks, monuments to war, and he smiled to himself, for he realised that man's desire to subjugate his fellow man had not diminished in the many millennia that had passed since his own original demise.

It reminded him of his father, and how he built temples proclaiming his prowess in battle, how he destroyed his enemies and triumphed over all of his adversaries to save Egypt's good name and sovereignty, so that it could remain a safe and prosperous land for his beloved and deserving people. He understood that his father was a braggart and egotistical, but he also knew that he loved him. However, he felt that all of this changed when Siamun fell in love with Amunet, and his father's eyes turned green with jealously. Maybe his father despised his youth, or the fact that he attained privilege without the millstone of responsibility; and this very fortunate act of birth, cut him to the core.

He smiled to himself, for he understood that with great powers come an even greater responsibility, a responsibility to uplift those in your presence and not demean them, not persecute them for your own failings. He above all others realised that freedom was a state of mind, yet his father was so engrossed in the infinitesimal turning of the political wheels of his country, he was constantly embroiled in the internal wrangling and petty in-fighting, so-much-so, that he perceived that everyone, including his own family, were as fickle as those whom he surrounded himself with.

Standing before the cenotaph, he lowered his head as his thoughts wheeled and turned in his mind. He allowed his eyes to fall upon the depictions of war that were emblazoned upon the cold granite surface, honoured by this sanctity to war. He realised, with a heavy heart, that man's lust for conflict would never be appeased, no matter how educated they misled themselves into believing. The truth was always the truth, and death was always death. And here he was, standing at an edifice erected to the passing of millions, the magnitude of which his ancient soul could not comprehend. In those battles endured by his father, hundreds, possibly thousands would perish, but the comprehension of what had passed in this modern era filled him with a true sense of the savagery of this time into which he had fallen. After a few moments he raised his head, smiled, and walked silently into the shadows and melted into the darkness of London's streets.

Abigail sat silently in her room, the clock on her mantle lightly struck 10:00 p.m. bringing to her the realisation that the day was almost over. Standing, she left the novel she had been so avidly reading open on her bed as she walked over to the window and drew back the heavy red velvet curtains, which were put in place to keep out the bitter chill of winter. As her eyes grew accustomed to the darkness, she stared, without direction, down the lonely street. All about the snow sat undisturbed. The road demonstrated witness to a few transgressions of the horse-drawn carriages; other than that, the world was silent and a little subdued.

Letting the curtain fall free, she turned and walked back to her bed. Sitting, she allowed her mind to wander back to the events which she recently experienced in the museum. 'Had she encountered an Egyptian fundamentalist?' she thought to herself, as dark foreboding concerns began to rise deep within her, sparking a tirade of dark images that washed over her thoughts and destroying the barriers of her rational mind. 'What if they had followed her home?' 'Knew her identity?' Abigail contemplated informing her father of her concerns, but then thought twice about this, for she knew that he would ask questions and the whole story relating to Siamun would unravel. She was impeached by her own actions, a victim of her presenting situation, and the dilemma which she experienced was compounding at the turning of each minute.

Her attention was soon distracted by the sound of the doorbell ringing. Urgently, she looked at the clock on her bedroom mantle: 10:05 p.m. Closing her recently purchased novel, 'Sherlock Holmes -The Sign of Four,' she stood and walked over to her bedroom door.

"Who could be calling at this time?" she said to herself, as she took her dressing-gown from the hook on the back of her door and placed it hurriedly about her shoulder. Urgently, she opened the bedroom door and walked briskly out onto the landing, below her, muted voices spoke in urgent tones.

THE MUMMY

"Is everything alright?" she enquired, as she made her way down the stairs and into the hallway. As her presence became apparent, Lord Cornwall turned from the stranger and looked directly at his daughter, offering her a broad, yet concerned smile.

"Henry's here, he's been telling me that there was an incident at the museum this evening. Weren't you going to inform me of this?" he enquired.

Pausing on the last few runs of the stairs, Abigail offered him a nervous smile.

"I didn't think that it was that important," she stated. Glaring at Henry and offering him a scolding glance.

Ignoring her manifest emotions, Henry stepped forward and took off his top hat.

"I was just visiting to ensure that the events of this evening had not unsettled you," he stated with a rather rictus grin.

"I'm perfectly fine," Abigail retorted, endeavouring to deter her guest from remaining a second more than she desired.

Lord Cornwall stared irately at his daughter.

"What?" she replied to his wrathful glare.

"All Henry was doing was ensuring your safe passage home, the least you could do was to offer him a little hospitality." Turning to his guest, Lord Cornwall smiled and placed a friendly hand upon his shoulder. "It's such a dreadful night, what with all of this snow, please remain for a little while and allow me to offer you a night-cap, something to fortify you against this bitter night."

"That is very congenial of you Lord Cornwall," Henry replied with a childish smirk.

Turning to his daughter, Lord Cornwall smiled.

"Would you ensure that the fire is well managed in the library, I think that would be a suitable place for us all to retire, and I know that there's a vintage malt just waiting for you to savour," he said, turning back to Sir Henry and pulling him a little close, in an almost jovial manner.

As Henry walked forward, Lord Cornwall stopped and looked at his daughter.

"Sir Henry, would you mind making your own way to the library, there is a matter that I must discuss with my daughter?"

Abigail shook her head in objection, but remained silent.

When Sir Henry was out of earshot, Lord Cornwall turned cautiously to his daughter.

"Remember dear, always keep your friends close, but your enemies even closer. Sir Henry is a petulant man, and now he is your employer, the last thing you want is to make him an enemy in both camps."

"That type of man was born to the shadows and very rarely steps into the light, he feigns his concern, but he would, in the blink of an eye, cast me to the wolves. I wouldn't trust him as far as I could…spit," she stated.

"Neither would I, but if he does throw you to the wolves, you learn by your mistakes and return triumphantly as leader of the pack," he firmly stated.

Realising the truth in her father's words, Abigail allowed the timbre of her armour to soften and she nodded her head.

"As always father, you're right," she replied.

"With age, comes a little wisdom," he retorted with a smirk. "And, I can gather information from him in relation to your future with the museum and if he knows anything about these incidents involving Lord Aster and Lord Hawthorn's daughters."

"Now who's being Machiavellian?" she stated.

"Only in a good cause," he replied, as they made their way to the library.

By the time they had entered the library, Sir Henry had already relieved himself of his heavy outer winter overcoat, which he had unceremoniously thrown over the sofa, and was standing next to Lord Cornwall's desk holding the whisky decanter on his left hand, which he had already retrieved from the tantalis, and was imbibing the delicate aroma of the vintage malt into his eager lungs.

"This smells like a fine vintage," he declared to Lord Cornwall, as he entered the room.

Lord Cornwall smiled.

"Oh, dear boy, that is a fine vintage malt, but that is for guests," he stated as he turned and walked over to the small cabinet that sat at the far end of the room. Retrieving a small key from his waistcoat pocket he turned to Sir Henry and smiled. "However, the whisky I have in here is for a much finer pallete, and is reserved for friends," he stated as he unlocked the cabinet and retrieved the single crystal decanter, holding it momentarily in the warm glow of the firelight.

Sir Henry smiled and placed the decanter he was holding back into the tantalis, before he moved closer to the warmth of the fire and sat arrogantly down onto the waiting sofa.

"You do me a great honour," he stated in an empty cold tone as he offered Lord Cornwall a hollow smile.

Pouring Sir Henry an ample serving, he offered him the glass, which he readily accepted, taking a considerable mouth-full, without waiting for his host to offer him salutations as a guest in his esteemed company.

"As you were explaining earlier in the hallway, something about a disturbance at the museum?" Lord Cornwall passively enquired.

Sir Henry's eyes lit up with a childlike glee, for he knew that he retained information desired by another, and he perceived that this acquisition maintained some form of insignificant power over his host, and he would relish this domain for as long as socially possible. He looked peevishly in Abigail's direction, who was seated demurely in a chair opposite, he offered her a rakish smile, the type that is exuded by one who understands more than they are committed to reply.

"I must say, this is a damn fine whisky," he briskly stated, as he drank the glass dry.

Realising his guest's voracity for his hospitality, Lord Cornwall stepped forward and poured him another ample serving of the aforementioned malt.

"I am only too pleased that it meets with your approval," he stated with a broad smile, endeavouring to socially manipulate his guests over-inflated ego in order to express the information which he retained.

Sir Henry smiled and took another ample mouth-full of the amber liquid as his host walked over to his daughter side and sat onto the vacant chair next to her. Realising that the short silence which followed this action was a social prompt for him to recant his eagerly awaited tale, Sir Henry positioned himself on the sofa and began his recantation.

"As you know, my father has acquaintances positioned high in our society, and he has been discussing the presenting intolerable situation that appears to have befallen all of us in relation to the attacks upon people of our social standing and the recent break-ins at the museum."

Lord Cornwall smirked at the thought that Sir Henry perceived himself to be a social equal to himself; he remained silent, and allowed the rendition to continue.

"He was in discussion with none other than Brigadier – General, Sir William Horwood, the recently retired Chief Commissioner of the Metropolitan Police. It would appear that there are suspicions that there could be a small faction of Egyptian fundamentalists who have infiltrated British society and are hell-bent on deterring any further expeditions into Egypt. Sir Horwood has allocated several plain clothed officers to the museum, who will be on duty both during opening hours and after dark, to ensure the safety of the artefacts and those working with them," he explained.

"How gracious, we get a mention," Abigail quipped.

Her father offered her a disparaging glance which stemmed her rebellious ardour.

"Please, go on," he requested.

Sir Horwood informs my father that he feels that these fundamentalists may have sympathisers within the higher echelons of our social strata. Thus offering them unfettered access to a majority of delicate areas which otherwise would be barred from their negative influence. Security has been increased around certain key areas, such as Parliament, Buckingham Palace, several of the predominant hotels, and other possible areas of terrorist interest," he highlighted.

"Does Sir Horwood perceive such places as being a possible target to these people?" Lord Cornwall enquired.

"Anything is possible," Sir Henry replied, relaxing into his chair and relishing his fleeting position of absolute power.

Lord Cornwall sat back in his own chair and turned cautiously to his daughter.

"Sir Horwood must also perceive that those individuals who inhabit this upper echelon of society are also at risk, primarily their children, specifically their daughters,' he stated in a leading manner.

"What do you mean?" Abigail enquired of her father.

"Well if we look at the evidence it is plain to see. First there was the attack on Lord Aster's daughter. Then the botched attack on Lord Hawthorn's daughter, where the poor maid was murdered." He looked pensively at his daughter. "You were present at this last encounter," he highlighted.

"Really!" Sir Henry interjected in surprise.

"It's nothing," she stated, momentarily glancing in Sir Henry's direction. "I was endeavouring to discover a suitable Christmas present for my father when I was passing the London residence of the Hawthorn's and I heard a scream. It was pure chance."

"Or coincidence," Sir Henry replied in a condemnatory tone.

Abigail pursed her lips and repressively smiled at Sir Henry.

"You should try it, being pleasant to others, it's enlightening for the soul," she retorted.

"I agree," he stated. "Only prior to this I was collecting my mother's present from Gerrard's, something which is a little lost on you," he replied in childish spite. Realising his less than social proclivity, Sir Henry stood and straightened his waistcoat before turning to Lord Cornwall. "I feel that my time here has come to a conclusion, I will see myself out, I do hope that the remainder of your evening is pleasant, and thank you for the splendid whisky," he said as he picked up his coat and briskly left the library.

"Pompous ass," Lord Cornwall stated.

"Father!" Abigail stated, in a chastising tone.

"Well, he is. He perceives that his inbred ignorance is an equal to my knowledge and understanding. He thinks that power brings understanding and insight, when in fact all it brings is aggression," her father replied.

"And you plied him with your best whiskey, what a waste," she stated.

Lord Cornwall looked at her in childish glee.

"Like hell I did. Do you think I would give a vagabond such as he, any of my good whisky? Perish the thought. He was given the cheap stuff, something kept for lowly relatives and tradesmen, for occasions such as this," he stated. Lord Cornwall endeavoured to stand, but quickly sat back into the sofa, his mind turning in alcoholic disarray. "It's strange, I spend all of this money on whiskey, and at my age all I have to do to experience the same affect is to stand up too quickly."

Abigail laughed.

"Father, your incorrigible. It's your blood pressure, you know what Dr. Jones said."

"I have my moments," he replied with a smile.

"I'm off to bed, it's getting late," she said, looking at the mantle clock.

"I know," he replied. "It's almost 10:55 p.m., and I have errands in the morning, and Christmas presents to buy, and before you ask, no, I'm not telling you what you're getting this year," he stated playfully.

Kissing her father on the forehead, she smiled.

"Whatever it is, I'm sure I'll love it, but I don't think you'll have any trouble sleeping, you know how that cheap whisky affects you, and don't take your blood pressure pills, you know what your doctor said about taking your medication with alcohol," she said, as she turned and left the room.

Slowly, she walked up the stairs to make her way to her bedroom, her mind contemplating the Christmas gift that her father was about to choose with love and affection. As she walked along the landing, her eyes fell upon the doorway to her room, which stood slightly ajar. Her mind began to slow as caution entered her thoughts. A shadow fell across the opening, cast by the light within, causing Abigail to stop dead in her tracks. As she placed the palm of her hand upon the flat surface of her bedroom door, exerting enough pressure to cause it to slowly open, she observed the shadow within as it moved without hesitation towards her. Her emotions built within, causing her to physically withdraw from its impending presence, as she stepped momentarily back into the shadows of the corridor.

"Are you not entering?" a seductive ancient voice enquired from within.

"Siamun?" Abigail enquired.

"Who else," he responded, as he looked around the door and offered her a broad smile.

Looking about to ensure that her father did not observe Siamun's presence, Abigail walked forward and placed her open palm on his chest and physically pushed him back into her room, closing the door behind her.

"How did you know where I lived?" she asked in confusion.

Siamun smiled.

"That night, when I was brought back from the underworld, I observed you at your chamber's window. The night that the clouds fell," he highlighted.

"Oh, the snow," she said.

"There are tales of it falling in my land, but it's occurrence is rare and only a few members of my people have observed it, and I must say that it is a delight," he stated.

Abigail shook her head in dismay.

"What are you doing here? My father might see you," she said, nervously looking about her room.

"I didn't think it would be a problem," he said in slight dismay. "It's not as though I know many people in this city that I can call upon to discuss my adventures."

"It's not you that I'm concerned about," she stated. "It is…" she paused for a moment as her mind crashed to an abrupt halt as her timorous thoughts collided. "It's socially unbecoming of an unmarried lady to accept guests, especially those of a male nature, into her bed chamber."

Siamun smirked.

Taken aback by his reaction, Abigail looked at him in slight bemusement.

"What's so funny?" she enquired.

Siamun shook his head as the broad grin spread across his lips.

"You are shy and fearful of how others may perceive you within your social circle, and you're standing here with a man who is almost as old as time itself. A man, who I may add, you have undressed and examined his body to a greater degree than my own mother."

Abigail's features turned to a flushed red, as embarrassment washed over her entire body, causing her senses to tingle in humiliation. After a moment she regained her composure and realised that Siamun was teasing her. Without consideration she hit him playfully on his chest with the back of her hand.

"I suppose when you put it like that, it does sound rather foolish. However, that does not detract from my own personal discomfort," she said.

"That is easily remedied," he stated.

Abigail looked at him cautiously, but did not speak.

Siamun elucidated.

"We should find neutral ground." Turning, he looked out of the window at the light fall of snow. "The evening looks inviting, should we not walk in its delights and savour this night?" he enquired.

Abigail shook her head in dismay.

"If it gets you out of the house, then yes," she replied, as she opened her wardrobe and withdrew a heavy winter coat. "We'll have to sneak out through the servant's entrance at the back of the house," she whispered as she listened up against the bedroom door for the sound of any activities that could be attributed to her father.

"Why?" Siamun playfully enquired.

Abigail looked at him in spirited contempt.

"One, you're a man and shouldn't be seen in a young woman's company, especially when her father is present and it's the middle of the night. And two, you're wearing 'that said' father's clothing, that he would recognise them in an instant, and that's an explanation that I don't want to get into," she highlighted, as she opened the door and peered into the shadows. "The coast looks clear, follow me and don't touch anything. If I hide, you do the same, and don't speak a word until we are outside of the house," she firmly instructed.

Siamun looked away, a broad smirk etched upon his lips.

"Yes ma'am," he whispered, as he followed Abigail out into the shadows. "I did not realise you could observe the coast from here," he mumbled to himself.

Tentatively, the pair walked down the stairs of the property and made their way silently to the back of the building. There, Abigail took the key to the backdoor which allowed them access into the garden at the rear of the house. There, she closed the door and ushered Siamun out into the alleyways that criss-crossed this part of the city.

"You really are a bad influence," she whispered, as they walked away for the protective light that issued from her home and into the dark shows that encircled London.

"From where I'm standing, it would appear that you require very little encouragement," Siamun stated with a grin.

Abigail turned and offered Siamun a playful yet withering glance.

"What have you been up to?" she enquired.

"I have been savouring the delights of your lovely city," he declared. "I have observed your monuments to your valiant dead, the building of commerce and law, the structures constructed for hypocritical endeavours. This world you live in is truly magical."

"As is yours," Abigail replied, her voice denoting an air of wonder.

Siamun smiled.

"I would hate to see my land now. Ravaged by these explorers of antiquity and those fundamentalists alike. To you it is ancient history, yet to me it is only a memory away." An air of sadness fell over him, as the dark clouds of remorse filled his soul. "How I yearn for those whom I have lost."

Abigail smiled and rubbed his arm in comfort. And to elicit warmth on this cold dark night.

"It is difficult; I understand what you're going through. My mother died and I still don't think that I have truly come to terms with her passing," she highlighted.

"That is sad, to lose someone so close to you," he softly replied.

"You don't get over it," she stated, "you just learn to accept it with the passing of each day."

"Were you close to your mother?" he asked.

"Yes, but I am also very close to my father. I don't think that I could have got through everything if it hadn't of been for him." She smiled to herself. "I suppose I took on my mother's role, following her death my father was a broken man, and I offered him as much comfort as I could at such a tender age."

"Did you understand death?" he asked.

"I don't think so, but what I did understand was the loss. How the very act rips out your heart and leave only a gaping hole where your soul used to be, and years later all of your emotions are as raw and tender as they day the event occurred." She shook her head. "Time doesn't heal your wounds; it only dulls your memories, it leaves you numb, as if a rudderless ship adrift in a social storm. You watch in pure dismay as others continue with life as though nothing has happened. It is only after this storm has ceased, do you realise that for every man on the street this storm has not occurred, and it is only personal and devastating to you, and you alone."

Abigail looked up at the heavens as the light drift of snow continued to fall.

"I suppose we need these experiences in our lives so that we can appreciate what could be described as 'good times,'" she said.

"You must miss her," Siamun stated.

Abigail thought for a moment before answering.

"Yes and no," she said. "I don't miss the fact that she was suffering near the end, but what I do miss is the experiences which I am presently encountering which she will not have a share in. She would have been so proud that I achieved a first class honours degree, and that I had attained employment at the British Museum, also, that I am an independent and honest working woman, surviving in a man's world."

Siamun laughed, not in ridicule rather in bemusement.

"Several millennia have passed, yet the world remains the same. Our aspirations are no different, and, although your society has advanced in so many ways, we are surrounded by mere mortal magic. Magic of a social construction. You may dress in your fine clothing and ride in your horseless chariots, but you are no different from my own kin. Objective, social ascension, and the accumulation of wealth, has always been man's downfall. Your world may have advanced within its sciences, however, man's understanding of man, appears to be as primitive as it has always been."

Abigail smiled.

"I think the problem isn't the understanding of man, it is the acceptance that we have not advanced emotionally or socially since long before even you were ever born," she retorted as she turned and walked into the darkness of the alleyway.

Siamun smiled but remained where he stood, watching Abigail as she was enveloped by the shadows, a single tear of remorse rolling down his cheek. Realising that her companion had not followed her, Abigail turned and observed Siamun enveloped in his own dark melancholy moment. Momentarily she remained stationary, hesitant to invade his solemnity.

"Are you alright?" she enquired, as she returned to his side.

"I feel an emotional, groundless pain, for events which occurred a multitude of lifetimes ago. It's strange, as a young man I thought I was immortal. The son of a pharaoh, a God. I thought I was invincible and so were those who surrounded me. How wrong could I be?" He shook his head. "With this arrogance comes blindness. I was a fool, I was driven by self-gratification, unobservant of the lives that faded all around me." He looked deep into Abigail eyes. "And here I am, my time limited and my family long since forgotten, and I now truly understand the value of life, friendship and family."

"Do you blame your father?" she asked.

"How can I blame him for something which he did not understand? My father had been Pharaoh since he was an infant, so to him it was all that he knew. His word was the law, his actions were unquestionable, his knowledge was unbound. As a child I wanted to be him, to illicit that same reaction which he evoked when he walked into a room. Kings would shudder and tremble in his presence, emissaries would scurry back to their lands with tales of woe, and stories of power and regal magnificence. And what was it all for? My father genuinely thought, or hoped, he was impervious to death, he truly believed he would rule Egypt forever. Yet, here I am, the consummate disbeliever, living in a time I should never have witnessed, and where is he? Long dead and forgotten."

"I'm sorry, I never considered that you would miss your family this much," Abigail said.

"To you, their passing was forever ago, something lost in the pages of history, but to me, it is only the blinking of a mortal eye which has passed, and their passing is as painful now as it was when history turned its back upon my mortal presence." He looked at Abigail as tears filled his eyes. "Strange, isn't it, this life, this time. It is only now, when I understand that my time is limited and my stay upon this earthly plain is brief, do I realise the value of my life and the time which consumes it. I ran around like a giddy child, blind to those within my life and how my actions could impact upon their own brief existence." He could feel the dark clouds of remorse drift over his soul as his heart began to beat with a dark rage in his chest.

"Amunet?" Abigail gently enquired.

Siamun nodded his head and lowered his eyes.

"If we had remained strangers, then she would not have befallen under the wrath of my father. Her life would have continued and neither Nehi nor myself would have suffered the dark fate that consumed us."

"You can't blame yourself for your father's actions," Abigail insisted.

"I don't," he stated as he looked wistfully up at the open moon that shone down from above. "I blame myself." Siamun let out a long and laboured breath. "Don't you feel that this opportunity is wasted upon me? This second taste of mortal life, although brief, it is rewarding, but I have little understanding of its purpose."

Abigail contemplated her next sentence precisely.

"I thought you assumed that Nehi had a hand in this, he somehow placed the spell with you, to protect you," she stated.

"I don't know, maybe I am assuming too much. As my time here has unfolded I have thought about my last few hours upon this earthly realm, and it is apparent that all is not as it would have initially appeared," he stated.

"How do you mean?" she asked.

"I don't know, but something doesn't appear correct," he highlighted.

Abigail looked at him in rather a sheepish manner.

"What?" he asked.

"When you recanted your tale of death, and the events which preceded it, something didn't sit right," she stated. "I have been contemplating that conversation for some time, and it don't feel comfortable with it."

"In what way?" he asked.

"Can you go through the events, as you remember them, and don't leave out anything, no matter how insignificant it may appear," she requested. Turning, she looked along the alleyway at the small public square that presented itself before her. There was the subtle light of the old gas lamps that offered a warm and welcoming invitation for them to enter its embrace. "There are seats in the square. Why don't we go there and sit, and you can tell me everything?" she requested.

Chapter 23.

As the snow gathered in its intensity, Siamun and Abigail sat beneath the sheltering branches of an old oak tree. An unnatural silence hung in the air, something rarely associated with this part of London. Siamun gathered his thoughts as his mind turned in mortal conflict, those ancient memories as fresh and as apparent as if they were forged yesterday, were in fact, manifested many millennia ago, and appeared unaffected by that colossal passage of time.

"I recall it as if it were yesterday. I was sitting in one of the gardens that surrounded the palace, overlooking the Nile. It was such a fertile place, blessed by the river gods and consecrated by the blessed touch of Ra. I discovered it as a child, and almost every day since that time I would venture there and spend some of my contemplative time within the lush embrace of its green slumber. It was my sanctuary, that place where you run to in life, where you would always feel safe. It was one of the first places I showed Nehi, and in time Amunet. As our collective friendship grew, we would spend whole afternoons sitting on the lush lawns, contemplating the world and suggestively planning our collective futures. It was whimsical, almost juvenile, but I knew that I would never be Pharaoh, for my ascension was far too diluted to be cognised, and my ambition was as objective as was my interest. I lived a life of pure indulgence, as was ascribed to one in my position, but I also recognised the injustice which this birth-right had offered me."

"Did your meeting Amunet change your relationship with Nehi?" Abigail enquired.

Siamun thought for a moment.

"No, I don't think so, after all, he was destined for the priesthood, so there wouldn't be any negative influence on his behalf," he replied. "Yes, we had disagreements, as do all brothers, but they were few and far between, and were quickly resolved."

Abigail's eyebrows knitted in concern, realising the confusion Siamun smiled nervously.

"What's wrong?"

"All you're offering me is supposition, conjecture, no true facts. These are merely your thoughts," she stated.

"Would it be easier if you asked questions?" he enquired.

THE MUMMY

"Possibly," she stated.

Sitting back onto the bench, Siamun smiled and awaited her first query.

Contemplating her first question, Abigail allowed enough time to formulate a cogent enquiry.

"Was there any ill-feeling between Nehi and yourself?" she asked. "Primarily around the time Amunet was introduced into the group."

Siamun shook his head in dismay.

"No! As I said, we were closer than brothers. In our time together we were inseparable, much to the jealously of my own true kin. He would protect me, honour me, and at time even lie for me," he firmly stated.

"But did this change when you began your relationship with Amunet?" she firmly reiterated.

"Well, no, Nehi was destined for the priesthood," he stated. "If anything, he became more protective."

"That's not what I asked," she firmly replied.

Siamun contemplated her words for a moment, elucidating their true meaning to his mind.

"Do you mean to myself, or to Amunet?" he asked.

"Well primarily to yourself, as Amunet was initially a newcomer to the relationship. But, you can highlight if his relationship with her was either cold or hospitable. As Sherlock Holmes so eloquently highlighted '… when you have eliminated all which is impossible, then whatever remains, however improbable, must be the truth…'" she stated.

"This Sherlock Holmes sounds like a wise man," he said.

"He's a fictitious character, from a book," she highlighted.

"I don't understand," he stated.

"He's a famous literary detective, he's not real, he's a work of fiction," she explained.

"No," he said, shaking his head. "I understand that, for I have observed his books in your bed chamber. What I am confused about is how you can use a fictitious character, as you call it, and place their ethos into a realm of truth and return with a suitable conclusion."

"I didn't know you could read English," she stated in surprise.

"I cannot, but I can look at pictures, as the language of my time was written in this form, and I surmised, as your Sherlock Holmes has, probability is the foundation for most of his investigations, and you appear to be an avid reader of these works, as there are a number of these volumes in your chamber. I then surmised that he would have an influence upon your own ability to reason and rationalise a presenting situation, and so, your ability to return with a suitable conclusion may be coloured by his imaginary influence and your own infatuation." Siamun smiled. "I understand the rationale to your questioning, but it is no more apparent than many of my people believing in gods and monsters."

"Didn't you believe in the gods?" she enquired.

"No!" he replied. "As many of my people didn't. Nehi was only undertaking the role of priest because he knew that it meant employment for life and he would not grow hungry. In my father's house he was no more than a servant, and my father's emotions could change as fast as a desert wind. His mother had him prepared for the priesthood before he was born, and he was to serve Amun until his dying breath."

"Here I was, thinking, that your lives were controlled by the gods and you were scared of death as much as we are," she stated.

"What the people were scared of was growing old and not having anyone to care for them, they were scared of not having enough grain to feed their family. They were scared of being robbed or having their reputations destroyed by liars or vagabonds. We were scared of the same things that you are. We weren't scared of death, for we knew that the rest from the rigours of our world was perpetual, we were in fact scared of life, which is why we had so many gods to protect us." He laughed lightly to himself. "There were gods of the trees, gods of the fields, of the rooftops, of the water, of the sun and the moon, of everything. There were thousands of them, all invented by a race of people who were too scared of their own mortality, and did not retain the inner sanctity of their own self-worth. It was all lies, there were no deities or magical beings guiding our lives," he stated. "It was all hapless chaos."

Abigail looked at him in a slight state of mental confusion.

"And yet here you are, anathema to your people's beliefs, an enigma to death itself,"

"What do you mean?" he innocently enquired.

"If there are no gods or magic, what brought you back to life?" she asked. "There is an empty sarcophagus in the museum that proves otherwise."

There was an empty silence as Siamun contemplated Abigail's heavy words.

She allowed him to wallow a little in his own personal dilemma regarding religious doctrine, before she presented her next question.

"To move this on a little, we need to be more specific about the situation which occurred around the time of your death," Abigail stated.

Siamun nodded, but remained silent.

"What exactly happened in relation to your father and the reason around your arrest and eventual execution," she asked.

"Nehi, Amunet and myself were, as usual, sitting in the garden next to my father's palace. It was late in the afternoon and the sun was already falling in the sky. The day had been uneventful and we had discussed the same mundane subjects that people our age were prone too. Just as we were about to leave, my father's guards entered the garden and we were taking into custody without question. Both Nehi and myself were taken by chariot to the place where we died, and Amunet was slain in the garden where she stood," he recanted.

"Sorry to interrupt," she said, raising a finger to pause the conversation. "But what did you observe?"

"Well," he continued. "We were taken through the desert to…"

"No, not that. What did you observe in relation to Amunet's death? Did you see her die?" she asked.

"No, the guards held my head and forced me to look in the direction they were guiding me. I heard a sword being unsheathed, and a scream which fell to silence," he stated.

"Go on!" she encouraged.

"Both Nehi and I were taken through the desert by the Medjai. When we reached the house of the embalmers, I was mistaken for Nehi and he dutifully assumed my role and the subsequent punishment decreed. The guards present informed him of my misdemeanours and he was put to death in such an appalling fashion, something I would never forget, I could hear his screams haunting me through time itself."

"Once again, I require you to be a little more specific, as I am a little confused," she stated. "I recall from our previous conversation that they plucked out one of Nehi's eyes. That must have been terrifying to witness?"

Siamun thought for a moment before replying.

"I did not witness this, I was already in the sarcophagus at this time, but I heard him screaming that they had cut out his eye."

"Once again, this is all supposition," she declared. Looking down at her watch she smiled. "We must return to my home; I can settle this quandary in a second."

"How?" he asked.

"I have a number of books that trace the lineage of the pharaohs and it also has detailed entries about their families," she stated with a smile.

"What about your father?" he pensively enquired.

"It's past midnight, my father will be in bed and probably in a deep slumber. While Sir Henry was visiting, they consumed a considerable amount of cheap whisky, and that has a nullifying effect upon my father, and it is guaranteed that his will wake late tomorrow morning with a considerable headache, and little recall of the events of this evening," she said.

"I don't understand. How you can even consider Nehi to be involved in anything untoward that could have occurred to me?" Siamun proclaimed.

"I am a very strong believer that at the precise moment loyalty dies, betrayal begins," she said as she stood.

"Is this another of the proclamations expressed by this fictitious character you so avidly read?" he asked.

"No, that is my own opinion and personal observation, I do have a mind of my own," she sharply stated as she turned and walked back along the alleyway which led in the direction of her home.

Chapter 24.

By the time they had reached Abigail's home, the house was drenched in darkness. She was relieved to discover that the back door to the property remained unlocked, and collectively both Siamun and herself made their way to the sanctity of her father's library, to begin their research into ancient history itself.

"Please, sit down," she instructed her guest, as she moved to the impressive, heavily-laden bookcase, that spread majestically across the walls of the room. Discovering her desired volumes, Abigail reached up and acquired several of these tomes, which she gathered in her arms, before taking them over to the sofa where Siamun sat patiently.

"Over these past few decades since Champollion deciphered the Rosetta Stone, we have been able to follow the family pattern of many of the royal families of ancient Egypt. I would say that your family reigned around the time of the 18th dynasty, if my supposition and time lines are correct," she muttered as she hurriedly searched through several pages of a particularly large volume. Shaking her head, she dismissed the book and retried another volume from the pile that rested on the sofa beside her. "I don't know if I can find you," she stated in dismay.

"Why don't you look for my father, or my grandfather?" he enquired.

Abigail smirked as she looked over to him.

"Well, that would be the sensible thing to do."

"My father was called Ahmose, son of Seqenenre Tao, brother of Kamose, father to his first born Amenhotep. My father sired many children in his younger years and, by the time I was mummified, he would have been close to his fortieth year and his wives still bore fruit," he explained.

"How old was your father when you were born?" she asked.

"No more than sixteen years, maybe younger," he said.

Abigail's eyes searched the pages before her, until they eventually fell upon their quarry.

"I think that your father would have been a considerable age younger than you surmise," she stated. "he was very young when he ascended the throne, and he died when he was about forty years of age. How old are you?" she asked, looking directly at Siamun.

"Twenty-three," he replied.

"So your father could have ascended the throne when he was about ten years of age, and from that time he would have been encouraged to undertake his royal duties, which included securing an heir to his dynasty," she said.

Siamun nodded his head in agreement.

Lifting her finger from the page, she raised it pensively to her lips and slowly turned to look at her guest. Realising her apprehension, Siamun offered her a nervous smile.

"What is the matter?" he enquired.

"There is no record of you, yes there is a highlighted birth, but apart from that, very little else. Also, it is highlighted that, if we calculate your age and compare it with that of your father, that he died not long after yourself, around 1515 B.C. He was then succeeded by his son"

"B.C?" he queried.

Abigail smiled.

"Don't ask!"

"Is there anything in there about Nehi?" he enquired.

Abigail urgently scanned the page, but her quest returned fruitless. Shaking her head, she offered him a pitiful smile.

"Nothing," she said.

"It's as if history has forgotten us," he whispered, as he pensively looked down at the floor.

"That doesn't mean that Nehi or your own history isn't there, it just means that we haven't discovered it yet," she stated, endeavouring to encourage Siamun, and lift his darkening emotions. "Archaeology is only in its infancy and we are discovering new facts on a daily basis, facts that force us to rewrite our own perception of your history on an on-going basis. After all, it has only been just over a hundred years since Champollion deciphered the Rosetta Stone, which gave us such insight into your lives. Before then, it was all guess work and supposition. Your father's mummy was discovered about 1881 and now resides in the Cairo Museum."

"They have desecrated my father's resting place?" he cried.

Abigail nodded her head, a little in remorse.

"Yes, but modern archaeologists don't consider it to be a desecration. He didn't have any living relatives, that were known, and for the advancement of science and our understanding of your world, we strive to discover how your lives turned and functioned all those thousands of years ago."

"He didn't have any family!" Siamun hissed. "Then what am I?"

"An anomaly. A quirk of fate. I don't know," she said as she took hold of his hands, endeavouring to comfort him. "I'm sorry, but you cannot mourn for a history that did not occur. You were not part of this, you had died and were only a memory to those who loved you. I'm sorry if I sound harsh and callous, but you have to be a realist, and you weren't there to prevent these events occurring, and even if you were, they may have been unpreventable."

Siamun shook his head as he strove to stem the tears that were welling in his eyes.

"I'm sorry, it is not you that I am angry with but myself, I should not be here to witness this, I am an abomination of nature. I cry for my father, for he would have been appalled at all of this." Siamun turned his head and looked into Abigail's eyes. "He had a fear of dying, of being mummified. He even constructed a plan with the chief embalmer, so that his body would be spirited away at the time of his passing and that the body of a commoner, who would be around his age, would be substituted, so he could rest with the earth touching his flesh."

"We have no way of discovering if it is in fact your father's body in the museum, but from our records, he died not long after you did, possibly in the same year," she highlighted.

Siamun looked to the ceiling and shook his head.

"If only he hadn't had been so impetuous, I could have supported him in his last days in this life and followed his wishes. Then Amunet and I could have faded from the pages of history and spent our eternity together as it was written in the stars."

"Your brother, Amenhotep succeeded to the throne," she stated

"Yamānuḥātap," he replied in confusion. "What of Ahmose-Akan and Ahmose-Sapair? They were my older brothers. It was their destiny to succeed my father, Yamānuḥātap was third in line to the throne, as I was the fourth."

Already knowing the answer, Abigail offered him a nervous smile.

"They both died before your father," she regretfully stated.

"It seems that you were correct in your previous supposition. 'When loyalty dies, treachery begins.' It would appear that somebody was killing off members of my royal household for power, or for something more. Possibly, the dark knowledge held by those who served them," he whispered.

"What makes you think that?" she asked.

"I don't know, but it's as if the cold desert winds are blowing across my bones," he replied.

"You miss your family, it's understood," she said.

"No, I fear that it is something more, I feel a dark foreboding, I understand that my time here is limited, but I do feel that it's conclusion cannot be attained quick enough. Although I am in wonder at your modern world, I am an interloper into this time, and I am exiled from my own territory, from a land that no longer exists. I have neither past, present, nor future. I am lost to the annals of time, forever disregarded onto the shores of life's unwelcome embrace." He looked pitifully in Abigail direction, his eyes unfocused and full of tears. "If you were the one who called me into this life, then who is to say that another cannot undertake that very same action in years to come, and I will have to relive the trauma of losing another person that I have come to know and understand. My mind will be a cluttered gallery of those I have loved and lost from differing times within this world's history."

He wiped his eyes and looked at Abigail, a dark intensity gathering in his eyes.

"Do you know how it feels to not have anybody? It's not as simple as losing a loved one, but to lose your whole history, to lose your identity? The positive thing about death is that those who have passed have attained a little immortality, for they survive in the memories of others, those who knew and loved them. I know that they're hieroglyphs depicting my father and my own history on the ancient temples in my home land, but I'm not talking about that. I'm talking about the fact that a memory would remain in a living person. An individual who could recall your laugher, your deeds, the way you walked, your smell, the way you loved and allowed others to love you. Don't you understand? After you have died, that is not your concern. You become stardust. You don't have to consider the impact that your passing has upon others. It is the one gift that death offers you. However, now, because of the meddling of magic, I am not even afforded this dark pleasure. Consider it, if I were to awake in another two hundred years. Where would you be?"

Abigail semi smiled and looked at Siamun in confusion.

"I would be dead," she stated.

"But I would not. I would be able to recall your face, our friendship, your fragrance. This is unnatural and against the desire of the gods themselves." He stood from the sofa and walked over to the dying fire, and stood silently, enthralled by the warming embrace of its glowing embers. "This whole situation flies into the face of human nature. We are born, we live, we die. Every part of that statement is permanent and irresolvable. We should not be called back from the great beyond to undertake the dark bidding of others."

"I didn't, it was an accident," Abigail proclaimed.

Siamun smiled.

"Not you," he replied warmly, "but others. We must discover who brought Nehi back to life and why, and in doing so, send him back into the underworld, and possibly discover a means of returning myself to my own dark slumber." He walked over to where Abigail sat, and lowered himself until their eyes were level. "Where is the spell that brought him back to life. We need to find it and destroy it so that his fate is sealed."

"It must back at the museum, in his sarcophagus," she replied.

"Then we must return there forthwith," he instructed.

Mesmerized by the beauty of his dark brown eyes, Abigail allowed her stare to linger a little longer than was socially acceptable, a subliminal consequence of a fragile heart.

"I will get a more substantial coat," she stated in a timorous voice, "the snow outside looks as though it is getting heavier."

Siamun stood and offered her his hand, which she took and delayed her departure for a brief moment longer.

"Is there something wrong?" he gently enquired.

Abigail shook her head.

"Only what life experience has taught me, and that sometimes your oldest friends can become your latest enemy. In your desire to discover your own dark history, do not discount anyone in your investigation, because of your own fragile emotions. For human emotion is always the first weakness which others will choose to manipulate, a dark lesson I learnt from my father."

Siamun nodded.

Realising that the conversation was taking a rather negative downturn, Abigail quickly interjected.

"Speaking of fathers, I'll go check on mine."

"Won't you disturb him?" Siamun asked.

"No, he always leaves his bedroom door slightly ajar, it's a habit that stems from my childhood. I was always afraid of the dark, and I guess when I became an adult he never got out of that routine."

Siamun smiled and let go of Abigail's hands, signaling to her the appropriate time to leave the room and check on her father's wellbeing.

Abigail smiled to herself as she ascended the staircase that led to the upper floors of her home. The lights from the lamps that were situated along the dark walls, offered a welcoming, but not a glorious light, to accompany her into the shadows as she approached her father's bedchamber. She smiled to herself as she observed a slight chink of light which was emitted through the slight gap between the door and its stanchion. She paused for a moment and smiled, as a feeling of warmth rushed over her body as she listened to the sound of her father as he snored quietly in his deep slumber. After a few brief moments she recalled the true rationale for her venture and raised her hands to each opposing upper arm and rubbed them lightly, for she could feel a defined decline in the overall temperature of the house, and surmised that the weather had emotionally darkened as the heavy blanket of snow descended. Turning, she made to walked briskly to her own room, however she was confronted by the decayed remains, and rictus grin of a mummy who stood less than a few inches from her own petrified face.

Chapter 25.

It was Abigail's muffled scream that brought Siamun rushing out of the library and up the main staircase of the property. As he reached the landing he could see the mummy bending over her lifeless body, as it released its grip upon her fragile throat.

"Nehi!" he cried, but the creature remained unresponsive.

Rushing over, Siamun pushed the creature with all of his preternatural might away from Abigail's lifeless body, sending the bandaged assassin stumbling blindly into the shadows that littered the corridor before him. Falling to his knees, Siamun listened intently, endeavoring to hear the slightest whisper of mortal breath as it escaped from Abigail's chest.

"I'm not having another death on my hands," he screamed, as he gathered her up in his arms and ran down the stairs to the library. Placing her body on the floor close to the fire, he turned and rushed over to the door, locking it as a precaution against the creature without, he returned to Abigail's lifeless body and stared bewildered at her cold form. "What should I do?" he asked himself several times, his anxiety rising deep within him. Lowering himself to his knees, he reached across her body and shook her violently.

"Wake up!" he cried in vain.

Realising that his actions were to little avail, he raised his hands, clenched in fists, and brought them angrily down upon Abigail's chest in mortal rage. Immediate she gasped as life returned to her fragile corporeal form. As she lay gasping, Siamun sat back as a feeling of relief filled his entire body, and the deep tension in his muscles began to fade. He watched as her chest rose and fell in a regular and assuring way, as consciousness returned to his beloved friend, emphasized as her hand was raised to her forehead. Turning to him, her eyes flickered open and she mouthed a single word. Siamun concentrated and eventually realised that she was endeavoring to say the word, 'Father.'

Moving forward on his knees, he offered her a smile and whispered tenderly to her.

"No, it's not your father, it's me, Siamun."

"No," she endeavored to reply, her voice broken and laboured. "Go check on my father, he's in danger if that creature is still in the house?"

Without hesitation, Siamun rushed from the library and out into the hallway. In rage, he propelled himself upwards until he came to the door where he originally discovered Abigail, lying in her slain pose. Slowly, he walked to where the door stood slightly ajar and peered into the room. Lord Cornwall lay quietly in his slumber, unperturbed by the dark events of that evening. Pushing the door slightly open, Siamun peered cautiously into the room only to discover that Lord Cornwall was in fact its only inhabitant. A sense of relief washed over him as he returned the door to its original position and made his way back to the library.

As he entered the room he observed Abigail sitting quietly on the sofa, gathering her fractured thoughts.

"Are you alright?" he enquired, as he rushed to her side.

"I'm fine," she replied. "How's father?"

"Fast asleep," Siamun replied with a smirk.

Abigail laughed and shook her head.

"That man could sleep through anything, I bet he took his blood pressure medication after I specifically instructed him not to." She looked at Siamun. "Where is that creature?" she enquired.

"I am about to look around your home, to check all of the chambers to ensure that he has gone," he said.

Abigail nodded her head.

"Good, I'm coming with you. I think to narrow down the search we should check the back door first."

"Why?" Siamun asked.

"Well, chances are, your friend Nehi, observed us outside while we were in conversation in the public square, and followed us back here. He saw how we gained entry and mimicked our actions," she stated.

"It would appear that your fascination with this fictitious character, may bear fruit after all," he said, offering her his hand.

Abigail stood and smiled at him.

"Thank you, but I feel well enough to gather my own strength. Please, follow me and we will discover your ancient brother's whereabouts. And tomorrow, when I return to the museum, I will destroy the incantation which brought him back to life. It's better to be safe than sorry, even though I would be destroying a precious ancient relic."

"More than you think," he whispered.

"What do you mean?" she asked.

"I don't know if I am connected to that relic, as you call it, I don't know if its magic would be diminished if it were destroyed and my immortal being would be sent back to the underworld also," he stated.

"Then we can't destroy it," she proclaimed.

"We don't have a choice," he stated.

Abigail looked at him with sorrow in her eyes.

"There's always a choice, the fundamental difference is that we have the ability to rise above others to discovering what that choice is, we have been blessed with education and the ability to recognise what is presented before us. My parents offered me an opportunity not bestowed upon others. The ability to evaluate life. Unlike Henry or Walter, I was not taught the price of a possession, but its value, I never wanted to grow up rich and titled, all I wanted to be was happy."

"I wish I had such blind fortitude and sense of probity," he stated.

"I'm not one for blind arrogant gestures, I leave that to Sir Henry and his father, but when I know that I'm right, it couldn't take a harras of wild horses to drag me away from my principles." She looked pensively upwards and took a deep breath. "We must stop this idle chatter; we have a mummy to find."

The rear door to the property stood slightly ajar and tracks initially leading to the home and those leading away were primarily evidenced by the dragging, almost pitiful movement of their perpetrator. Both Abigail and Siamun followed the tracks as they wound their way along the pathway and out into the back-lane that cut adjacent to the rear of the property. Abigail held her hand up to Siamun, requesting silence as she lowered herself to the ground and attempted to read the patterns left in the snow.

"It looks as though your friend followed us from the square, and probably watched us as we entered my home. However, exiting the property, it looks as though he has chosen to go in the opposite direction from which he initially came," she highlighted.

Siamun looked along the alleyway to his right, then turned his gaze to the left and smiled.

"I would surmise that he is returning to the museum," he stated, looking directly at Abigail.

"I think that your right, but I am concerned," she highlighted.

"Why?" he asked.

Looking down at the snow-covered alleyway she pointed to the fresh imprints made in the virginal fall.

"If you look here," she requested. "These are evidently both your and my footfall, made when were both left the house and returned. I would deduce that from the fact that there are only two sets and they leave and return and appear to be freshly made." Looking up she smiled. "If you look at the rear of Mrs Birkhouse's property, there is a fresh layer of snow, every evening during this time, Mrs Birkhouse instructs her footman to clear the snow, and if you look, there is a recent fresh covering, which denotes that any impression made upon its surface must therefore be recent, or within the last period of snowfall, which I would say is within the last two hours."

"I agree with your deduction," Siamun stated with a smile.

"So, if we use that as a basis of my presented hypothesis, then we must conclude that, if there have not been any other wanderers vacating the square, then we must surmise that Nehi was not here alone."

"What make you think that?" he enquired.

"Look," she said, pointing to a place close to the backdoor of her home. "Nehi's footprints are evident, as they initially make their way from the community square to this point, here they enter into the grounds of my home. But now if you look and observe, when Nehi exited my property, they turn to the left and are met by two other sets of footprints, which then make their way in a northerly direction, and as you state, possibly towards the museum." She stood and looked along the alleyway. "There are three distinctive sets of footprints moving in that direction," she said, pointing into the darkness. She turned and looked back at Siamun and smiled.

"Let's follow," she whispered, her mind burning with intrigue.

"Stop a moment," he urgently requested. "Before we go running after my friend, don't you think that there is a more predominant factor that you have not considered?"

Abigail turned and looked at him, an air of slight disarray clouding her mind.

"I can't think of anything," she stated.

"How about, why was Nehi at your home? And what was he after?" he coldly stated.

Abigail looked cautiously at Siamun, but could not offer him a tangible answer.

Chapter 26.

As they made their way to the museum, a cold silence hung heavily in the air. Abigail's mind was abounding with unanswered questions, as her thoughts collided in disarray and confusion.

'Why had Nehi attempted to kill her?' 'Was it connected to the murders of the servant girl, Rose, and Lord Aster's innocent daughter?'

As they stepped from the curb onto the road opposite the museum, Siamun stopped and looked directly into Abigail's sorrowful eyes.

"I do feel that my presence has brought you untoward danger and a risk that appears insurmountable," he stated.

Abigail smiled.

"I think you'll find that it was my meddling and unwarranted intervention that brought you back to life. If there is any blame in the travesty, then it should be placed firmly at my shoulders and not at yours. My father always told me that eventually, 'curiosity would kill the cat,' and here I am a shining example of that idiom coming painfully true."

As they crossed the deserted road and stood before the iron railings protecting the museum, Siamun offered her a word of caution.

"I would suggest that you remain here, and I will return to Sir Henry's examination chamber within the museum. I will endeavour to discover the spell from the sarcophagus, and return forthwith."

"I'm a bit worried about being left alone, here, outside of the museum," she stated. "After all, we did discover two extra sets of unknown footprints in the snow. How do we not know that these individuals accompanying Nehi, are not observing me as we speak?"

"Would it not cause concern for you to enter the Museum after dark?" he enquired.

"I can't see why, after all, I met Johnathan in the depths of night retrieving documentation for Lord Karvahill and Sir Henry, and that does not appear to have presented as a concern," she stated.

Siamun nodded, but did not reply, as he walked into the grounds of the museum.

"I will do as I have observed others, and make my way to the rear of the museum and request that one of the night porters allow me access. I understand that they receive shipments at all hours of the day and night and the presence of one other person will not spark curiosity, it appears as though it is a matter-of-fact occurrence," she highlighted.

Siamun smiled.

"I agree, but it also highlights to others that you were here, and so your whereabouts can be tracked. If you are following an adversary, then surprise and subterfuge, along with surreptitiousness, are your closest ally and best defence. You only ever allow others to see what you want them to see, otherwise you leave yourself vulnerable to their deceit and lies, this was a lesson I learnt all too quickly in my father's presence."

"It sounds as though your father's court was a lovely place to be," she sarcastically highlighted, as Siamun pushed the lower part of the sash window open and stepped inside of the building. Pausing for a moment, his body half ensconced within the museum, he looked playfully at Abigail.

"You don't know the half of it, but that tale must be told at a less perilous time," he said just before he fully entered into the examination room.

All about, the shadows huddled and conspired as an eerie silence filled the air. It was at this moment that Siamun paused in his endeavours, for a dark sense of vulnerability washed over him. It was not the fact that he had entered this dark unobserved chamber, or the fact that he was placing Abigail, her father and himself in the pathways of certain danger. The concerning dilemma that consumed him was the fact that he could hear his own breathing, slow, low and mortal. A sound that he had not experienced for several millennia. He stood for a moment, transfixed by his own vulnerability, a slave to the savagery of time. His senses were heightened by an emotion he had not experienced since the time he took his dying breath, and that emotion was fear. For it was at this precise time that he thought about his family, and as most impetuous young men, he thought only of that moment in which he lived. It was only through this realisation did he truly understand that in the briefest flicker of time, does that cherished moment become a mere memory, a thought, something that haunts the mind with its harrowing remorse.

Walking slowly over to Nehi's open sarcophagus, he smiled at his brother's decorated prison, for it was as if this humble casket had offered his bloodless kin a sanctuary, against the torturous savagery of time. After a moment he reached out his hand and allowed his finger tips to trace across its smooth and highly decorated surface. Its presence was both a comfort as well as a measure of his reformation. He allowed his fettered emotions a brief transient moment of release, and this revealed to him a deeper and darker fear, for he felt truly alive. However, his joy was to be short lived, for he knew that death was but a breath away. A constant spectre that rested wearily upon his shoulders, whispering its dark intent as the sands of time upon this earthly plain slowly fell through the hourglass of his plagiarised life.

Closing his eyes, he permitted a single emotional tear, filled with regret and remorse, to fall onto his cheek. Lowering his head, he allowed the palm of his hand to lay flat against the warm surface of the sarcophagus. Holding the moment, for he could feel his emotions turn, he smiled to himself, for a feeling of deep gratitude engulfed him, for he felt truly blessed for this brief moment stolen from time itself.

It was the sound of Abigail's whispering voice that broke him away from the spell that he was casting over himself.

"I can hear someone coming, hurry up," she urgently pleaded.

"I will be but a moment," he replied, endeavouring to reassure her. Gathering his thoughts, he focused himself upon the task at hand, and he allowed his fingers to search the casket for the secret chamber that contained the papyrus. As his fingernails discovered their objective, he smiled as he gently lifted the tiny secretive lid of the concealed compartment. However, upon doing so, his eyes return to him a disparaging sight, for the compartment was barren of all content, and once again Siamun's heart sank in dismay.

"What's wrong?" Abigail urgently enquired. "You're taking too long," she stated as she looked into the room through the window. There, she observed Siamun standing silently in the shadows, lost and alone. "Are you alright?" she enquired as she stepped over the threshold of the window's ledge and into the dark room.

Turning, he offered her a weak smile.

"It is gone," he stated in a forlorn voice.

"What's gone?" she asked in confusion.

"The spell, it has been taken, the compartment in which it lay for many lifetimes is now barren, as is my hope," he stated.

"What's wrong? It's only an incantation," she said, placing a hand on his shoulder, endeavouring to reassure him.

"It isn't," he said as he turned his head away from the sarcophagus to look directly at her. "If that spell is destroyed, then so am I. If I am lucky, I will be returned to the underworld and my mortal remains will turn to dust."

"And if you're not?" she pensively enquired.

"I will truly die. My body shall be as lost as if the sands of the desert, and my soul shall be devoured by the gods. I shall no longer exist in word or mind." He looked emotionally into Abigail's eyes. "The power of the spell is what binds me, if it is destroyed, I will not have anything, and my existence will no longer be justified."

A cold silence filled the room, holding a desolate council of the soul. Abigail could feel the tears of dark remorse well in her eyes, for no sooner had this newfound friend entered her life, then he was about to be so cruelly ripped away. Stepping forward she embraced him, holding him in her bittersweet embrace, a portent of what could never be.

"Couldn't we tell someone?" she gently enquired.

Pulling out of their embrace, Siamun turned and looked out of the window, in order to conceal his rising emotions.

"It would only compound our problem," he stated.

"How?" she urgently asked.

"Who could we possibly turn to in such a time as this?" he replied, answering her proposed question with one of his own.

"I don't know. My Father?" she replied in disarray.

"And how would your father help? Is he an expert in ancient Egyptian spells? Does he have insight into the machinations of the underworld? Could he go to Horus and beg for my mortal life or plead for my immortal soul?" he humbly enquired. Shaking his head, he turned to Abigail and offered her a weak mortal smile. "No, I am damned. The only desire that forged my way and compelled me though this darkness called death, was the thought of seeing my Amunet once again. But now, with the loss of both spells and their possible misuse, I am living in a period between times. I am neither alive nor dead. I neither have constitution nor valour. The living world would not have me and the underworld would destroy me. I am a prisoner of fate, existing only in this brief moment," he said.

"As do we all. There are no definitive in life, other than its demise. In our world we have recently experienced a battle which we called the Great War, where millions upon millions of innocent men were slaughtered in the name of political gain. Every family in this land and those across Europe, India, Australia, New Zealand, and many more experienced death's cold touch. The destruction that consumed this world was heart breaking, and will echo through time for as long as history itself." She took hold of Siamun's face and turned it to her own. "Nothing is assured. I truly understood this the day that I lost my mother. I realised that if I awoke in the morning and my body did not ach, then I was truly blessed. Life is so fragile, as are our emotions, and if you are driven by your sentiments rather than an urge to savour the former, you are on the pathway to disappointment. Your history is only there to be pondered and reconsidered, never to be lived in, never to be desired. You must feel blessed that both you and Amunet experienced your brief moments together, and if fate were to wipe your existence from the pages of history, then so be it. You cannot be afraid of fear itself, for fear is created by your own insecurities. Live for now, cherish this moment, and let the future be damned, for it has not yet been written."

Stepping back, Siamun offered Abigail an uncomfortable smile.

"I know you are right, for I have tasted life, as well as death, but I have never experienced non-existence. A time when I will not be, a time when there is void."

"But you will exist," she stated. "You will live within my memories, and when I pass onto this next life, your memories will surely follow,"

"A hollow memory of what once was," he coldly stated.

"A memory just-the-same," she replied.

"It's getting late, we must get you safely back to your home," Siamun instructed, endeavouring to defer his thoughts away from the dark images that were gathering in his mind.

"What of the strangers, those belonging to the footprints in the snow?" she asked.

"I don't understand?" he replied.

"Well surely if Nehi's body returns to the museum, then they won't be too far behind," she highlighted.

"A very legitimate deduction," he replied.

"Then what are we waiting for?" she said, as she reached for the handle of the door.

"Don't be so impetuous," he instructed as he reached for her outstretched hand.

Abigail quickly withdrew her hand and blushed, for the touch of warm flesh upon her own, excited her tender skin.

"Lead the way," she instructed with a discordant smile, her pure emotions in disarray.

As Siamun exited the room, Abigail closed her eyes and held her hand close to her heart.

"Get a grip, young woman!" she muttered, chastising herself, before she stepped out into the corridor, following Siamun along the dark shadowy passageway.

As they reached the door to the main corridor primarily reserved for general public, Abigail held her finger to her lips, requesting Siamun to remain silent. Reaching forward, she turned the door's handle, and upon hearing the gentle click of the locks release, she allowed the ingress to swing freely open.

"Where could Nehi be?" Abigail enquired.

"I don't know," he replied. "Maybe, Sir Henry has had him moved to a more secure part of the museum, after all, he does perceive our presence in a monetary value."

"You might be correct in that assumption, but then that would leave a question as to why you remained in an examination room which has windows at both the front and side of the museum, which are easily accessible, as we have both recently demonstrated."

"We only gained access because I left the lock free on the window's frame, as I required discreet admission," he stated.

"I agree, but that also leave the vulnerable access point open to others, and with the recent thefts from the museum, I would have thought that both Sir Henry and his father would have been more diligent in relation to security," she highlighted.

Walking to the centre of the room, Abigail observed a thin sliver of ancient linen discarded on the floor, reaching down, she retrieved her desired goal and held it close to her eyes, studying its integrity intensely.

"This looks like a small section of mummy wrapping," she declared, turning to Siamun.

"Do you think that this could have been torn lose in the struggle with yourself?" he enquired.

"I don't think so, I didn't struggle, it was all too quick," she replied.

"They couldn't have started unwrapping the bandages here, could they?" he enquired.

"If they have, then they are doing so in a rather unprofessional manner, this linen looks as though it has been torn or ripped from the mummy, rather than being cut, in an investigative way," she surmised.

"How could that have happened?" he asked.

"There are several possibilities," she replied. "They could be retrieving the artefacts placed within the binding at the time he was mummified. After all, these alone, could be worth a small fortune. Sir Henry may have begun his actual investigation, and, as he is a very competitive soul, he may be rushing his work, and in doing so, missing strategic information which would give us a greater insight into the lifestyle and funerary rituals of your people."

"Do you think Sir Henry is aware that Nehi has once again become sentient?" he enquired.

"I have no idea, but if he has not, then he is in considerable danger," she stated.

"Do you think that they will move my sarcophagus to a more secure location?" he asked.

"After all, Nehi's sarcophagus remains where Sir Henry placed it, but the mummy has been physically removed. Possibly to a place of safety."

"I don't know, I haven't considered that," she replied in surprise.

Siamun mind turned and he then contemplated Abigail's situation for a brief moment.

"Do you consider that you will be safe returning to your home this night?" he asked.

"I can't see why not," she replied. "There are plenty of carriages outside of the museum, I can procure one of them and return home directly. Why, what are you considering?"

"I will accompany you to the front of the museum, and then return to my casket after securing the windows. If I am there tomorrow morning, you will realise that there have not been any further developments in relation to our discovering a solution to this conundrum. However, if I am not present when you return, it would mean that I have been relocated, and if this is so, I will wait for an opportune moment to avail you of the information relating to my whereabouts," he instructed.

"Only if you are sure?" she replied.

"I cannot see any other way of discovering a solution in relation to the events which are occurring," he said.

"I agree," she stated. "Meanwhile, I will endeavour to formulate a contingency plan in relation to discovering the rationale as to why and how your friend is haunting this city, and also consider the possibility that another may be manipulating him for their own desire. However, there is a greater need, because of the theft of the spells, I understand that time is neither on our side, or our friend. And its dark presence casts an urgency upon our proceedings. I will endeavour to discover if there is a spell that can block the negative intentions of others in order to provide us with a little more precious time."

Siamun smiled and lowered his head as a wave is dismay washed over him.

"I'm sure we will succeed," he stated with a smile.

"God willing, I will see you tomorrow," she whispered.

Chapter 27.

That following day, as she alighted the carriage, Abigail's mind was in consummate dismay, a thousand unanswered questions rampaged through her dark thoughts, demanding recognition and recourse. She was lost to the world around her as the hustle and bustle of life surged onwards, blind to the emotions of their fellow man. As she stepped into the courtyard of the museum, Abigail was greeted by the warm and welcoming smile of her friend Johnathan, his enthusiasm for life appeared unbound.

"You appear to be unhealthily buoyant this morning," she stated.

"It would appear that my luck has finally taken a turn for the better," he proclaimed.

"Would you like to elucidate?" she enquired.

"You know how I have taken lodgings with an elderly uncle of mine?" he rhetorically enquired. "Well, during our evening meal, he asked me a little about the circumstances surrounding my father's death and why I undertook employment with Lord Karvahill. I could not see any tangible reason to dilute the fact that I was paying off another family member's debt to his Lordship, and this was solely undertaken through family loyalty rather than some disproportionate or shameful ownership of guilt. It was then that he opened up to me and informed me that he and my father were very close when they were young, and it was my father's good-will that enabled him to start his very lucrative business, which has continued to develop and grow, even to this very day. My uncle has always been very philanthropic in his daily life, supporting those who were not born to privilege, be that financially or educationally. And, he felt that the debt which has been incurred in my father's name is not only my responsibility but his own. For it was my father's act of kindness which offered my uncle this present favourable fortune to spread the good-will to those whom he encountered through-out his life."

"I'm pleased for you," she replied.

"However, it is tinged with a little sadness," he said. "My uncle is in ill health, and I discovered last night that his time is now limited, and unbeknown to myself, he has bequeathed to me all of his worldly goods, and stated that he wanted to observe my good fortune in life, rather than from beyond the grave, which is why he has been so financially benevolent."

"I wonder how Lord Karvahill will respond to your good fortune, as this would mean that you would no longer be financially encumbered to him?" she asked.

"He took it quite well," he replied.

"You've already told him?" she asked in amazement.

"Not only told him, but I have already paid off my father's debt," he stated, with a tinge of triumph in his voice.

Abigail smiled, her heart slightly shaken.

"So you'll be leaving us?" she asked with a nervous smile. "Now that you're not bound to your father's liability?"

Johnathan returned her smiled.

"I am a free agent, and will remain where I choose. I have instructed Lord Karvahill that I am no longer in his employ, however, I did state that I would remain working with yourself for as long as is required."

"And how did he react to that?" she asked.

"He agreed, and as a matter of respect, he stated that my wage is to remain as is," he said.

"How noble," she replied rolling her eyes.

"I'm amazed that Lord Karvahill took this news so well," she stated.

"He didn't, but I offered him a further £10, and this sweetened my departure, as well as his disposition," he highlighted.

"What a cad," she stated in disgust.

"Don't worry, I would have offered him more, if it would have secured my father's debt," he stated. "Lord Karvahill and Sir Henry are as they are. They are very much a law unto themselves. I would not wish to change them, but also I would not choose to freely elect to be in their company." He smiled at Abigail. "The thing that sets us apart, is that I will follow on my uncle's philanthropic endeavours, and demonstrate to the world that money may also bring enlightenment and life is not directed primarily through wanton greed. I love my fellow man, and do not perceive them as social leaches, who devour the limited resources of our society. Money is not the root to all evil, the intentions of man are."

"You are an inspiration, my friend," she said, as they walked up the stairs to enter the museum. "For lunch I propose we visit the café and order a thousand sugary delights, as a means to celebrate your good fortune," she said. "And I insist that this treat is upon me."

"Thank you," he said, as tears of joy welled up in his eyes. "You always treated me as an equal," he said.

"I wouldn't go that far," she stated in jest. "You could never be the equal to a woman," she said, with an impish smile, as she turned and made her way through the doors and into the museum, closely followed by her colleague and friend.

Inside the examination room, the air hung heavy with a stilted silence. Abigail stared at the desiccated corpse of her friend as she contemplated the injustice of his brief existence.

"Have you discovered any more information about our guest?" Johnathan enquired, nodding in Siamun's direction.

For a moment Abigail was transfixed by her ancient compassion, but she recognised the necessity for a reply, she turned to Johnathan and smiled.

"Oh, just the usual stuff. He was about 25 years of age when he died, the usual funerary customers were not adhered too, he was generally fit and healthy at the point of death," she half-heartily replied.

"Have you any idea where in history this mummy can be placed?" he enquired.

"I think this is the son of a pharaoh, possibly from the early Eighteenth Dynasty. Possibly the son of Ahmose the First," she replied.

"Didn't Sir Henry state that he was a high priest?" Johnathan said.

"And we all know that Sir Henry is an aficionado of all things Egyptian. He can't even decipher a simple cartouche. He has only succeeded because of the endless financial enticement offered by his father to those around him," she harshly replied.

"And it would appear that you are impervious to that incentive," Johnathan gleefully stated.

"As are you," she replied with a broad smile, highlighting the fortitude of Johnathan's presenting situation.

"Tell me, what is to become of him?" Johnathan enquired.

"Who? Sir Henry?" she enquired in confusion.

"No, the mummy," he said, looking into the sarcophagus.

"I don't know what you mean," she stated as her confusion deepened.

"Well, knowing Sir Henry, and Lord Karvahill as I do, they would not keep him here unless he could make them money. Their world revolves around cold hard cash," he stated.

Abigail could feel her heart pounding in her chest, as fear began to rise from deep within her heart.

"I don't know," she whispered, as an urgency consumed her mind. "I think that someone may consider purchasing this artefact from Lord Karvahill directly. To keep it within the protective custody of the museum. He can't become a part of some circus sideshow, or a travelling vaudevillian attraction."

"It seems that you have grown a little attached to our friend," Johnathan said with a smirk, as he took off his outer coat and placed it upon the hat stand.

Abigail did not react to his words, for this would have betrayed her true emotional feelings towards her ancient friend.

Realising that his jibe had little effect, Johnathan walked quietly over to Abigail's side and offered her a smile.

"Whatever you choose to do, I would recommend that you do it quickly."

In her confusion, Abigail looked directly at him.

"What do you mean?"

"I heard Sir Henry discussing the fate of the mummies with his father this very morning. He was stating that they had invested too much money into their procurement and he didn't want it to be a financial burden," he explained.

"And how did Lord Karvahill react?" she asked.

"He didn't, he just dismissed his son's concerns and continued with his morning routine," he said, "an action that considerably angered Sir Henry. I think that he feels that his father second guesses all of his business transactions and monitors his financial affairs far closer than any business partner would ever consider."

"Maybe all he is doing is protecting his investments," she surmised. "Do you know how much Lord Karvahill paid for this mummy?" she pensively enquired, pointing to Siamun.

"I don't really know, but realising his depleted value-base, he would have attained the deal of the century, or he would have been taken to the cleaners and paid way over the odds, either way, he would want a considerable amount in return," Johnathan elucidated. He then paused in his explanation and looked Abigail directly into the eyes and offered her a playful smirk. "Please tell me that you're not considering purchasing these mummies?"

"No!" she quickly replied. "Not both of them, just this one," she stated, pointing directly at Siamun.

"But, why?" he enquired.

"Why not?" she retorted. "I know I have only been working with our friend for a few days, but I have grown accustomed to him, one could even go as far as to state that I am quite fond of him, and the thought of some other archaeologist pulling off his bandages and placing him into a display case for all-and-sundry to stare at, seems a little garish, a little inhumane."

"It's only a mummy," Johnathan stated with a smirk. "He's long dead and I'm sure he doesn't mind."

"He was some mother's son," she stated harshly rebuking him. "He was once living flesh, just because time has passed and he no longer has any descendants who have a living memory of him, doesn't mean that his life and death are any less valued than someone who has recently passed."

Johnathan smiled, more out of an uneasy emotional state, rather than satire.

"I think you have become too emotionally attached to our friend," he stated. "It's early and I think I'll make us both a refreshing cup of tea, to set us up for this morning, until we visit the café and eat our body weight in cakes."

He smiled sympathetically at Abigail before he quietly turned and left her alone in her silence in the examination room. The winter sun was reaching half-heartily over the skyline and its weak, yet delightful shades of flickering morning light streamed into the far corners of the room, through the vast windows of the museum.

"He does have a point," Siamun stated, his vibrant interjection causing Abigail to physically jump in surprise.

"Don't do that, you startled me," she said, rushing over to the sarcophagus. "Johnathan is just outside, in the kitchen, and he may be able to hear you."

"Which is why you are whispering?" he stated mockingly.

Without replying, Abigail twisted her facial features, demonstrating her displeasure, but this was soon replaced with a comforting smile.

"I searched the museum for a majority of the night, but could not discover the whereabouts of my friend, Nehi. It would appear that your Sir Henry has mysteriously 'whispered' him away."

"I don't know; I have been considering all of the possibilities until my mind is positively numb. From the moment I closed my eyes last night and from the second I opened them this morning, all I can do is think of is, 'What. Where. Who and Why.' What is the rationale behind these murders? And if I cannot discover a reasonable hypothesis, then I'm afraid I must cast my investigative mind further afield, no matter how preposterous or supernatural my suppositions may be, in order to gain a little insight into the rational for these attacks," she stated.

"Do you think that you should inform someone of the attack last night?" he enquired.

"I have considered that, but it would only raise more questions than answers," she stated.

"But it could also give those investigating the attacks a deeper insight into the quest they are chasing," he highlighted.

"I will consider it," she whispered. "But the problem is, my innocent confession could unravel everything and place us both in a greater danger. Sometimes silence is a prudent friend."

Siamun sat back into the sarcophagus and smiled.

"How much?" he whispered.

Abigail looked at him in confusion.

"How much what?" she innocently enquired.

"How much would you consider paying Lord Karvahill for me?" he asked with a winsome smirk.

"I didn't realise you understood my language," she enquired with surprise.

"The nights are long, and this museum is full of spirits, and they whisper to me, translate your conversations," he highlighted.

"They speak ancient Egyptian?" he enquired in amazement.

"The language of the mouth is a construct of man, the language of the spirit is constructed by the universe," he stated.

"At this rate, I'll pay him to take you off my hands," she quipped, raising a finger to her lips, requesting silence, for she could hear her friend Johnathan returning with the refreshments.

Turning, she observed the door handle of the examination room door turn which allowed the door to swing slowly open. Anticipating Johnathan's return, Abigail stepped forward with a smile and a welcoming hand to offer him assistance with the beverages. However, instead of encountering her friend, she was confronted by the enraged features of Sir Henry.

"He's an absolute buffoon, taking this fatherly guidance to its most extreme and debilitating extent," he cried, entering the room and discarding his coat and hat onto the table. "I know that he's my father, but there are times when he simply infuriates me."

Abigail stood in silence, her mouth slightly aghast as she observed her employer parade before her in his pompous demeanour.

Sir Henry then, realising his situation, turned and looked Abigail directly into the eye.

"My father has decided to offer one of the mummies to some museums in Paris. The Louvre, I think, and he has taken it upon himself to choose which, without consulting me, and only offering me a dictate."

Abigail looked pensively in Siamun's direction, she could feel the tension rise within her heart as her throat dried, and fear rose from deep within.

"And now all we are left with the priest," he announced casting a dismissive wave in Siamun's direction.

Abigail let out a relieved breath.

"This is preposterous, every time I try to break away from that man's controlling actions, I am snared and pulled deeper into his stifling ways," he cried.

"Is there anything I can do?" Abigail enquired in a rather submissive, disarming tone.

"Not unless you have a spare £500 locked away in your night stand, then no I don't consider that you have the ability to help me," he spitefully replied.

Abigail smiled.

"Would you like that to be in cash or a cheque?" she lightly remarked.

"What are you blithering on about?" Sir Henry snapped.

"The money," she calmly replied. "Do you require cash or would a cheque suffice?"

Sir Henry ceased his pompous parade and turned slowly to look in Abigail's direction.

"Are you telling me that you want to buy the pharaoh's mummy off me?" he cautiously enquired.

"No," she quietly replied. "What I am saying to you is that I want to purchase 'that' mummy," she stated, pointing directly to Siamun. "And I will offer you £300, take it or leave it, it is a one off offer, I understand if you have to consult with your father in relation to this matter, but I am prepared to wait."

"My father has interfered in my life one too many times," he bellowed.

"I will give you time to consult with him, to ensure that you're making the right decision," she stated, knowing full-well that she was already stoking the fire of dissention between Sir Henry and his father by making this overtly enticing and generous financial proposal.

"No! I accept your offer," he bellowed in delight.

"Good, I will contact my bank and request an order to be drawn up, and this will be released to you immediately after you have signed a contract from my solicitor, denoting the transfer of ownership," she calmly stated.

"To expedite matters, I will contact my solicitor and draw up the documents," Sir Henry stated with a broad grin.

Abigail smiled.

"No, thank you, I will leave forthwith and request Mr Meadows, my father's solicitor to construct something absolute and binding, I'm sure it will be prepared before lunchtime. I will also ask a representative from Coutts to draw up the bank draft."

At that moment Johnathan entered the room, encumbered with two large workman mugs of tea.

"I'm sorry but these were the only cups I could…" Realising the Sir Henry was present, he made to leave, but was stopped in the actions by a request proposed to him by Abigail.

"Perfect timing, Johnathan, as you are no longer employed by Lord Karvahill, and appear to be a free agent, I am requesting that you support me by being a witness to a legal document which is to be signed this afternoon," she requested.

Realising that she was taunting Sir Henry, Johnathan remained silent for a moment before he smiled and replied to her request.

"I would be delighted. However, I must inform you that I cannot remain for long as I have a personal errand that I must complete. Would this undertaking be before or after our luncheon?"

"Oh, after," she teasingly replied. "I never undertake business transactions before lunch, it would be frightfully uncivilised."

"Well, at least the museum will not have lost a mummy," Sir Henry bitterly replied.

"On the contrary," she stated. "This mummy will be in my personal possession, and in signing the papers, this will denote it as being so. Therefore, I will be the sole custodian, and in being so, will dictate its whereabouts."

THE MUMMY

Sir Henry pursed his lips and furiously gathered his belongings.

"So be it, I will return at 1:30 p.m. and I expect everything to be in order."

Abigail stared at him, without compassion or ridicule, for at that moment his humanity had faded, to demonstrate his own true colourless hew.

"As you wish, 1:30 it is. I suggest we meet at my solicitors to reduce the requirement for subterfuge," she stated."

With these words, Sir Henry bolstered out of the room, leaving those present to bath in his cold distain.

"I don't know what shook him the most, the fact that I offered him £300 for the mummy, or the fact that you were no longer encumbered to his father, and are now technically a free man," she stated.

"I think Lord Karvahill will be enraged beyond endurance by Sir Henry's actions," Johnathan stated.

"I don't particularly care, for I don't think he will inform his father until after the deed has been done. He's proud to renege upon his word, and too arrogant to risk his father's wrath, he will wait until he has the money in his cold sweaty hands to plicate his father's rage," she calmly highlighted.

Johnathan smirked.

"If it ever reaches him," he flippantly stated.

"What do you mean?" she innocently enquired.

"There are a hundred bordellos and gambling houses, between here and Lord Karvahill residence, and Sir Henry has a weak constitution."

"Once he has signed the papers, he can throw the whole god-damn lot into the Thames for all I care," she replied.

"I do hope this transaction won't leave you financially bereft, or place you in disagreement with your father," Johnathan stated cautiously.

"Don't worry about me, my mother ensured that I was well catered for, the sum of money I offered Sir Henry is mere chicken feed and I could have offered him ten times the amount and I would not have missed its presence. As for my father, unlike Lord Karvahill, my father is a gentleman, and he respects the wishes of others. I would not consider broaching the subject with him, as it is neither his concern, nor mine to burden him with," she replied.

As she walked to the door, Abigail turned and smiled at Johnathan.

"If you don't mind, I'm going to the offices, I understand they have a telephone there. I'm going to call my father's solicitor and request they draw up a contract regarding the purchase of the mummy. I will also contact Coutts Bank, and inform them of my request in relation to the forthcoming transaction. Would you be a darling and look after everything while I'm gone, I should only be 30 minutes or so, no more."

Johnathan rolled his eyes to the ceiling and smirked.

"No problem, and I'll make you a fresh mug of tea when you return."

"How very civil of you," she replied, as she kicked her heels and left the room.

Chapter 28.

The transaction had been completed as smoothly as was humanly possible, especially in relation to Sir Henry Karvahill's constant and inaccurate nit-picking, as he half-heartily read through the hastily drawn up contract, grumbled about certain aspects of the document, but signing it anyway, with great disregard. Observing this, Johnathan made his excuses and departed, leaving Sir Henry eagerly awaiting his reward. He then held out his eager hand in anticipation of the banker's draft, while casting the signed document into the waiting hands of the legal clerk who stood anxiously beside him, turning, he offered the boy an understanding glance. Upon receiving the banker's draft, he offered Abigail an arrogant smile, before he departed her solicitor's office and was lost, for that moment, in the throng of pedestrians that flooded the streets at this festive time.

"I must apologise for him, his arrogance knows no bounds," she stated to the solicitor and his clerk.

"It's alright, it appears to be a family trait," the solicitor scornfully replied, ushering the clerk out of the office.

Requesting the contract to be secured in her solicitor's safe, she bade him a fond farewell and meandered slowly back to the museum, as wistful thoughts danced through her mind. All about, the Christmas cheer appeared to be lifting everyone up into its festive arms and carrying them into a world of wonder and anticipated delights. It was at this very moment that she thought of her mother, and the altruistic endeavours that she would undertake on a daily basis to ensure that those who were less advantaged than herself, experience a little kindness at such an emotionally bitter time of year.

Just as she turned the corner to face the museum, she observed Johnathan stepping onto the pavement before her. Upon recognising their encounter, he offered her a broad and welcoming smile.

"I was just popping out to the shop to purchase a little something for my uncle, as a means of saying thank you for his generosity," he explained.

"How very thoughtful of you," Abigail replied. "Would you like a woman's opinion on whatever you purchase?" she enquired, linking her arm into his.

"That would be delightful," he replied with a smile.

"Well, if I'm doing you this favour, maybe you could consider supporting me in one of my endeavours," she requested.

"With pleasure," he replied.

"You don't know what it is yet," she playfully stated.

"True," he replied with a jovial laugh.

"I have withdrawn an extra £10 from my account, and I don't know if this is partially guilt over being so extravagant, or my strong desire to continue with my mother's benevolent works, but I do feel that I should give 'something back', something that has a tangible affect upon those people who surround me. I feel that I should venture to the East-End, and visit some of the rundown slum areas, where the people are hard-working but still experience a subsistence existence, living from hand-to-mouth. I know that I have only £10, and it is a mere drop in the ocean in relation to the poverty which haunts this land, but it is something, and I hope than the kindness I offer will be welcomed in its true intent," she said.

"You can do a lot with £20," Johnathan replied.

Abigail looked at him in confusion.

"You forget, I have a spare £10, which was given to me by my uncle, in case Lord Karvahill incurred further interest upon my father's debt," he stated.

"I thought you were going to purchase your uncle a present?" she said.

"I am, the comfort of others, I shall undertake this endeavour in his name, after all, I can't do anything about yesterday, as it has gone, tomorrow is yet to come, but I can, as a forthright man, make changes to the here-and-now, if those around me allow it," he replied.

"You truly are a kind person, let's celebrate both of our good fortune by spreading a little Christmas cheer," she said, as she pulled him a little closer to herself as they walked along the slush filled streets, towards the Christmas market.

Chapter 29.

By the time Abigail returned to her home, her father was deep in conversation with the detective who had called previously. She could hear their mutterings as she closed the front door and made her way to the library. Listening for a moment, she could hear the detective explaining to her father the theories relating to the murders which had taken place over the past few days.

"We have the impression that the attacks are related to fundamentalists, those who are not pleased that we are funding expeditions to their country and, as they put it, plundering their history," he highlighted. "It was only two nights ago that the police endeavoured to apprehend an individual leaving the Museum's grounds, dressed solely in black. There was a telephone call less than an hour later highlighting a further issue within the museum itself."

"I understand, but why do you think that my family or myself are connected to this?" Lord Cornwall enquired.

"It's not that we think that you're connected, but it is a fact that your daughter has recently acquired employment within the museum, in quite a senior role, and prior to this she was a mere student," the detective stated.

"Are you endeavouring to tell me that you think that my daughter is connected to these fundamentalists?" Lord Cornwall asked in dismay.

"No," the detective implored, "All I'm saying is that she may be an unwitting pawn, who could be manipulated by others for their own desires."

"Such as?" Lord Cornwall enquired.

"Sir Henry Karvahill," the officer replied.

"Don't be preposterous!" Lord Cornwall firmly stated, chastising the detective.

"If that were so, then can you please tell me why she handed Sir Henry the sum of £300, earlier on this afternoon?" he enquired.

There was a cold silence that hung accusingly in the room.

Abigail took a deep breath and closed her eyes for a brief moment, as she endeavoured to summon up her mortal courage, before entering the affray. Pushing the door urgently open, she stepped into the soft light of the library and looked at the detective directly.

"I would like to know how you came about this information," she urgently enquired.

"I'm not at liberty to inform you of that Ma'am," the officer replied, as he sat opposite her father, his notebook open in readiness.

"Whatever it is, it is a gross breach of confidentiality and I will make enquiries immediately with both the bank and my father's solicitors, to discover how this has occurred," she stated.

"How do you know that these establishments are the source of our information?" he asked with a mischievous smirk.

"It is either there, or one of the secretaries within the museum. There cannot be anyone else," she said. Abigail glared at the officer as she sat on the sofa next to her father. "Please tell me what evidence you have of this financial transaction."

"I'm not at liberty to divulge my source or to highlight the information given," he stated.

"Then I am not at liberty to reply to your questions detective," she firmly stated.

The detective smiled and flipped his notebook closed.

"That is your prerogative, but hampering an investigation is an offence," he highlighted.

"How do you know that I am hampering your investigation, when you don't know what I have done?" she asked with a smile.

The detective sat back on the chair and smirked.

"May I ask of you a simple question? Did you furnish Sir Henry with a banker's draft for the sum of £300, this afternoon?"

"I will answer your question if you answer mine," she replied.

The detective contemplated her proposition for a brief moment.

"Off the record, yes."

"Quid-pro-quo," she said, "It means…"

THE MUMMY

"I know what it means," the detective sharply interjected. "My father taught Latin and Mathematics at Oxford."

Abigail appeared physically shocked at this revelation and smiled apprehensively at the detective.

"Why, you appear a little taken aback by this revelation," the detective stated. "We're not all lumbering ill-educated misfits, who 'get-off' investigating grisly crimes, Miss Cornwall. Some of us have integrity. Now, if you don't mind, may we return to this, 'something for something' contract. After all, the passing of this information is contingent upon the satisfaction of the other. Is it not so?"

Abigail remained silent, but nodded.

The detective raiser the index and middle finger of his left hand and opened them into the sign of a V.

"You have two questions, which I will endeavour to answer without contaminating evidence or placing my source at risk," he stated. "Choose wisely, you only have two questions which will remain off the record."

Abigail smiled.

"As do you," she replied. Abigail contemplated his advice for a few pensive moments, before she raised her eyes and smiled at the detective. "In the spirit of fairness, I propose that we offer our questions alternately, and as these are advanced times, I also propose that, as a lady, I will consider it a grace if you offer the first question," she requested, knowing full well that this question would be direct and require little consideration or evidence to prove.

The detective smiled.

"Very well, did you give Sir Henry a large sum of money today and if so what was it for?" he asked.

Abigail smirked.

"Are you asking both of your questions at once she enquired?"

"No," he retorted. Realising his purposeful indiscretion, he smiled and refined his questioning. "Did you give Sir Henry £300 today?"

Abigail raised her finger to her lips and contemplated the question proposed.

"Yes," she firmly stated.

The officer smiled.

"And now my first question." Abigail stated. "Is your informant male or female?"

"I don't see the relevance…" he stated.

"I'm not bothered about what you perceive; I am asking a simple question. Is your informative male or female?" she reiterated.

The detective took a deep breath and shook his head before replying.

"Male," he stated.

Abigail smirked gratuitously.

"And now my second question," the detective stated. "Why did you give Sir Henry the sum of £300?"

"For the purchase of an ancient Egyptian mummy," she calmly stated.

"Is that the only reason you gave Sir Henry the sum of £300 and request he sign a contract?" he asked.

"No," she replied.

"Then why else?" he asked.

"No, as in, no more, you have asked your two questions, I have a second question which I must propose," she said, searching her mind for a suitable source of enquiry. Realising that she had discovered her quest, she smiled at the detective. "Is your source under the age of twenty?"

"I don't see the relevance of that question," he stated.

"You don't have to understand the relevance only the knowledge to answer the question proposed," she stated.

"For what good it will do you, the answer is yes," he replied.

"Then you have informed me of everything which I need to know," she said.

"I don't understand," he said.

"Evidently," she replied.

"Would you like to enlighten me?" her father enquired.

THE MUMMY

"Only if you answer one of my questions," she asked.

"Of course," he replied

"Does Sir Henry use your solicitor?" she asked.

"No, but his father does, this doesn't matter," he insisted, "Please go on with your supposition," he urged.

"In front of detective, Mr…" she said, turning to the police officer.

"…Holmes," he said.

"Really!" she stated in surprise.

"Yes, Edward Holmes," he stated, in slight dismay.

"It's just that I'm a fan of the literary detective Sherlock Holmes and your name was a little amusing considering the line of work in which you are entailed."

"You have me at a disadvantage, I've never heard of him. If he is from a work of fiction, I avoid them like the plague, I'm only interested in factual publications, everything else I find mentally tedious," he stated.

"Maybe you should try them, it may sharpen your investigative skills," she stated with a slight sliver of sarcasm.

"Please, enlighten me," he requested.

"Well, if you look at your two answers, they can be broken down into certain elemental factors. My first question proposed was, is the informant male or female. You answered male, this then narrows down the list of possible suspects. The only people I spoke to in relation to this transaction were in Coutts Bank, and my father's solicitors. Now if I had been overheard by the secretaries within the museum, as they were present when I made the initial telephone calls, and, as all of those were female, this precludes them from my own enquiries," she stated.

"And the age?" he asked.

"Well, if the informant is male then it could only be the solicitors or the bank. For they do not employ females, and if the person is under a certain age, then this can also narrow the list of suspects even further down," she stated.

"How so?" he asked.

THE MUMMY

"Coutts do not employ anyone under the age of twenty-five, and the only person within my father's solicitors who is under the age of twenty, is the great nephew of Lord Karvahill, who was recently employed as a clerk, very much at the request of Sir Henry himself, a way of possibly monitoring his father's affairs. Also, nobody at the bank or in the museum knew that Sir Henry had signed a contract relating to the transfer of £300. Thus giving motive, evidence and suspect, in one fell swoop," she triumphantly stated.

"Maybe I should start reading these mystery novels you previously referred to," the detective stated with a smile.

"Maybe you should," Abigail replied, in a lighter tone.

"However, your premise does easily fall asunder," the detective retorted.

"In what way?" enquired with a smile.

"That I was telling you the truth," the detective stated.

Abigail looked in aghast at the detective, a possible victim to her own arrogance and naivety.

"May I ask a question?" her father enquired, endeavouring to discover more appertaining facts in relation to this conundrum.

"Why were you giving Sir Henry £300, I do hope he wasn't blackmailing you," he urgently stated.

"Father! He would have no reason to blackmail me," she replied. "It was a genuine transaction. I purchased a mummy from him."

"Now that's where the problem arises," the detective stated.

Abigail looked at him in curiosity.

"It appears that the finances initially procured to purchase those artefacts came directly from Lord Karvahill himself and not his son, and so, those artefacts were not Sir Henry's property to sell," the detective highlighted. "But also, the artefacts were initially procured for the museum, thus making their ownership rather circumspect."

"Which is why Lord Karvahill contacted yourself," she stated resolutely.

"What does Lord Karvahill want to do about this whole situation?" Lord Cornwall pensively enquired.

THE MUMMY

"Nothing," he stated.

"You mean he wants the mummy returned?" she asked.

"No," he replied.

"I don't understand," she highlighted. "He wants to keep the money?"

"No," the detective stated.

"Then what?" Lord Cornwall asked.

"Lord Karvahill was more concerned that his son had in some way pressurised you into purchasing the mummy. If this was so, he would himself, return all the funds, for he was under no illusion that his son would have frittered away a considerable amount of the money already procured, also he did not want any bad blood between your families, especially that contrived by his son."

"And now you understand that the transaction was undertaken by my daughter's own free will?" Lord Cornwall enquired.

"Then the contract remains as is," the detective stated.

"I don't understand," Abigail indicated.

"It means that the contract is binding, and is to be honoured by both Sir Henry and Lord Karvahill alike. To all intents and purpose, that mummy is now in your possession, and it belongs solely to you," the detective highlighted.

"I don't understand your interest in this," Lord Cornwall highlighted.

"Me neither," the detective replied. "My only interest is in the apprehension of these fundamentalists, but when you are requested by a higher source to follow an alternative lines of enquiry, then it is not for me to question why."

Lord Cornwall smiled and lowered his head, as the answers rushed frantically into his mind.

"Brigadier – General, Sir William Horwood," he muttered.

Without replying, the detective offered him an understanding smile.

"Friend of Lord Karvahill," Lord Cornwall muttered disparagingly.

"May I ask you another question," Abigail asked, "This can be either on or off the record."

The detective nodded.

"Do you think that the people undertaking these attacks are fundamentalists, or should we be looking a little closer to home?" she asked.

Detective Holmes contemplated his reply for a few brief moments.

"Anything is possible. At this point in time I wouldn't be ruling out any possible avenue of investigation."

Abigail looked contemplatively into middle distance, her mind turning in its eternal machinations.

"Do you think that there could be a more concise rational attributed to these attacks in London? After all, the victims appear to be considered and precise in their selection," she stated.

Detective Holmes sat back in his chair and contemplated her words.

"In what way?" he enquired. He leaned forward and raised his index finger. "I am intrigued by your answer, and I do not mean that in a patronising way, for it is apparent that you have considerable insight and an inquisitive mind that any detective would be proud to aspire to attaining."

"If we look at the basic facts, and break them down into their lowest common denominators. What do we have?" she rhetorically highlighted. "These three attacks took place in London, all within a short distance of one another. They were perpetrated upon affluent families, or to put it precisely, the daughters of those families. Could there be a connection which you have not thought of in relation to those females?"

Detective Holmes smiled.

"I feel that you understand this situation a little more than you are revealing," he stated.

"I don't understand," she furtively replied.

"Oh, but I think you do, Lady Abigail," he highlighted.

She could feel a soft expanse of warmth flutter up her throat, as a red sea of embarrassment consumed her.

"I'm a little lost, please enlighten me to my mistake," she requested.

"I only know of two attacks, yet, at the beginning of your recantation, you stated that there had been three," he highlighted.

An uncomfortable silence hung impatiently in the air.

"My mistake," she said pursing her lips.

"I doubt that Miss Abigail," the detective replied. Knowing full well, that any individual, no matter how articulate, would stumble within the realm of self-assurance or arrogance. "I have only known you for a brief moment, but in that time it appears that you are not only precise, but very practiced in the art of academic conversation. After all, was it not your forte at university, languages?"

Abagail turned and looked sheepishly in her father's direction. Who in turn searched her expression with fearful eyes.

"It would appear that you are not the only sleuth within this room. Is there something that you're not telling me?" he parsimoniously enquired, now wishing to discover the truth within her answer.

"It would appear that you have done your research," she stated to detective Holmes.

"A few basic enquiries. Primarily information given to me by Lord Karvahill," he stated.

"Lord Karvahill. It would appear that all roads lead back to him," she said.

"Abigail," Lord Cornwall said in a rather stern voice. "Answer the detective's question."

"Very well, but you may not like my response," she highlighted to her father.

"I'm sure I'll cope," he said, asserting his parental domain.

"After we were visited by Sir Henry last night, where both he and yourself consumed a considerable amount of whisky, I was about to retire to bed," she said.

"What time was this?" the detective asked, as he took out his note book from his breast pocket.

"At about 10:30 p.m. possibly 11," she replied.

"Go on!" he instructed.

She took a deep breath.

"My father had retired to bed about 30 minutes prior to myself and it was while I was walking up the stairs when I noticed a strange shadow on the wall. It appeared to be that of a possible intruder. Initially I thought it was my father, but then I realised I could hear him snoring and so I could not attribute this anomaly to him," she explained.

"So what did you do?" the detective enquired.

"I shouted at them, asked them what they were doing in my home," she stated.

"Go on," the detective encouraged.

"Then nothing, the stranger raced passed me and knocked me off my feet on the first floor landing on the stairs, by the time I caught my breath they had gone. I ventured out into the lane behind the property, but all I could discover were footprints leading away from our home," she deceptively explained.

"And none leading to your property?" the detective asked with a wry smile.

Abigail looked at him without consideration or compassion, for she felt lost in her own lies.

"There was a fresh snowfall, and any previous impression would have been masked by that downpour," she stated.

The detective smiled and stood.

"Thank you for your…honesty," he stated, snapping closed his notebook and placing it back into his breast pocket. "You have my card. If you recall anything else, please don't hesitate in telephoning me." He offered Lord Cornwall a respective bow. "Don't worry, I'll see myself out." He said as he walked briskly out of the room.

After they heard the door close, Lord Cornwall turned to his daughter.

"There's more to this than you're saying," he quickly highlighted.

"Father…" she began in protest.

"Don't 'father' me. I want the truth, and I want it now," he sharply declared.

Abigail stood from the sofa and walked over to the fire, the warmth and light that issued, touched her features and offered her cheeks a soft redness that softened her demeanour, contributing to the frailty of her soul.

"In relation to the mummy," she began. "It was my choice and I was not coerced or emotionally manipulated in any way by Sir Henry."

"Go on," her father instructed.

"I cannot tell you everything, but what I can promise is all that I do inform you of shall be purveyed with the unvarnished truth. Please, do not push me for details, for at present I do not feel that I can furnish you with any more information than that which I am about to freely give," she firmly stated.

Lord Cornwall smiled and nodded his head.

"My assistant," she stated, but then corrected herself. "My work colleague, Johnathan, has been indebted to Lord Karvahill since the death of his father, who worked for his lordship, had accumulated a considerable amount of debt and following his death, his son accepted that obligation and felt duty-bound to repay in full his father's liability. It would appear that there was a turn of fate, and Johnathan's uncle, his father's brother, discovered this obligation and interceded and gave him the financial whereabouts to fulfil this dark responsibility. It was as he was undertaking this final duty, when he overheard Lord Karvahill and his son discussing their collective finances, and it appeared that they are in a considerable mess. His Lordship even contemplated selling one of the mummies, which he had purchased at the request of his son, for the museum."

"Why didn't the museum purchase these artefacts originally?" her father enquired.

"I don't know, but if Sir Henry is as appalling with the museum's money as he is with his own, then there could be a whole plethora of lawsuits and tales of embezzlement which would pepper the tabloid press if this information were to be made public," she highlighted.

"And you discovered that Sir Henry was in a financial predicament and decided to purchase one of the mummies?" he father sceptically enquired. "And at some considerable amount."

"Yes father," she firmly stated. "But I did not purchase the mummy for that reason. Also, in relation to finances, I consider it to be an investment. The mummy is worth £500 and I purchased it from Sir Henry for little over half that amount."

"May I ask you a question?" he enquired.

"Of course," she replied.

"Is the aforementioned mummy in the same physical condition as it were at the initial inspection undertaken at the original sale?" he asked.

"Well, no," she stated. "I have taken off a few layers of bandages," she highlighted.

"Then it is not worth what Sir Henry or his father paid for it, and so your purchase may not be as lucrative as initially surmised," he said.

Dismissing her father's pessimism, she continued.

"It was agreed with Sir Henry that I would pay him £300 for the mummy and there would be a contract drawn up by our solicitor and he would sign this, granting me sole ownership of the mummy, and neither he nor his family could place any future tenure upon him," she highlighted.

"Him?" Lord Cornwall stated. "It appears that you are becoming increasingly fond of this swathed cadaver. Your first period of employment and already you are mixing your personal life and that of your professional, so much so that it concludes with the police turning up at my door. Something I could never have attributed to one such as yourself."

Realising the shame that she had brought upon her father, Abigail remained silent, and without protest, lowered her head.

"I understand that you are a grown woman, but you are naive in relation to the world and its turning. Spending such an amount upon such an object is inexcusable, and, before you object, the spending of the money is not the issue, for it was bequeathed to you by your mother to do as you wish. All she requested was for you to attain a strong and robust education, this you have dutifully fulfilled. My concern is that you have entered a financial contract with the Karvahills, and in doing so, you have unwittingly bound our families together. Society will view this in a negative light, if it were to become general and common knowledge. All of the nefarious assignations and underhanded dealing which have been attributed to that family's business dealing over the past fifty years could also haunt our good name. The old saying, 'there's no smoke without fire,' is untrue, but can be severely damning. Why do you think Lord Karvahill is endeavouring to bury the news of this transaction before it has drawn its first breath? His actions are simply damage limitation. If the museum were to discover this, then you all could be embroiled in this dark affair and encircled by the whisperings of embezzlement and misappropriation of official funds, thus drawing to yourselves the attention from those neither of our families would desire inquiry. Accounts would be investigated and it would come to light that Sir Henry is an incompetent and has been mismanaging the museum's funds for years. And, as you are his employee and our families are superficially connected, assumptions would be made and that smoke, would reappear, without any evidence of that aforementioned fire," he coldly highlighted.

"But I have a contract," she urgently stated.

"Please tell me daughter. Who would care? Once the gossip has reached the ears of those too lazy to socially stand on their own two feet, do you think that the mention of a legal document would quell their repugnant lies? The genie would be out of the bottle, and as with smoke, it could never be fully returned. Your life would be socially ruined, your name, as well as mine, would be scorned." Lord Cornwall rose from the sofa and walked over to the door. "I do not know what spirit compelled you to undertake this foolish endeavour, and I pray for your sake that this matter is truly buried, for if not, all of the finances at my disposal could not save you from the all-consuming wrath of this cruel and unforgiving social collective which we inhabit, for they are as vicious as the wolf, and as dark as Satan's soul, they will emotionally tear you asunder without a by-your-leave. Do not let their smiles deceive you, for its veneer conceals a soul unbound in its desire to destroy those who inhabit their social circle, for the she-wolf would turn for fear that its place upon the precipice of destruction were uncomfortably close to your own." He reached for the door handle and turned it, before turning back to his daughter. "Why offer those hungry for flesh your own, when a naïve victim, such as yourself, would taste all the more succulent?" He swallowed hard, as if his next words were vicious and barbarous. "I know you daughter, better than you think. Yet I cannot comprehend what action could have compelled you to undertake such a foolish action. Yet, no matter how much I tell myself that you are so akin to your mother, and these thoughts are comfortably distracting, I find that at this very moment in time, my assumption is wholly untrue. For you mother would never lie to me, or withhold her secrets. We were as open and as honest as the sunrise at dawn." A single tear of remorse ran down his cheek. "I will retire to my room, for I feel that this day has become unbearable, and so, I bid we speak no further upon this subject."

Abigail watched in horror as her father silently left the room, closing the door gently behind him as he exited. Closing her eyes, she sank emotionless to the floor, her heart broken, numb to her own selfish desires.

"Oh, father. What have I done?"

Chapter 30.

Lord Karvahill circled his son, his mind a rage with anger and distaste.

"Are you a fool? Bringing this innocent girl into your pantomime of deceit and treachery? Don't you realise that you will draw attention upon my financial transactions and suspicion will fall upon me, besmirching my good name, a name that has taken me years to forge through the blood and sweat of others?" he shook his head in displeasure. "Selling that mummy to a work colleague, to someone who actually works within the museum? I can't believe the levels to which your crass stupidity will stoop. And what am I supposed to tell that French museum that was going to purchase the mummy for a tidy profit? Sorry, I lost it? Sorry my idiotic son sold it for below the price his father procured from them?" He turned upon his son and looked feverishly into his hollow eyes. "You don't realise what I have done for you, do you? If everything were to come to light I could go to prison, or worse, I could swing from the gallows." He shook his head, endeavouring to release the dark images if his imagination that hung harrowing in his mind. "Believe me, if I do, beloved son, I will have a companion to enter through the gates of Hell with me."

"But father, I have your money," Henry implored.

"All of it, all £300?" he replied.

"Well, I had to pay off a few debts," Henry protested.

"My debts, or your debts?" his father coldly enquired, hissing his words through his thin lips.

Sir Henry endeavoured to hand his father a small bundle of bank notes. Observing his son's trite actions, Lord Karvahill brought his hand mercilessly into contact with that of his son's, sending the notes cascading into the air and fluttering down in a fiscal snowstorm.

"Keep your damned money," he screamed. "Our debts are at present the least of your worries. Just wait until they start to investigate the sale of that wretched mummy. If they look into the purchases undertaken in your name for the Antiquities Department, it wouldn't take a genius to discover that most of those acquisitions were procured by yourself. Scratch a little harder and it becomes glaringly apparent that these artefacts were sourced by myself. All it would then take is for those investigating to contact the original suppliers and they would discover that the museum was paying, at times, over twice as much for their artefacts as their original purchase, and the money I was using to purchase these items was attained under false pretences."

Sir Henry looked at his father in dismay.

"What?" Lord Karvahill screamed angrily. "You appear offended that your life is based upon a foundation of lies. Welcome to the real world and stop being so naive. What do you think paid for your plush university education? What bribery do you think attained your first class degree? My financial interests in the underworld of this society which have afforded you a kinder life. The finances attained from the opium dens and bordellos, along with my interest in the Far-East, have made your life a privileged and comfortable one" He paused as bitterness dripped from his lips. "And now I want something in return. I need you to go to the museum tonight and destroy all of the evidence that could possibly point the finger of suspicion to myself. Take everything, burn it, burn that blasted museum down if you have to, preferably with you in it, to protect me from your incompetent arrogance. You're a total liability, both socially and economically. Now get out of my sight," he commanded.

"But what about the contract I signed with Lady Cornwall?" Henry cried.

"Don't worry, my nephew is seeing to its tenure, and soon there will be no evidential trail to follow," Lord Karvahill stated with a slight tinge of glee.

"What about that police officer, Holmes, he knows about these events," Henry highlighted.

"Yes, I agree, and he is also under my employ. As with Pringle, young Miss Abigail's assistant, he is indebted, and would not dare to cross me," his father replied.

"What about the police investigation?" Henry implored.

"What police investigation?" his father snapped. "There is no police investigation. Holmes works for me." Lord Karvahill shook his head. "This has always been your problem; you are a one-process thinker. You can never plan ahead and imagine how your actions could affect others, and in doing so influence their reactions. Now get out, and do not return until your task is completed."

"Father, please don't dismiss me as though I were some underling or servant," he pleaded.

"To me, my servants are not as troublesome or the liability you appear to be," he snarled.

"You think that you know me? You understand me? Because you're my father, you have a right to judge me?" Henry shook his head in dismay. "When in fact you have no idea who I am."

"Oh, I know you. I know you only too well," his father replied. "Your problem is you don't learn from your actions and keep repeating the same mistake over and over again. You don't take into consideration how your actions or words could affect another person; you negate to realise that this life isn't always about you."

Lord Karvahill sat back into his comfortable leather chair and withdrew a large Panama cigar from his top pocket. Biting off the stub, he spat it onto the floor at his son's feet and lit a match before burning the tip and disrespectfully blowing the smoke in his son's direction.

"Are you still here?" he bitterly enquired.

Without another word, Henry Karvahill momentarily closed his eyes and turned away from his father, wading through the ocean of finance discarded on the floor. As he reached the door, he opened it, and with the intention of fulfilling his father's final wish, turned his back upon that dark domain which was so comfortably inhabited by many generations of his family.

Following his son's departure, Lord Karvahill rose from his chair and made his way to the fire surround, there he pulled the chord requesting his butler's attendance. Within a few moments the door to the library opened and in stepped a smartly dressed servant.

"Watkins, build up this fire," Lord Karvahill demanded. "Also, bring my large attaché case from the office, the black one next to the safe."

"Yes Milord," Watkins dutifully replied.

"Oh, and bring all of the files appertaining to my son's accounts, there on the book shelf next to the safe," he instructed. "Primarily those associated with the museum."

"Very good Milord," Watkins replied.

Chapter 31.

The museum was dressed in shadows, as the night gracefully fell towards dawn. It was almost 3:00 a.m., and the clouds above were taking on a rich umber hew, denoting the impending deluge of snow that was forecast for that very morning. Looking to the skies, Sir Henry stepped from his carriage and marvelled at the wonders of this world, and at that very moment realise how complex his mundane life had truly become. He had chased adventure and risk at every turn, longed for intrigue and mystery, however, all that this left was a bitter sweetness that haunted his soul and left a great chasm in his heart were love refused to reside, he was truly alone.

Nodding for his driver to remain, he wrapped his scarf around his chin, to protect him from the bitter winds that blew along the deserted roadway and onto the naked, unprotected areas of his flesh. Reticently, he made his way around to the rear of the museum and tentatively withdrew a large selection of master keys from his pocked. After several moments endeavouring to discover his anticipated goal, he eventually retrieved the desired key, which he urgently placed into the lock, which would grant him unfettered and unwitnessed access into the museum. Turning the key slightly, he heard the familiar click of response as the door swing freely open. Looking about for evidence of observation and realising that none was forthcoming, Sir Henry briskly stepped into the darkness of the corridor and closed the door quietly behind him, now, with these actions, forever damning himself to his own lost world.

Inside, he made his way surreptitiously along the deserted corridors and up the main stairs that led to the first floor, and the section of the museum that was not generally open to the public. Briskly walking down the corridors, he came to a door which had written in bright white writing upon its middle panel, 'Private,' he reached down and gripped the brass handle. Gently, he turned it until it relinquished its tenure and swung freely open, the hinges squeaking slightly in their journey. Inside, he walked along the inner corridor until he discovered the door to the finance department. Looking about, he realised that his intrusion had not been revealed, and so he entered the inner sanctum of the museum's financial world, and searched eagerly for his father's desired goal.

Walking tentatively over to one of the administration desks, he lifted an ornamental Christmas candle from where it rested and withdrew his

THE MUMMY

cigar lighter from his pocket and ignited the wick of this mundane festive decoration. This insignificant infusion of light, illuminated only the barest of images that haunted the room. He walked over to the bookshelves, laden with heavy ledgers denoting years of precise inventory. His fingers ran urgently along the leather spines, spanning the decades of financial accoutrement and expenditure. His fingers rested on that year, 1928. Placing the candle on the shelf above, Henry withdrew the ledger and opened it at the last entry, his eyes searching for his own name denoted next to any acquisition. It did not take him long to realise his own misgivings, for there, several lines above the last entry read the name 'Sir Henry Karvahill – purchase of two mummies for the sum of £500 – and the company Millwood and Pinchin. A company whose silent partner was none other than his own father, Lord Karvahill. He turned the crisp heavy pages over and over, as the company's name screaming at him from every leaf of this heavy and incriminating tome. Henry closed his eyes and allowed the ledger to rest on the table by his side. Opening his eyes, he then withdrew the second ledger dated 1927. A dark sense of remorse filled him, as a fearful anticipation haunted his mind. Opening the ledger, his eyes were immediately beset by the name Millwood and Pinchin, screaming at him from the crisp white pages, written in black ledger ink, meticulous and condemning.

Henry took a deep breath and placed the book onto the table next to the first ledger, his mind in disarray, as confusion through anxiety gripped his thoughts and for the first time in his insignificant life he felt genuine fear. A fear that was unbound and unsalvageable.

Observing the drawers on the desk he offered this his undivided attention as he lowered himself to his knees in order to pry open the drawers and discover what damning evidence could lie within. Realising that they were locked, his nails searched the top of each enticement, endeavouring to seek entry, but none was forthcoming. Angrily, he beat his fist upon the desk and stood and returning his attention back to the ledgers that lined the shelves before him.

Henry's eyes searched the shelving, desperate to discover further evidence that could incriminate either his father or himself. His eyes searched back and forth, lost in their despair as the sense of urgency consumed him and thus turned to blind rage.

"Where is it? Where is it?" he cried, as a sense of deep tension rose from deep within his core causing him to shudder uncontrollably with rage. "Where can it be?" he whispered, his eyes endeavouring to penetrate the gloom of the office. He shook his head in dismay as a feeling of remorse echoes through his heart. He made to turn but at that moment his eyes fell upon the safe that sat at the back of the room. A wry smile broke upon his lips as he felt a slight tinge of hope. He made to step forward, but something preternatural, something primal and protective censured his advance. His eyes peered into the darkness, at the shadows that littered the area next to the safe. There it was again, that unnatural movement, the loss of innocence, the shimmer of dark light from the shadow world.

"Is there someone there?" he enquired.

A deafening silence responded to his question.

Realising that his question held little declaration, he smiled to himself and shook his head.

"Is anyone there?" he stated mockingly. "Yea, its three o'clock in the morning, the only idiot that would be here is an idiot like me," he lamented.

From the shadows there came a sound, muffled at first, but apparent. The sound of cloth shuffling upon the cold wooden floor of the office. Henry could feel an anxious warmth rush across his body, which was closely followed by an unholy chill, that froze him to the very core.

"Show yourself!" he demanded, more in fear than arrogance.

The sound increased as the source moved unhealthily closer, cutting through the shadows. The white of the linen was reflected in the shallow light which was emitted from the sole candle that shone on the bookcase above, this advancing apportion caused Henry to inhale a sharp breath. Stepping backwards, he knocked the bookcase with his back, causing the candle to shudder in its position and fall forward onto the ledgers resting on the desk. Immediately, the crisp white pages turned an unhealthy sombre colour, as the flame ravaged their integrity and devoured their purity from within. In mere moment the growing flames were conspiring against Sir Henry's desire to quell them, as he hit down upon the pages with the flat of his hand, sending small ignitable strands of ash floating into the air. Realising that his actions were compounding the effects of the increasing fire, Henry stepped back and stood in disarray for a few brief moments. His mind impotent against all that was good as his own selfish emotions rose, and the only passion that consumed him was that of his own self-preservation.

His eyes searched the room and quickly focused upon the exit point, the door through which he entered, he took a deep breath and made to rush to expedite his own safety. However, his actions were quickly thwarted as a mummified hand reach out of the shadows, and gripped him firmly around his throat, thus preventing his assured escape.

Chapter 32.

Abigail had been experiencing a restless slumber, her mind tormented by her own betrayal, she could feel her own insincerity gnawing her emotions to the core. Here she was, an educated and privileged woman, lying to the man who had demonstrated nothing to her but love and compassion. 'How betrayed he must feel', she thought in her shallow dreamlike world. 'How disappointed,' he was of this selfish daughter who turned her back upon his advice and withheld her own dark secrets from his comforting wisdom and council. Opening her eyes, she sat up in bed and looked to the small carriage clock that sat on her bedside table. 3:10. a.m., she let out an exacerbated breath and lay back onto her bed, her bleary eyes searching the shadows that littered her ceiling. It was only after a few moments did she realise that one of the shadows appeared familiar, fatherly, and she sat up once again as her eyes searched the darkness within her bedroom.

"Father?" she whispered.

After a moment, the shadows acquiesced their son and Siamun stepped apprehensively into view.

"Siamun," she whispered, as he strove towards the bed. "My father can't discover you here, he already disapproves of me to such a degree that this encounter would send him over the edge."

"I must see you," Siamun protested. "The museum is on fire."

Abigail sat in shocked silence, her world turning in dismay.

"I don't understand; how can it be on fire?" she whispered.

"I don't know. I was outside of the museum, exploring your world, when I noticed the familiar reflection of a fire's illuminating presenting at one of the first floor windows," he urgently stated.

Rising from her bed, Abigail rushed over to her wardrobe and flung open the doors, lifting the garments she had worn that previous day she looked at Siamun and glared.

"What?" he enquired.

"Turn around so that I can get dressed," she sharply replied.

"Oh, sorry," he said, as he clumsily turned and faced the door. He could hear the sound of rustling material as Abigail disrobed from her nightwear and put on her social clothing. At that moment he observed the door handle to Abigail's room turn as the door was slowly pushed open, revealing the figure of Lord Cornwall, standing motionless in the corridor.

Realising the severity of the situation, Abigail pushed her way past Siamun and rushed towards her father.

"Father, it's not what you think, I need your help and you must hurry, I want you to dress and accompany me to the museum, this friend has come here to inform me that the museum is on fire."

"Without hesitation, Lord Cornwall turned and made his way back to his room and dutifully dressed and within moments was standing at the main door of the property waiting for his daughter and her companion to join him.

As they ascended the stairway and stepped into the hallway, Abigail observed her father as he courteously opened the door and ushered the group out into the cold night air.

"I've called for a cab to take us directly to the museum," he stated as he looked both up and down the street, endeavouring to discover the whereabouts of the vehicle.

"Father, I must explain," she said, endeavouring to focus his attention.

"My dear girl, there is no need for an explanation. I have contemplated my actions and I feel that it is I who is in the wrong. You're a grown woman, and you should have your secrets. You're not my little girl anymore, and I should respect you for that." He said, looked roguishly in Siamun's direction.

"No father, you don't understand," she implored.

"I do understand," he stated with a reassuring smile. "You're growing up, and that's alright, I have to accept that. I can't be there to protect you all of the time, and maybe I should hand that mantle over to someone else, someone younger," he said, as he looked at Siamun then apprehensively along the dark street. "Where is that damned cab?" he protested. "You would have thought with all of this modern technology, such as the telephone, that these services would run a little quicker. It would have been easier if I had run to the end of the street and haled a cab personally."

"Father, you're not listening!" she protested.

"I am listening darling and I understand," he stated with a submissive smile.

"No you're not," she stated turning to Siamun. "He's the reason why I spent all of that money on the mummy," she proclaimed.

"You purchased the mummy for this man?" Lord Cornwall enquired in a curious tone.

"No father, I didn't." she stated, as an anxiety began to build deep within her.

Lord Cornwall's eyes began to narrow, as a deep sense of realisation dawned upon him.

"Why is he wearing one of my old suits?" he slowly enquired, looking curiously in his daughter's direction.

"Father, listen to me," she urgently demanded. "He's not the reason I bought the mummy, he 'is' the reason."

"You're not making any sense," her father proclaimed.

"Father! He 'is' the mummy!" she cried.

In the distance, the sound of horse's hooves striking the cobbles broke the reserved silence of the city street.

Lord Cornwall looked at his daughter with a sense of shock etched upon his features.

THE MUMMY

Chapter 33.

The group sat in silence until the cab pulled up outside of the museum. As they alighted, the light from the first floor window gave credence to Siamun's account, and so presented the group with a daunting dilemma.

"Do we wait for the authorities?" Lord Cornwall shouted as he observed the smoke seeping through the lower broken pane of the office window.

"Siamun can gain access, and we could make our way to the office and tackle the blaze before the fire brigade arrive," she highlighted.

"Shouldn't we wait?" her father enquired.

"Father, if we don't do something, all of those artefacts which have given us knowledge of the ancients, will be destroyed forever," she cried.

"I understand, but you could be hurt, or worse killed. I've lost your mother and I'm not prepared to lose you," he said.

"Siamun will help me," she stated

Lord Cornwall looked pensively in Siamun's direction.

"Then we will all go," he stated.

Abigail turned to Siamun and smiled.

"Hurry, you must get us into the museum and to those offices as quickly as possible, otherwise everything could be lost," she urgently requested.

"Follow me," he commanded as he rushed to the rear of the museum and to the window he had left slightly open to aid his passage to and from his makeshift abode. Inside, the smell of acrid smoke was already seeping down the stairs and long the corridors towards the back of the museum, its presence tangible as it bit deep into the back of their throats. Hurrying along the corridor, they came to the stairway that led to the first floor. Siamun strode up the steps two at a time, eager to support Abigail in her request.

As they raced through the private areas of the museum and quickly approached the partially closed door to the finance office, they could feel the heat emanating from within. Siamun turned to Abigail and held out a hand, requesting for her to stop and remain where he stood.

"Allow me to enter the room and survey the situation, do not worry, I will not place myself in any danger and will return forthwith," he said.

Abigail nodded her acceptance, and watched as her friend slipped into the office through the slight opening in the doorway, dark plumes of smoke dissipating out through the gap as he entered.

"I do hope he's going to be alright," Abigail whispered to her father.

"As I hope we will all be," he replied, his eyes focusing upon the dark figure that stood some distance along the corridor, staring intently at them.

Abigail followed the direction dictated by her father's stare until they rested upon the stranger.

"Madjai," she whispered.

Inside the office, the smoke was black and acrid, its presence detrimental to all lifeforms. Siamun searched the area until he discovered Sir Henry's almost lifeless body laying where the creature had discarded him. Realising that some earthly spirit remained, he lifted him from the floor and carried him to the doorway, there he was met by the gnarling presence of the mummy.

"Nehi," let me pass. This man will die," he pleaded.

The creature remained silent and unresponsive to his command.

"Nehi, I implore you, please step aside, otherwise we will all re-enter the underworld," he angrily stated.

The creature remained stoical, staring at him with its rictus grin.

"Nehi," he screamed.

"There is no point shouting at him," a voice stated from the shadows, speaking in his native tongue. "He can't hear you, he is no more than a murdering fool."

Turning, Siamun faced the direction of the voice, but as the smoke was so thick he could not perceive the features of the instigator of these words.

"Who are you?" he demanded, "Show yourself."

"With pleasure, dear brother," he said, stepping from the smoke infused shadows.

Siamun stood momentarily in shock, his mind turning in disbelief.

"How? I heard you die. How can this be?" he asked.

"You heard what I wanted you to hear, that was all. There had been a plot to destroy your family's dynasty for many years, and it was only my subtle introduction, with a little help from my mother, that set the damning wheels in motion which eventually tumbled your corrupt empire," Nehi coldly stated with a soulless smile.

"I don't understand; how can you be here?" Siamun enquired.

Nehi smiled.

"You're not the only one with a benefactor who has the ability to speak our language and tinker with the odd mystical spell or two."

Siamun looked down at Sir Henry.

Nehi laughed.

"Don't be so preposterous," he stated with a smirk. "Look to the older generation," he highlighted.

"Lord Karvahill?" he stated.

"Exactly," Nehi replied.

"But why?" he asked.

"Why not? Who better to front all of his untoward business transactions? It would appear that Lord Karvahill has expressed an interest in the occult for many years, and since acquiring a few artefacts from Lord Carnarvon, and a little cumbersome knowledge, he brought us all back from the dead," Nehi highlighted.

"He didn't bring me back from the dead," Siamun stated.

"No, he didn't" Nehi replied, raising his left hand and revealing that he was holding that very life-giving spell between his thumb and forefinger. "That was your lovely Abigail, one of Lord Karvahill's intended victims."

"I don't understand," Siamun stated.

Lord Karvahill was so twisted by his own black history that it followed him like a dark shadow, infesting everything which it touched. So much so that it prevented his family alleviating themselves of the one true liability they possessed. Lord Karvahill took this personally, very personally," he said.

Siamun looked down at Sir Henry.

"Lord Karvahill was the one killing all of the young women in society, because they had rejected his son's marriage proposal."

Nehi smiled and gently nodded.

"So why?" Siamun asked.

"So why what?" Nehi replied.

"Why did you betray me and my family?" he asked.

"Power. That was all, pure and simple. Ironic that we should all meet now," he stated.

"What do you mean?" he asked.

"Well, if I'm me, and I'm standing here," he stated, raising his eyebrows. "Then who is he?" he enquired, nodding towards the mummy.

"I don't know." Siamun highlighted.

"Oh, how I love family reunions," Nehi sarcastically replied.

A wave of recognition swept over Siamun's mind as a deep sense of realisation confronted him.

"Father!" he whispered.

Observing a flaming ledger on the desk beside him, Nehi placed the spell precariously close to the naked voracious flames, so much so, that the material began to smoulder the instant it made contact. Turning his attention back to his brother, Nehi smiled.

"However, your reunion shall be rather short lived."

"Thank the gods that Amunet isn't here to see this," Siamun stated.

There was a cold protracted silence.

"Oh, but she is, she's outside, totally unaware of your presence. In all the time we have been here, in this newfound world, she believed that you were dead and long forgotten," Nehi stated with a, unemotional smile.

"So here you are now, the snake in the shadows. Manipulating everything from the side. Whispering in the ear of Lord Karvahill," Siamun stated.

"They all make it so easy. I knew that if you plant the seed it will eventually come to fruition. I knew that if Lord Karvahill informed his worthless son of the police's investigation that he would go straight to Lord Cornwall and inform him of the events. Thus setting the wheels of intrigue in motion. They are all puppets dancing upon my stage," Nehi highlighted.

"I don't understand, why are you here? Why are you the age you are at the time we died?" Siamun innocently asked.

"The cruel hand of fate, dipping my toe into the pool of risk one too many times. First I killed you, then your father, and your brothers, until only Ramose remained, but he was clever and quickly discovered my treachery and dispelled me to my own just and dark fate. And there I remained until this hapless Lord Karvahill awoke me, and in doing so, allowed me to bring back those I desired," Nehi stated.

"Allowed you! I would say that he had little choice," Siamun spat angrily at his brother.

"We all have choices," he indignantly replied.

"Did you give Amunet the choice? Does she even know a fraction of your deceit?" he irately enquired.

"No, and you won't be around to tell her," Nehi stated, as he watched the flames devour the papyrus, sealing Siamun's eternal fate.

"I don't understand, why now?" Siamun asked.

"You were the fly in the ointment. You weren't supposed to be brought back to life. However, the bumbling intervention of your friend, brought this act about. And, rather than raising suspicion, it was decided that she should remain within the employment of Sir Henry, so that his father could keep a watchful eye upon her activities. If he were to immediately dismiss her, this would only draw attention to his actions. Why do you think that he encouraged her colleague to work so closely with her? He is besotted by her presence, and Lord Karvahill hoped that he would sweep her off her feet and take her safely away from his nefarious activities. But, being a woman, she couldn't stop meddling. Picking at the wounds until they bled."

"And what if I were to go out of that door and inform Amunet of your actions. Your pretty little quiet life plan wouldn't come to fruition then, now would it?" he highlighted.

"Be my guest, you wouldn't last long, the spell which brought you to life is destroyed, as you will be in a moment or so. And, I don't think that you will get past your father. He's very obedient. Like a friendly Jackal, only a little more vicious," Nehi stated with a cold smile.

Siamun turned to his father and searched his blind stare for any remanence of compassion.

"Father, please let me pass," he urgently requested.

The creature remained emotionally unmoved.

"This destruction has to stop, for everyone's sake, we must all rest," Siamun cried at his brother.

"You may feel that way, but I am sure I have a lot more living to do, and with the beautiful Amunet by my side, anything is possible," he stated.

"You can tell that you are not a descendent of royal blood," Siamun spat at his brother. "My father should never have allowed a viper such as yourself into our home. My father may have been strict and unyielding, but I knew he loved me and for you to let me believe that he had instigated my death, is beyond reproach. You turned the love that I had for that man and allowed it to fester and turn to hate, pure and unadulterated."

"There are casualties in every war," Nehi hissed, and you my poor brother, are just one, as will your friend Abigail and those who accompany her." He turned to the mummy and hissed. "Kill him, and when you have finished, kill the others."

The creature remained motionless, its expression unchanged, its mouth opening and closing as it attempted to muster its strength to speak.

"Look at the fool: endeavouring to communicate without his tongue," Nehi mockingly highlighted.

"Leave him alone," Siamun cried as he stepped forward towards his bastard brother. Nehi raised his hand and held a small papyrus spell between his fingers.

"Ah-ah," Don't be a fool," he said.

"If that is the spell that keeps me earthbound, then destroy it, my life is already over," Siamun triumphantly declared.

Nehi laughed.

"That has long since been destroyed," he coldly stated. "No, this, this is the spell that keeps your beloved Amunet alive. And, if you do not do as I say, and die as requested, then she will endure the same fate I have degreed for yourself.

"You wouldn't be so cold," Siamun said.

"Companionship is fleeting, I'm sure I could find another willing victim to follow me through time," he stated.

"Oh, your compassion knows no bounds," he mockingly replied.

Nehi smirked and shrugged his shoulders.

"It's alright, in a few moments your fate will be sealed and you will return to dust, and Amunet will never know that you were here."

"Bastard!" Siamun hissed.

"As we all are," Nehi replied.

From the shadows a quiet and comforting voice echoed.

"Son?"

Nehi allowed his smile to fall from his face as he turned to the mummy.

Siamun nervously smiled and faced his father.

"Yes father, I am here," he whispered.

The mummy endeavoured to smile, but its jaw had long since been dislocated. A tear of remorse ran down its cheek and onto the bandages.

"I love you father," Siamun whispered.

"Son," the mummy stated a second time, as he stepped to one side to allow Siamun safe escape.

"No!" Nehi bellowed, but his objection was too late to be considered, for Siamun brushed passed his father and out into the smoke filled corridor, Sir Henry in tow.

Nehi, screamed in rage and raced towards the doorway, however his exit was blocked as the creature returned back to its original position, blocking the doorway.

"Get out of my way, you idiot," he screamed, but at that moment he realised that the expression of placidity has changed in the creature's eye, and had turned to that of pure hatred.

The creature elevated his head and looked Nehi directly into his fearful eyes. Raising his hands, he lunged forward, screaming as he did so.

"Die!!!" he cried, as he pushed Nehi into the searing flames, embracing him as they fell to the floor, his linen bandages igniting with avarice.

THE MUMMY

Chapter 34.

As Siamun stumbled out of the room, he fell into a scene of further turmoil, before him stood Abigail, protected by her father, in combat with a sole Madjai. Instantly recognising her stance, he requested her attention, as he placed Sir Henry onto the floor of the corridor.

"Amunet," he cried, his voice echoing around the museum walls. Immediately the figure ceased in its advance and turned to Siamun. Its eyes searching his face for recognition.

"Siamun," she whispered, "How can it be?" she asked, her hand raised to her head and removing the apparel of the Madjai, revealing her true beauty.

"Amunet?" he whispered, as tears of joy fell from his eyes. "I can see you for one final time before I am eternally banished to the underworld."

Amunet stood in sheer amazement, her heart pounding with pure excitement in her chest.

"It can't be, you are dead. Nehi told me that your father had you killed, he pleaded for your life, before he escaped, and we fled from his court for a year until his mother requested we return. It was soon after that your father died, as did your brothers," she stated, dropping her headgear to the floor and stepping closer to her beloved. Raising her hand, she gently placed her open palm upon his cheek. "It is you, it is my Siamun?"

"Yes, it is I," he whispered, as tears ran down his cheeks and he embraced his beloved. "I'm sorry to say but Nehi had all of my family killed, and he stole your innocence."

"I never thought I would see your beloved face again," she whispered, as they sank to their knees in their final embrace.

"The spell that contains us is broken, we have only a few moments remaining until the underworld calls us," he whispered.

"I don't care, as long as I have you. A second in your embrace is worth a lifetime of loneliness," she said, burying her face into his chest.

From the bottom of the stairs there came a commotion as Lord Karvahill accompanied by Johnathan raced into view.

"Is everyone alright?" Lord Karvahill cried.

THE MUMMY

"No thanks to you," Siamun replied.

"What do you mean?" he angrily retorted.

"I didn't know you could speak ancient Egyptian," Abigail stated.

"There's a lot of things I can do, young lady, and I'm not answerable to you," he stated in a chastising tone.

"And if you're asking about your son, he's doing fine," Lord Cornwall highlighted. "But you will be answerable to the police."

"The son that you sent here to die," Siamun highlighted. "Along with those who accompanied him." He nobly stated to those gathered. "You see, Lord Karvahill was responsible for the murders which recently took place in London. He manipulated my father who undertook these actions in his lordship's name, he was killing those women who had declined his son's request for courtship. It appears that Lord Karvahill's bitterness runs very deep. He was also responsible for all of the nefarious transactions in relation to the acquisition of artefacts for the museum, his son was innocent, an idiot, but innocent none-the-less. Everything can be attributed to his lordship."

"You have no evidence," Lord Karvahill stated, nodding towards the smoke filled room, a sardonic smile breaking across his lips.

Johnathan stepped from behind Lord Karvahill and pulled his hands apprehensively behind his back, securing him until the authorities arrived.

"Apart from that evidence that I have been amassing for years, as a contingency against you allowing me to be freed from my contract. Monkey see, monkey do." Johnathan stated with a smile. "You should always learn from those who deceive you, it prevents it from occurring a second time."

It would appear that the evidence is slipping away quite quickly, you could say it has all gone up in a puff of smoke," Lord Karvahill highlighted.

"What, all of the papers which Watkins presented to you to burn?" Johnathan enquired. "They were your household purchases over the past four years, placed in the files labelled Millwood and Pinchin. You see Lord Karvahill, when you retain staff through blackmail and fear, they will eventually turn against their nemesis, for fear fades and ambiguity fills that void. You beat them down to such a degree that their self-worth evaporates and the only thing that remains, is blind hope. Watkins, myself, and a thousand others, do not care what happens to us, all that we do know is, we don't want this to happen to anyone else."

Siamun smiled and looked at Abigail, offering her a cheeky wink.

"You have an honourable and kind man, there," he said, nodding in Johnathan's direction.

"I don't feel as I should," Amunet whispered to Siamun.

"I know my dear, it is the underworld calling, be brave it will be over in a moment," he replied in a calming reassuring tone.

Siamun looked tenderly at Abigail and smiled.

"Please, do not mourn my passing, for I have been blessed. I beg of you not to waste your life in the pursuit of another's dream. Be selfish and live for yourself, for you only have one life."

With these words Siamun closed his eyes in anticipation of the inevitable, a warm smile pressed upon his lips, as if welcoming the kiss of death's bitter allure.

Abigail watched as the sands of time fell from his features and in a few brief moments both he and Amunet were reduced to a small pile of insignificant dust, that was blown across the museum's floor by an unobserved ethereal wind.

Within the hall below their erupted a commotion as the authorities fought their way into the building and made their cumbersome way towards the source of the fire. The firemen were closely followed by the police, primarily, Detective Holmes. Upon observing his ascent up the staircase, Lord Karvahill offered him a knowing smile, which was returned by a stony, emotionless expression.

"This man is responsible for the murders which have recently taken place, he is also responsible for the fire which almost took his own son's life. He is also responsible for embezzlement and a number of other illegal transactions associated with his company, Millwood and Pinchin, and this museum," Johnathan proudly stated.

Detective Holmes looked to his officers and motioned for them to take Lord Karvahill into custody.

"You haven't seen the last of me," Lord Karvahill declared.

"Oh, I think we have," the detective stated as he leaned forward and shook Johnathan's hand. "Good work Detective Pringle. Sterling undercover job."

Johnathan smirked as he looked at Lord Karvahill's' pitiful face as he was unceremoniously dragged away by the police, protesting his innocence as he descended the staircase, impugning his son for all of his ill-fortune.

At that moment, Sir Henry rose from his smoke inhaled slumber.

"Have I missed anything?" he enquired.

"No, not much," Johnathan replied with a smile.

Epilogue.

The winter sun was melting low above the trees as Abigail walked hand-in-hand with her beloved. Johnathan smiled as he clutched her fingers tightly, as if a child disbelieving that they had attained the prized toy, which all of the other children coveted.

"It's true what they say, when they highlight that one friend can change your whole life, and that's how I feel about Siamun," she stated.

"It sounds as though you had a special bond," he replied.

"I suppose we did, it must be akin to those emotions experienced by siblings, protective yet nurturing. I know that he was in my life for a brief period, but his presence taught me so much about myself," she said.

"I wish you had confided in me," Johnathan stated.

"As you did with me, Detective Pringle," she sarcastically replied. "I suppose it was you who informed Detective Holmes about my financial transaction with Sir Henry."

"It was the only confidence which I broke, but as it was the pivotal point in our investigation, I felt honour-bound to inform my colleagues about the situation. You have to realise, everyone who has been mentioned during the course of this extensive investigation, from myself to Brigadier - General, Sir William Horwood, were in some way negatively indebted to Lord Karvahill," he explained.

"And you all collectively gathered Lord Karvahill's dark information and disposing of it aptly, so much so, that it will probably never see the light of day ever again. Was this a way of wiping the slate clean? No more blackmail? No more debt? A line drawn under the corruption in the Met?" she asked.

"I suppose so, I had been working undercover for almost three years, I was even there when your Siamun was shipped into England. Lord Karvahill requested my presence, which played perfectly into the authority's hands. I was able to survey everything from both sides. I do regret a little of the subterfuge, the fact that I had to keep the truth from yourself, however, everything else which I told you was factual. About my father and his debts, the financial burden which my father further endured in Lord Karvahill's employ, which ironically benefited me in my investigations and allowed me access into the Karvahill inner sanctum. My uncle, who is benevolently still with us, the only thing I omitted to inform you was my true employment status," he said.

"So, that night when I encountered you outside of the museum, laden with documents, they were copies of those papers which Sir Henry would eventually endeavour to destroy on his father's behalf?"

"Yes, the museum allowed me complete access to their documents, once they discovered the truth about the embezzlement," he replied.

"So the museum knew about all of Lord Karvahill's nefarious transactions, and all these tales of fundamentalists were contrived by him as a smoke screen, to defer prying eyes against the true events?" she asked.

"I'm afraid so, and as for the museum, they only discovered this a few weeks prior, but they were fully complicit with our requests, it was only your employment that threw a spanner in the works, which is why I was so fastidious about protecting you, as you were wholly innocent in relation to these events," he highlighted.

"My hero," she mockingly stated, gripping his fingers a little tighter.

"I persuaded Lord Karvahill to allow me to assist you, and he thought that this would free up his son to continue undertaking his dirty work," Johnathan explained.

"Let's not talk about that man, the very mention of his name makes my skin crawl. To think he was endeavouring to kill all of the women in London who had demeaned his masculine character and denouncing his son as the impotent fool he really was. Lord pity the young filly who would have accepted his proposal, she would have endured a lifetime of emotional torture and social ridicule," she highlighted.

"Speaking of Sir Henry, has anyone seen him recently?" Johnathan enquired.

"Socially," she enquired, shaking her head. "No, there is a rumour that he has gone to the Americas, possibly to make a man of himself, away from his father's and his family's negative influence. But no, he no longer resides in any of his family's properties. The museum has offered me his position, which I am still contemplating, but I don't know whether to turn my back upon their offer and start a new life somewhere else," she stated.

Jonathan smiled and looked deep into Abigail's soft brown eyes.

"I suppose Henry would have felt blessed and betrayed by his father's passing. Justice was never truly served as mother nature demonstrated the upper hand. I suppose his life of excess and betrayal eventually caught up with him, and the Devil required his attendance in hell," he stated.

"Well at least he died of natural causes and his passing was not a burden upon his family or the state. A prolonged court case would have titillated society, but it would have also destroyed the reputation of many an innocent bystander. The legal investigation left Sir Henry financially ruined, but he threw money at his solicitors to ensure that he didn't follow his father's pathway into prison, or at worse, onto the gallows," she highlighted.

"Well, it's one less family to invite to our wedding, should save on the cost of sending the invitations out," he glibly stated.

Realising that she was the brunt of his humour, Abigail elbowed him in the ribs and smiled.

"Keep going on like that and I won't be inviting you to the wedding," she playfully stated.

"Really!" he stated, as he began to tickle Abigail around her waist.

"It's nice to see that you haven't let this incident affect you, as it becomes so easy to hate those who conspire against you," he said.

"I can't be bothered to hate. If anything, this adventure has taught me that you only have one life, and I cannot spend it hating myself, or crying over others, or chasing people who really don't give a damn about me. I'm spending all of my energies on those whom I love," she playfully highlighted.

"And I love you Mrs. Pringle," he whispered.

"Err, no. That will be, Mrs Cornwall - Pringle, if you don't mind," she stated, playfully correcting his misdemeanour.

"Is this how our married life is to start, a battle of attrition?" he playfully enquired.

"Of course not, as long as you behave yourself, and do as your told," she impishly highlighted.

Laughing hysterically, they both walked happily into the distance as the sun slowly descended upon the day.

The End

THE MUMMY

Lightning Source UK Ltd.
Milton Keynes UK
UKHW020755230320
360729UK00016B/427